Dane asked as he strode to the kitchen, "How about a glass of wine?"

"That will be fine."

Dane picked up a remote and the voice of R Kelly floated in the air. He went into the kitchen and poured two glasses of wine.
When he reentered the living room he stopped dead in his tracks.

Eden stood in the center of the room naked except for her candy-apple red stilettos.

Dane dropped the glasses he was holding. Ignoring the shattered glass and liquid on the hardwood floor with lightning speed he rid himself of his clothes.

Eden watched her prey. The nipples on her plump breasts were dilated from a combination of complete control and excitement.

Eagerly Dane grabbed her.

Eden reveled in the onslaught of his mouth.

Dane's hands cupped her full buttocks and pulled her closer to his body.

Suddenly, Eden freed herself from his roving hands and stepped back. "We need to talk," she said, and the deliberate throatiness of her voice sounded foreign to her own ears.

Eyes That Lie

Michele Cameron

ACKNOWLEDGEMENTS

I would like to take this time to thank the following people:
Author Deatri King- Bey for helping me without benefits, Sidney
Rickman, my editor, Daetriel Ortega of
http://simplybookformatting.com/services
my virtual assistant, Lynel Washington of
http://lynelwashington.com , and Jeff Lancashire, my graphic
artist.
Website: http://www.adjacentdesign.com

But most of all, I want to thank my mother, Martha Jane
Montgomery Cameron for instilling in me the love of reading at a
very young age.

Chapter 1

Sybil Masterson sat in the front row of her afternoon physics class. Her stomach growled and she glanced around anxiously, hoping no one had heard her body protesting the fact that she'd missed breakfast. Surreptitiously she reached inside her book bag and pulled out a king-sized Baby Ruth bar. Holding the bar underneath her desk she tore the wrapper off it and bending, bit a huge chunk out of it. *Thank God for vending machines.* Quickly she polished off her breakfast and then refocused her attention on Professor Wainright as he stood in front of the podium.

"I will not accept late papers. Even if there is a death in your family and you have to leave town, your paper if not your body must be present." He stared ominously at them. "Class is dismissed."

With solemn expressions students filed out of the classroom, completely silent until they reached outside. Skirting the grumbling students, Sybil walked down the steps. She spied Peyton Monroe, her roommate who was as usual flanked by two men.

Not wanting to be privy to the continuing saga of 'Who can screw the cheerleader tonight?' Sybil turned and started to walk to the student union to get something decent to eat before she went back to her dorm and tweaked her paper. Then she heard her name being called.

"Sybil, come over here."

Sybil turned back and looked at the trio.

Peyton was excitedly waving her over to them.

When Sybil looked more closely at Peyton's companions she recognized the twins, Kane and Dane Hamilton, two of the most notorious studs on campus. She'd never met them, but their reputations preceded them. Peyton was batting her eyes at Kane. *She is so dumb. How many times is she going to let herself be used by guys that don't have the decency to call her the next day?* With resignation she walked over to them.

"Kane and Dane, this is my roommate Sybil Masterson," Peyton said enthusiastically.

Dane Hamilton spoke first. "How are you doing, ma'am?" His heavy Texas accent was surprisingly melodic to her ears.

His brother Kane said nothing, just brazenly looked her up and down before turning his attention back to Peyton.

Now it was Sybil's turn to give them a once-over. Kane had steel blue eyes while Dane's were emerald green. They were fraternal twins with very different demeanors. Dane's stance was confident yet not intimidating. Kane, on the other hand, projected a bad boy image as he stood with one leg thrust out in front of the other and his thumbs hooked into the pocket of his jeans. They both wore cowboy boots. *Who the hell wears cowboy boots?*

With obvious excitement Peyton said, "We were just getting ready to go and eat at The Outback. Do you want to join us?"

Denial instantly formed on her lips. "No thank you."

"C'mon, Sybil," Peyton pleaded in a cajoling voice. "There's too much testosterone between these two cattle rustlers for me to handle all by myself."

Dane's eyes crinkled with mirth and he took his hand and pushed back a lock of jet black hair. "We'd be pleased if you'd join us, Sybil. Besides, I'd really like to get to know you." His smile dug huge dimples his cheeks.

"Why?"

Dane seemed taken aback by her bluntness. "Umm," he paused, "We have a couple of electives together."

"We do?" Sybil exclaimed.

"Hell, yeah. You sit all the way in the front and I sit in the last row by the door."

Sybil cast a wary look at Kane who was staring at her. Ignoring his lack of manners, she said to Dane, "Okay, but I can't stay too long because I have to wrap up my paper for Professor Wainright."

"I have that class next semester. I'll pay you for your paper and change the words so Wainright doesn't figure it out," Kane said, his lips twisted to one side.

Sybil gave him a scathing look. "Yeah, that's gonna happen."

Peyton laughed nervously, trying to break the tense atmosphere. "Come on. I'm starved." She linked her arm into Kane's and began tugging him down the sidewalk.

Even though it was still August, autumn leaves fell from the trees and fluttered around their feet as they walked. As Sybil brought up the rear she gathered her sweater closer around her. The wind was unseasonably chilly. After a short walk, they reached a small, black Mercedes.

Dane opened the car door for her and she slid into the back seat. Then he walked around to the other side and got in, letting Kane and Peyton take the front.

On the short ride to the restaurant Peyton chattered nonstop.

She's trying too hard.

"So how do you manage to ever get a word in edgewise with her?" Dane quietly muttered to her.

"I don't," Sybil whispered back. "But I'm used to it. We've been roommates since freshman year and she's real cool people. I overlook the fact that she never shuts up."

"Well, she and my brother won't get along for very long because he always has to be the center of attention."

Sybil smothered her laughter. Jokingly she countered, "Maybe they'll annihilate each other."

"They just might do that." Dane sank back into the luxurious leather of the back seat with a quirky smile on his mouth at the thought.

At the restaurant she sat on the inside of the booth next to Dane. He draped his arm casually on the ledge behind her. They were sitting so close the clean smell of his cologne invaded her nostrils. His thigh touched hers and she felt something like sparks of electricity running up and down her leg.

Nervously she inched farther away from him practically hugging the windowsill.

On the other side of the table with his arm slung around Peyton's shoulder, Kane said, "I'll have a slab of ribs with the fries and slaw."

"That goes for me too," said Dane. "And also bring a pitcher of beer."

"I'll have what they're having," Sybil said, handing the waitress her menu.

Peyton studied the menu and absently chewed on a piece of her wheat blond hair. "I just want a garden salad with fat free dressing."

Damn! I can't believe she did that shit! Now I look like a hog. Sybil scowled at her.

After Peyton handed the waitress her menu, she locked eyes with Sybil and silently pleaded for understanding.

"Honey," Kane drawled, "you don't need to watch your weight. You should have some ribs."

"Oh, I don't eat meat," Peyton denied.

You eat meat all right. You just vomit it up later that night when you think that I don't hear you. Sybil felt Dane's eyes on her and when she turned her head his face was only inches away from hers. Long ebony eyelashes fringed his emerald eyes. She felt her body respond to his attractiveness.

"You're not wearing contacts," he breathed in amazement. "One hazel eye and the other one honey. I've never seen anyone with two different colored eyes."

"It's a family thing." Her voice sounded like a mere whisper.

"Very interesting," Kane drawled in a bored voice.

Dane shot him an annoyed look.

During lunch, conversation floated from one subject to another. Dane's eyes honed in on Sybil as he licked barbeque sauce off his finger.

"What do you plan on doing after you graduate?"

"I want to get my Masters of Social Work from Harvard and be a Director of Case Management at a hospital," Sybil answered. "What about you?"

Kane interjected before Dane could answer her. "My dad has a medical practice in Dallas with several locations. Dane and I are going to be the resident doctors in a couple of them."

Dane bristled. "You are, but I haven't agreed yet."

"You'd better get used to the idea, boy." Kane glared at Dane. "Grandmother's trust said that we have to keep the family business going or we don't get a dime."

"With a degree in medicine from an Ivy League school, I might not need her money," Dane replied with a jagged edge to his voice. "I'd like to work in the trenches for awhile. Maybe I'll volunteer at an inner city clinic or something."

Kane gave a deprecating snort. "There's no money in that." Then Kane turned to Peyton and asked suggestively, "How would you feel about being the wife of a rich doctor in Dallas, Texas?"

Peyton's cheeks flushed red with pleasure and she again batted her eyelashes at him. "I think that's a role I would really enjoy playing."

"Yeah, you seem just right for it too, darlin'. Hell, you may as well go on and start thinking about the kind of wedding you want, an inside one or an outside one at our ranch. It's up to you."

When Dane heard his brother's words Sybil felt his thigh next to hers tense up, and she immediately knew that Kane was full of it. *I need to talk to Peyton because once again she has stars in her eyes. Kane is just playing with her.*

*****

Later that night, Sybil woke when she heard Peyton creep into the room. She was obviously tiptoeing so as not to disturb her and suddenly shouted, "Ouch!"

Sybil turned on the lamp and the room was flooded with light.

Peyton stood on one foot nursing her other foot with one hand. She looked apologetically at Sybil as she sank onto her bed. "I was trying not to wake you."

"Mission unaccomplished," Sybil said in a drowsy voice. "I was only half asleep anyhow. I wanted to talk to you about Kane."

"Oh my God," Peyton gushed. "He's adorable, isn't he? I mean, I've liked him since freshman year, and I can't believe that we finally got together."

Now fully awake Sybil began in a warning tone, "But Peyton..."

Peyton held her hand out as if trying to ward off bad news. "I know that you're going to say that I slept with his frat brother Tristan, but that was a while ago. Kane and I've talked about that and he understands that's a thing of the past. We all have a history," she added defensively.

"But Peyton..."

"I also know that you're going to say that I slept with Kane too fast. But I've talked to him off and on for years. But lately, he's shown a real interest in me." Peyton gave her a long look. "Time's running out for me, Sybil. We have only ten months until graduation. I'm sure as hell ain't going back to that one horse town I was raised in. I'd shrivel up and die an old maid there. I'm gonna get me a husband before I leave this place."

"I can't believe that you think so little of yourself that you feel incomplete without a husband."

Peyton shrugged her shoulders defensively. "That's the way I was raised. You're nothing without a man and I don't want no damn coal miner."

"Just because you were raised that way it doesn't mean that you should feel that way. Those ideas are passé, Peyton. You're going to graduate with a Business Administration degree. You don't have to go back there to live after graduation."

"I'm at the bottom of our class. I never belonged here," she said bitterly. "My SAT scores weren't up to par, but the school lifted the guidelines to let me in because I can do seven back flips in a row without falling. And then I got injured so I can't cheer anymore. Thank God my grant money came through or I would have had to leave the end of sophomore year." Peyton stared Sybil dead in the eye and said in her forthright manner, "Who the hell is going to hire a has-been cheerleader?" In a bleak voice she said, "I'm going to take a shower."

Sybil lay in the darkness and listened to the shower water running. *Oh, Peyton I'm so afraid for you. I have a very uneasy feeling about this Kane Hamilton.*

*****

Sybil was readying her desk in order to take notes when a body plopped into the desk next to her. She looked up and saw the red eyes of Dane Hamilton. His hair was uncombed and it looked as if he had on the same jeans he'd worn to lunch the previous day.

"I don't have any of my stuff with me. Can I borrow some paper and a pen?"

"Sure." Shaking her head she said in a teasing manner, "Is your iron on strike?"

"Funny! I got this shirt out of the trunk of the car. I didn't even get a chance to shower this morning. I took off last night and stayed at a friend's because I got tired of your roommate screaming her pleasure. I could hear her from one end of the apartment to the other."

"Peyton was home by three o'clock this morning."

"Hmm." Dane rubbed the small scruff of black hair on his chin. "So he didn't let her stay the night. That figures."

A sinking feeling enveloped Sybil. "What do you mean?"

"He only lets the ones he really likes stay the night. Trust me, when you sleep with someone and they won't stay the night or vice versa, it's just a bootie call."

Sybil's bottom lip protruded as she listened to Dane's assessment of Kane's treatment of Peyton.

Watching her, Dane got an uncomfortable look on his face and then his eyes shifted from hers. "Don't tell Peyton that I told you that. Kane would kill me."

"You two are twins yet you seem very different." She studied Dane. "Which one of you is older?"

"He is by seven minutes." Dane grunted his dissatisfaction. "And ever since we were children he's tried to dominate me because of it."

Sybil felt compelled to say, "You guys sound like you should be named Cain and Abel instead of Dane and Kane."

"I think that I'll probably end up being the Prodigal Son." A wistful look flitted across Dane's face. "I wanted to go to Brown, but Father insisted that I go to the same school as Kane."

"I'm surprised that your brother chose this school instead of Brown. I mean, if you have the money and can get in there you're golden."

"We have the family money, but no matter how many palms my father greased, Kane didn't have the SAT scores."

She cocked an eyebrow at him. "But you got in?"

"Yeah I got in," he replied shortly. "My father feels that because we're twins we should be joined at the hip for life." He sighed. "I can't wait until I graduate."

"Me either," Sybil agreed. "Hopefully I'll get a job with a salary that will enable me to buy my grandmother the things she deserves."

"Money isn't everything," Dane said with a crooked smile.

"Rich people always say that," Sybil retorted in a sardonic voice.

"I don't have any money."

She scoffed, "I heard that you're from one of the richest families in Texas."

"And for me to get any of that money I have to deal with all the strings that go along with it." With a brooding look he asked, "Why do you think that Kane and I have to share a car?"

"I hadn't thought about it."

"It's one of my father's ways of controlling us. That's also why we share an apartment. I wanted to stay in the dormitory, but they couldn't guarantee that we'd be roommates."

With eyes opened wide, Sybil protested, "You and Kane aren't little boys. Why does he insist on keeping you two together like that?"

"Father would never admit it, but I'm here to watch Kane. He's always been a hellion and got into some trouble back home." Dane's eyebrows were drawn together in a frown. "I resent that I had to give up my dream of going to Brown."

"I would have gone where I wanted and bump that shit."

"With what?" A look of embarrassment flitted across Dane's face. "As I said, I have no money of my own."

"Have you never worked?"

"During the summers Kane and I have worked at my father's offices, but we didn't get paid for it. We have accounts for our needs, but they can be cut off at the drop of a hat. I'd be destitute if that happened."

"I wouldn't want to live with something like that hanging over my head. Nanny always let me be independent."

"So you see, the grass isn't always greener on the other side."

Their Juvenile Law teacher, Professor Lehman, entered and walked to the microphone. A hush fell across the room.

Throughout the lecture, Sybil was very conscious of Dane sitting next to her and several times she felt his eyes on her.

At the end of the lecture, Professor Lehman said, "You have a project to complete before Christmas break."

Immediately a groan circulated throughout the room. He said brusquely, "You may pick a partner to work with for the research part of it, but you each have to turn in a separate finished product. If you don't cite your references it's an automatic zero." He waved a bunch of papers in his hand and then placed them on the desk. "Pick your handouts up on your way out the door."

"I'm so fucked," Dane muttered vehemently. "As it is I'm already behind in my Anatomy IV class." He looked earnestly at Sybil. "Will you partner up with me? I promise that I'll pull my own weight."

"All right." She added in a warning tone, "But don't try and give me all the hard stuff to do or I'm going to cut you loose."

"I won't," Dane promised. Lumbering to his feet he returned her pen. "I don't need to take notes." He took his forefinger, touched his temple and grinned. "I'm smarter than the average bear."

Sybil chuckled. She didn't realize it, but her eyes followed Dane as he disappeared out of her sight as quickly as he'd appeared at her side.

*****

When Sybil got into her dormitory room, she found Peyton viewing the contents of her closet with a critical look on her face.

"What's the problem now?" Sybil teased.

17

With her brow furrowed in frustration she said, "I can't find anything to wear that Kane hasn't already seen me in."

Sybil gave a shrug. "I would lend you something, but it would just fall off of you. You're all skin and bones. "

"It doesn't matter that you're heavy, Sybil. You have a beautiful face, and with that haircut you look like Halle Berry." Peyton continued in a soothing tone, "On top of that your mocha colored skin is a gorgeous contrast with your eyes."

Even though Sybil knew that Peyton was only trying to make her feel better she seethed at the implication that her body was not what it was supposed to be. She snapped, "I may not be as skinny as you but at least I'm healthy."

"I didn't mean that the way it came out, Sybil," Peyton said in a contrite voice.

"I'm sorry too, Peyton." Then she added with some hesitation, "I shouldn't snap at you because you do what you feel necessary to keep your body runway slim. It *is* your life."

Peyton bent her head, ashamed because she realized that Sybil knew how far she'd gone to stay thin. "Well, after I marry Kane I won't feel the need to be so skinny. And I'll probably put on weight after the babies start coming."

"Has Kane asked you to marry him?" She stared at her with a shocked look on her face.

"No," she replied with confidence. "But he will. I think that he's going to talk to his father about it when he goes home for Thanksgiving."

Watching Peyton closely she asked her, "Why don't you ever spend the night at Kane's apartment? We don't have a bed check or anything here."

"It's because Dane is there." Irritation flashed in Peyton's blue eyes. "Honestly, I think Kane is as old fashioned as his daddy is supposed to be but he'd die before he'd admit it." She said in a musing voice, "I don't think Kane likes his father very much, but he tries to get along with him because he holds the purse strings."

So he's blaming it on Dane. I should tell her that he's had some women spend the night but she won't believe me, or she does and she'll confront Kane. He'd only deny it and she'd believe him and end up resenting me for questioning his intentions towards her.

"When are you going home with him to meet his parents?" Sybil probed carefully.

"I don't know. I think that he doesn't want me there when he talks to them. It's better that he softens them up first."

"Oh," Sybil replied in a noncommittal voice.

"I'm going home when we break for Labor Day." A delighted look settled on her face. "My brother Conrad will be there on military leave. I haven't seen him in such a long time."

"I'm going home myself. I want to check on my grandmother. Last summer when I was home she felt bad too many days for my liking." Her face brightened in anticipation. "I also get to see my high school friend Chloe."

"Is she still living in Scranton?"

19

"Yes she is. We're going to have a girls' night out and I'm really looking forward to that."

*****

Sybil sat at a table in the library. Various textbooks were strewn across the top.

Tristan Glass sank into a chair in front of her.

"What's wrong with Peyton?" he said without preamble.

"What do you mean what's wrong with her?" She was immediately anxious.

"I tried to talk to her today and she snubbed me."

Sybil looked into Tristan's warm, brown eyes and felt a tug of sympathy for him. "Oh," she said relieved that it was nothing more serious. "What do you mean she snubbed you?"

"You know we have the same lab class." Tristan's eyes narrowed as he watched Sybil. "I asked her to be my partner and she said that she already had one."

"Well, maybe she did," Sybil offered gently.

"But she didn't," Tristan denied. "So I paired up with Becky Davis. Because there are an odd number of students in the class Peyton then had to latch on to another group."

"She did?" she said. Sybil shook her head in disapproval. "I'm sorry that she hurt your feelings, Tristan. I think that you're a really sweet guy."

Tristan gave her a look of gratitude. Then he said, "Don't feel sorry for me. Feel sorry for Peyton. She joined Penelope

Sotheby and Kane Hamilton. All through class their group argued and in the end didn't get their assignment done."

"Kane Hamilton's in that class?" Sybil asked. Trying to hide her expression she looked down and muttered, "I didn't know that."

"Yeah," Tristan said with a scathing look in his eyes. "He's my frat brother and all but he can be a real asshole. He was really mean to her and by the end of class Peyton was crying."

"What were they arguing about?" Sybil probed.

"I didn't hear all of it," Tristan said crossly. "But I do know that he called her stupid."

Sybil stared at Tristan's cheeks flushed with anger. "It's obvious that you still care for Peyton," she said quietly.

"I do." Then he said abruptly, "Why doesn't she return my calls?"

"Are you honestly trying to tell me that you don't know who Peyton is dating?" Sybil scrutinized Tristan's face and saw confusion in his eyes.

"No," Tristan said slowly. "I didn't know that she was seeing anyone. Who the hell is it?"

Sybil simply stared at him.

A dawning realization struck him.

"Are you trying to tell me that she's dating Hamilton?"

Sybil nodded her head in assent.

"No wonder she got so upset today when he acted like he didn't want to be her partner."

"I know that it's a bad thing that they're dating, but how about you telling me why you think the same."

Tristan looked away, avoiding Sybil's gaze. After an uncomfortable silence he mumbled, "I can't. He's my frat brother. There's a code."

Sybil studied Tristan's strawberry locks that curled around the nape of his neck. Then she felt her attention being drawn away from him to a spot on the other side of the library.

Dane was leaning casually on the side of a vending machine watching them. Their eyes met and he strutted towards them.

"You're in my seat, man," he drawled to Tristan once he stood behind his chair.

Tristan looked up and when he saw that it was Dane a look of resentment settled on his face. Quickly masking it he stood. "I was leaving anyhow, Hamilton." He cast Sybil a look of caution. "I'll talk to you soon."

"See you, Tristan," she said with a soft smile at him.

Caught off guard by Dane's high-handed behavior she glowered at him as he settled in the seat Tristan had vacated. "What in the world would make you think that's your seat?"

"You agreed to be my partner on our research papers," Dane answered smoothly. "Too many people can't have the same information or Professor Lehman will flunk us."

"That's not what Tristan was talking to me about," she sputtered.

"Then what did he want?" Dane asked.

Sybil's eyebrows rose in surprise. "None of your business," she retorted.

"Not yet," Dane said. With agility he rose and confidently walked off, hitting the exit door with the flat of his hand disappearing as quickly as he'd appeared.

Sybil's mouth gaped open as she watched him. *What the hell?*

Chapter 2

As the train rumbled through the middle of Scranton stopping traffic, Sybil glanced at her watch and shook her head in frustration. It was getting late and she knew that her grandmother would be worried about her because it was almost dark and she didn't like Sybil driving at night.

A mixture of dust and dirt from the grinding wheels drifted inside her car and made her cough. During her drive, she'd been alternately rolling her windows up and down as she'd tried to adjust to the changing weather pattern from New England to Scranton.

Once the train track gates lifted, she hit the gas and her car stalled. When she turned the key in the ignition, her Ford Focus sputtered and then jerked into motion.

In her grandmother's gravel and sand driveway, she shut the car off and swallowed a lump in her throat. Thanks to her grandmother, the small gray house had been a haven to her after she'd been abandoned by her father. She'd never realized what it meant to be discarded.

Immediately the screen door was flung open and Nanny Masterson stood on the threshold hugging her arms around her to ward off the chill. Smiling lips revealed teeth that were stained from lack of dentist visits. Nanny wore a red, checkered seersucker housedress with a gray sweater pulled over it. Bedroom slippers and a checkered scarf on her head completed her outfit and to Sybil, she looked absolutely beautiful. Leaning heavily on a stick, Nanny started toward the front steps.

Hastily, Sybil got out of the car and slamming the door rushed up the steps and threw her arms around her grandmother's waist.

Sybil's grandmother embraced her, hugging her tightly.

Finally they broke apart. "Nanny, I've missed you much," Sybil exclaimed.

"Me too. I ain't seen you in six weeks."

"It seems like a lifetime," Sybil replied.

Nanny studied her granddaughter thoroughly and pleased with what she saw, she smiled. Nanny's smile was so bright it lit up the grey evening that had dark clouds hovering on the horizon. "You look good, Sybil."

Sybil gave a self-conscious shrug and shook her head sadly. "You just say that because you love me. Every time I come home I'm bigger than the last time you saw me."

Nanny led her inside the house and to the kitchen. "There's nothing wrong with having some meat on your bones."

"There is in today's world."

"Who would even notice your size when you have those eyes that people would kill for? I'll never forget the first time I saw you. Your daddy brought you here for a visit. Before he could tell me who you were I looked into those eyes and held out my arms for you. I knew that you was his."

"Is that why he chose to dump me on you and never return?" Sybil asked harshly.

Nanny stood in front of the stove and turned the knob. The eye on the gas range lit and almost immediately the old kettle as it heated began to rock. Throughout Sybil's childhood the sound had represented good times of hot tea and cinnamon toast as she sat at the table doing her homework.

Nanny gave her a stern look. "That was over eighteen years ago, Sybil. You have to learn how to let things go. If people hurt you and you let it fester inside of you you're only hurting yourself and they win."

Sybil bit her lip and turned her head away to stare through the open door that led to the living room. She hid a smile when she saw her grandmother's ever present plastic slipcovers on her sofa.

"He's gone to a better place, Sybil. You have to let it go."

"That's easy to do," Sybil replied shortly. "It's not hard to forget someone who was never a part of your life."

Nanny's steady gaze captured Sybil's. "He paid for whatever he did to you and your momma before she passed," she said in a grave voice. "When I went down there to Macon to identify your daddy's body, they had to pry his eyes open for me to see if it was him. I'm lucky that his eyes were mismatched. Otherwise he would've been put in an unmarked grave as an indigent."

*****

Sybil and Chloe sat at a small table in the barely lit speakeasy on the outskirts of town. Cigarette smoke swirled in the air and Sybil's eyes began to water. She rubbed her eyes with her fingers trying not to completely rub off all her makeup. "I don't think that I'm going to stay here much longer. My eyes are beginning to sting."

"If you leave now, you won't get to see Aramis," Chloe protested. "He usually drops in after his shop closes. He's always asking me about you. It might be worth the wait for you to stick around."

"Hell, I don't want to see no damn Aramis." Sybil gave a derogatory snort. "He's a married man and I don't sleep with them. I mean, what's the point?"

"You mean to tell me that you don't know?" Shocked, Chloe stared at her. "Aramis and his wife split up."

"They did?" Now Sybil's eyes opened wide with speculation. "That certainly was a short-lived marriage."

"They said she was cheating on him with some young boy. I can't imagine anyone cheating on Aramis' fine ass self. They say she said that all he did was work all the time and she was tired of being home alone."

"That's crazy," Sybil protested. "I mean, if he was working hard in order to provide for them I think she was pretty selfish."

"Well, bad news for her might be good news for you. You know how crazy Aramis was about you. He was pretty upset when you went away to college."

27

"Yeah, we had a big fight." Sybil added in a somewhat bitter tone, "Then after he cooled off he said that he'd wait for me and the next thing I knew he up and married Jolene."

"I think that he did that out of spite. He told his cousin Benny that he didn't think that you'd ever want to come back here to live and he was just a small time boy in comparison to the kind of men that you would be meeting in that fancy school in New England."

Sybil made another snort of derision. "There are more men to choose from here than in New London. There are only twenty black men at my school and every last one of them has a white girl hanging on his arm."

Chloe's mouth fell open from surprise. "Damn! I didn't know that the pickin's were that slim. But why do you have to go with a black man? If they can get a white girl, you can go with a white boy."

"I've gone out on dates since I've been there but nothing serious ever came of them." Sybil shrugged her shoulders. "I'm not really their type. They all like those anorexic looking women."

Chloe eyed her friend's figure. "Girl, that's the trend everywhere. Besides, you ain't all that big. What size are you now?"

"I'm a ten going on a twelve," Sybil muttered.

"Well," she drawled, "what goes for big up there is skinny down here. I'm a size fourteen, but after I slap this snapping ass pussy on a man he forgets all about the folds and keeps coming back for more." Then she lifted her glass and chugged the liquid down in one swoop.

Sybil picked up her glass and after taking a sip looked over the rim at Chloe. She said with a gleam in her eyes, "Aramis just walked in."

"You really should do him while you're in town." Chloe slammed her glass down on the table. "I mean, why the hell not?"

"Even though it's been too damn long since I got some, I don't think so. Besides, why should he get away with what he did?"

"Aramis will be thinking that it's all about him and you haven't met anyone who can match him. But it will also be a way for you to figure out if you have any lasting feelings for him." Chloe shot her a sidelong glance. "You were pretty crushed when you found out he married Jolene."

Sybil looked down at some imaginary stain on the table.

"I admit he made a huge mistake, Sybil. But don't do it for him. Do it for yourself. A night with Aramis will do one of two things. You can settle your past. Or the two of you can restart a future. Don't be afraid to find out which is right for you."

Sybil sat quiet for a moment digesting the validity of Chloe's argument. Finally she admitted grudgingly, "Aramis *does* have the longest penis I've ever had, but I've got a problem with him. He doesn't like to do," she paused and gave Chloe a look full of meaning, "the thing."

"Oh my God!" Chloe leaned forward and said, "Aramis doesn't do the thing?"

"Nope."

"Well, he really needs to do the thing," she drawled. "Otherwise he'll never be able to keep a woman."

"You're probably right. Because once you've had that it's hard to go without it."

Chloe gave a tinkling laugh. "Maybe *that's* why Jolene was cheating on him. I hate to say it, but I understand. But seriously, Sybil, don't know how to make a man do that? You know when they're kissing you on your stomach you take your hands and cradle his head with a firm grasp and you push it down there."

"I've tried that with Aramis, but he resists, popping his head up like a jack-in-the-box so I just give up."

"Try him tonight; if he really wants to hook you. He'll get right on down there."

Sybil gave her a look full of doubt.

"Listen, if he acts like he doesn't want to, then you tell him that you've changed your mind. You don't want to fuck him. I bet he'll get his tongue down there in a hurry."

Sybil chuckled at Chloe's mischievous expression.

"Sybil, when it comes to sex women have all the power and its right between their legs. Men will do whatever they have to do to get some good sex." Then Chloe quipped, "Uh, oh! Here comes your future candy licker."

Aramis made his way over to them, weaving his way in and out of people who stood around chatting or walking to the dance floor. A tall, leggy, light-skinned looking woman with shoulder length hair stopped him. Sybil saw the flash of his pearly white teeth as he smiled at whatever she was saying. Then he gave his head a negative shake and resumed his stride in the direction of Sybil and Chloe.

Sybil took a sip of her rum and pineapple juice as her eyes drank in Aramis' body. She felt heat stirring in her loins with the memory of the time they'd been lovers. Aramis had filled out considerably since she'd been his high school sweetheart and he looked yummy as he swaggered toward them in the gait she knew so well.

Once he reached their table he flashed them his million dollar smile and sat in the empty chair. "I heard you were in town."

Aramis' voice was warm and sensual.

Suddenly Sybil squirmed in her seat from pent up sexual frustration. Batting her eyelashes seductively at him she breathed, "Who told you I was here?"

"My mother saw you and your grandmother in the grocery store yesterday."

"Why didn't she stop and say hello?" The minute the words were spoken she wished she could retract them. She knew that the reason Aramis' mother hadn't made her presence known to her. His mother had never liked her. When Sybil met Aramis during their sophomore year of high school he'd been dating

Sapphire, the daughter of a prominent lawyer in town and his family thought that he'd hit pay dirt.

Then he'd fallen head over heels in love with Sybil and dropped Sapphire. When Sybil got a scholarship to college and made plans to leave, Aramis' mother had been very vocal with her displeasure, thinking that Sybil had ruined his and her only chance of climbing the social ladder in Scranton.

"I think that she was in too much of a hurry." Aramis' eyes shifted uneasily. "She had an appointment at her hairdresser's or something."

Sybil let his flimsy excuse pass without a comment. *Hell, I'm leaving tomorrow. I don't want to rehash that old dirt. I just need to get laid before I go.*

Aramis looked at Sybil and Chloe's empty glasses. "Would you ladies like a refill?"

"Sure, why not? I'll have another rum and pineapple juice."

"Thank you, Aramis," Sybil said. "I'll have the same."

Grinning at them he said, "I'll be right back."

Once they were alone Chloe leaned over and said, "He looks good doesn't he?"

Sybil raised her eyebrows in her usual mannerism. "He damn sure does. I'm glad that you drove tonight. I think that you might be right. Maybe I should spend a little alone time with him."

Aramis reappeared with lightning speed and placed two glasses on the table saying, "Drink up, ladies."

The music in the speakeasy was a combination of oldies and goodies. Suddenly the newest version of the electric slide music began to play and the dance floor was soon packed as women who hadn't been asked to dance all night jumped up to participate.

Jumping to her feet Chloe said, "Let's join the fun."

Aramis stood and held his hand out to Sybil. When he hoisted her out of her seat, she felt a shiver of anticipation run up and down her spine at the gesture.

Dutifully she let her hand be enveloped into Aramis' calloused one as he put his stamp of ownership on her. By doing so he squashed the hope of any man in the club who might be waiting for a chance to talk to her.

Chloe got in the front line and Sybil stood next to her with Aramis on the outside. They fell in step and mentally Sybil counted her steps. *One, two, three, slide, one, two three, and dip.*

All of a sudden, Aramis moved from her side and got behind her. Instead of getting in the horizontal row, he placed his hands on the side of her hips and planted his body flush to hers.

Sybil felt Aramis' rock, hard dick as it was sandwiched between her cheeks and she felt turned on by her own sexual power. They moved in unison and the deejay played the song consecutively three times. All the while they danced Aramis' penis didn't subside.

*****

Sybil and Aramis stood outside in the darkness by Chloe's car and waited for her to join them.

"I know that Chloe told you that I'm divorced from Jolene," Aramis said in a sad voice.

"Yes she did," Sybil responded honestly. "Are you okay?"

"I will be," he said. "I'm just glad that that Jolene can't have children. That would've made things so much harder."

"I guess that is a mixed blessing," Sybil said doubtfully.

"When are you leaving?"

"I'm going back to school tomorrow afternoon."

"My place isn't far from here." He asked with a quizzical smile, "Would you like to go and see it?"

And there it is... "Sure, why not?" she responded lightly. Burying her hands deeper into her blazer pockets she said, "Let me go and tell Chloe that you're taking me home."

"I'll wait right here," Aramis said with a pleased expression.

When Sybil reentered the club, Chloe was talking to the club's owner. Sybil tapped her on her shoulder.

Chloe looked at her and said loudly, "So you're leaving with Aramis."

"Shush," Sybil said. "Don't put my business in the street like that."

"Oops, I'm sorry," Chloe said without a bit of penitence in her voice. "But you got to know the way you two were all over each other on the dance floor that everyone in here pretty much figured out that y'all gonna fuck tonight."

"Stop being so coarse, Chloe," she chided her. "He wants to show me his new house," Sybil explained with dignity.

"He wants to show you more than his house." Chloe's raucous laugh filled the room.

"And I'm ready to see everything he has to offer," Sybil said dryly. "Listen, I don't think I'll get another chance to see you before I go so I want to hug your neck before I leave."

Chloe stood and practically towered over Sybil's five feet seven inch frame.   She reached down, gave her a mammoth hug, and whispered in Sybil's ear, "Have a good time with Aramis. Always remember, the pink stuff holds the power."

Sybil smothered laughter and she gave Chloe a hard squeeze, released her, and went back outside.

Aramis stood waiting by his car, impatiently shifting from one foot to the other, eager to get her out of the cool air and into his house.

The drive on the small, curvy road was a short one, but it seemed way too long for Sybil. Suddenly Aramis slowed and turned into a housing development. He parked his car outside a small duplex. "We're here," he said in a voice filled with pride.

"I like it," she complimented.

Aramis proudly opened the door and she walked into a foyer. Obviously, Aramis had left the heat on while he was gone because the house was quite warm. To the left was a room devoid of furniture. He said a little self-consciously, "Jolene took all of the furniture. It was easier for me to let her have it than to argue about it."

She cheated on you yet she gets everything. I would never let anyone get away with that. Off to the right was a bedroom that was also empty and then Sybil followed him into the kitchen that housed a small kitchen table with chairs and two bar stools at a snack bar. She turned to Aramis and teased, "I see that you made sure you have something to sit on while you feed your face."

His eyes twinkled with amusement. "That's a necessity, not an option."

When Aramis looked at her like that it seemed as if he hadn't changed at all from the teenager she'd been so crazy about four years earlier.

"Let me show you my other bedroom," he said. His voice sounded comforting and familiar.

Sybil followed Aramis down the hallway and found herself inside a bedroom with a king-sized bed. She saw an adjoining bathroom and with a small smile left his side to take a peek. It was bare but clean.

She turned and found herself against Aramis' body because he'd followed her. His breath fanned her face and she could smell the chewing gum he'd plopped into his mouth earlier in order to freshen his breath.

"Oh," she gasped, "I didn't know that you were behind me."

"I've always been behind you, Sybil," he whispered in a serious undertone. He put his hand in the small of her back and propelled her back into his bedroom. Aramis pulled back the sheets.

With a feeling of anticipation she lay down on the bed. Sybil watched Aramis in the dimness of the room. Light from a streetlamp filtered through the room illuminating Aramis' form.

Speedily, he pulled his shirt over his head and then bent and unbuckled his trousers. He kicked off his shoes, and then slid his pants and underwear down in one motion. When they were gathered around his ankles he stepped out of them. When he straightened he spread his legs and anticipation ignited in her gut at the sight of his penis. Fascinated she watched it twitch as it rose and remained pointed in her direction.

Aramis walked over to the side of the bed and looked down at her as she laid completely still waiting for him to join her. "I think about you all the time, but I never thought that we'd be like this again. It's a dream come true for me."

Sybil gave a start of surprise. *I hope he doesn't read more into this than it is.* Not knowing what to say she chose to remain silent, not wanting to spoil the mood.

Aramis reached down and began to pull at her dress. She lifted her hips and then her arms, eager to help him. He tugged at the sides of her underwear. Her thong easily broke away from her and she smiled with satisfaction. When she settled back down on the bed, Sybil drew her knees up and let them fall open.

Aramis took his fingers and parted the lips of her vagina. The he inserted his middle finger. Very slowly he slid it up into her and she got wet and it made a squelching sound. He slid his finger in an upward and downward motion, and when he removed it there was another squelching sound.

With eyes closed she writhed at his touch.

Then with his other hand Aramis unclipped her front bra closure and her breasts bounced once they were freed from their prison. Not withdrawing his finger from inside her, Aramis joined her on the mattress.

"Kiss me, Sybil," he demanded in a throaty whisper.

Sybil took her arms and placed them around his shoulders, at the same time lifting her mouth to meet his as it descended towards her. When their mouths met and she felt his tongue, she seemed to step back into time.

Aramis explored her mouth as if it was new territory to him and she felt her sexual frustration begin to mount as she let him drink her in. Then slowly he withdrew his mouth and planted his lips on the side of her neck. He planted warm kisses and with the palms of his hands began to knead her breasts.

Then Aramis stroked the midnight nipples on her breasts.

Sybil gasped from pleasure.

He murmured, "Your breasts are so full." Aramis scooted down until his head lay on her stomach. Aramis slid the palm of his hand under one buttock and kneaded it. With the other hand once again inserted his finger in her and played with her.

Sybil cradled Aramis' head. Then she lightly applied pressure as he began to kiss her stomach. She applied even more pressure. She felt him tense up and try to move his mouth back up to her breasts, but she didn't release the hold she had on him. She pushed him farther down. She felt his resistance fade and she loosened her grip on him. He moved his mouth to the bottom of her stomach. Without releasing her hold on him, she spread her legs.

Aramis slowly withdrawing his finger tasted her with his tongue.

"Oh, that's right, Aramis. Lick me," she breathed. "That's what I need."

Upon hearing those words, Aramis plunged his long tongue inside her and pulled her legs up, burying his face between her thighs.

Sybil felt his breath fanning her womanhood and she relaxed, letting her thighs open as wide as they could.

Aramis began to lick her. At first his tongue was slow, but then a moan of sheer awe from him reverberated into the room as he began to devour her. At first he suckled her gently. Then his tongue became more intense. Aramis explored her in an upwards direction and when she felt the tip of his tongue tickle her clit; she spilled her desire into his mouth.

"Yes, yes, yes, Aramis. That's the way to do it to me," she screamed. Time seemed to stand still for Sybil. Her head lolled on the pillow as she tried to hold back her next orgasm, not wanting to end this pleasure but when Aramis once again took his tongue and held it motionless in her center she exploded, drenching his face.

Reaching down to the floor to the shirt he'd earlier discarded, Aramis wiped his face. Then in one fluid movement he entered her slick, wet, saturated body.

"Oh my God, Aramis," Sybil screamed.

"You're the best lover I've ever had," Aramis grunted over her as he moved inside her.

Sybil arched her back to him and met stroke after stroke. He ground into her, releasing her fluids as he filled her with his sex.

*****

Sybil woke to a strange sensation that she was being watched. Blinking sleepily she looked around the unfamiliar room.

Aramis stood in the doorway and watching her.

She smiled at him.

"Is it my imagination or is that the best sex we ever had?" he said.

"It's not your imagination," she responded softly,

"I should have been going down on you a long time ago. Maybe then you wouldn't have left me," he teased.

"Maybe not," she said, joining in the light banter. Sitting up she looked around. "Where are my clothes?"

"I hung your dress up in the closet. Bacon and eggs are ready for you in the kitchen."

When she was dressed, she padded barefoot out into the kitchen and sat at the table. "This is very thoughtful of you, Aramis." After she drank some orange juice and took a bite of eggs, she said, "After I eat, I need to get out of here. I haven't even packed."

"You can't leave before we make some decisions."

Confusion clouded Sybil's face. "What do you mean?"

"I mean that what we have is too beautiful to let go. I think that we have a second chance to get things right."

Uh-oh! It was good but not that damn good. I'm finally ready to move on. She silently dug into her food. Once finished, she picked up her plate and went to the sink filling it with water and dishwashing liquid.

"See," Aramis said as he watched her with satisfaction. "You look so perfect here. We can do this."

Once the dishes were on the drain-board she sat down next to him and watched him manipulate the controls of the video game he'd started playing while she'd cleaned up the kitchen.

She said gently, "Aramis, I'm in college in New London. After I graduate I want to pursue my master's degree. How do you think that we could possibly have a relationship?"

Aramis got a stubborn look on his face and said, "I know that it would be hard but we could do it. We're older now, and more mature."

"We're not that old," she denied.

"I've opened my own shop and hired a mechanic to work for me. I could fly up to see you and when I can't come I'll send for you."

"I wouldn't have time for you to visit or for me to come and see you," she responded gently.

"You would if you wanted to." The words seemed to burst from his bowels.

"But I don't want to. We were together and you up and married another woman." She gave Aramis a look of controlled censure. "It took me close to a year to get over your betrayal, but I did get over it and it wasn't the end of the world for me. So I'm not willing to go the extra mile for someone who has already done the unforgivable."

Aramis's countenance looked like a thundercloud. He was livid that she'd brought that up. "I married Jolene because I felt abandoned. You need to take some of the blame for that."

"I refuse to feel guilty because I wanted more. When I was offered a scholarship it was a godsend for me. Education is the road to the successful life that I envision." After a long pause she said glaring at him, "You didn't even have the decency to call and tell me that you'd gotten married. You left it up to Chloe to do it."

He looked away, avoiding her condemnation.

"But all of this is a moot point because I don't want to come back here to live."

"So you're saying that Scranton is too slow for you?"

"It's not the size of the town but what goes on in it." She added for emphasis. "I want to go to Harvard for my Master of Social Science Administration."

Aramis snorted derisively. "Everybody wants to go to Harvard so don't be start packing your things just yet."

"I have a good chance of getting in," Sybil retorted with confidence. "If I keep my G.P.A. up this term, I have a real good chance."

Aramis spat out, "So you used me for sex. That's all last night was for you?"

Sybil placed her hand on his knee in an attempt to soften the blow. "Last night was great, but let's not read more into it than it was."

He knocked her hand off of him. "I did things to you last night that I've never done for another woman!"

"Well then," she quipped. "I've introduced you to a brave new world."

"Brave new world," Aramis repeated suspiciously. "What's that? Some college book I haven't read?"

"Actually," she said, "It's usually read in high school." Sybil retorted with a bland look on her face.

He turned accusing eyes to her. "You always did think that you were too good for me."

Sybil heaved a sigh now tired of the conversation. "What do we have in common, Aramis?" She stared at his head that was again averted. Then she said very slowly as if speaking to a child, "I don't even like video games."

On the ride back to her grandmother's house neither she nor Aramis spoke. She glanced at his stern profile. His eyebrows were drawn together in a frown and his mouth was clenched tightly from anger.

Barely giving the car time to stop she opened her door and got out.

Without uttering a word he reached over and slammed the door.

Sybil watched him back out of the driveway, his tires screeching and kicking up the dust and gravel. She didn't know it but a curl of satisfaction hovered around the corners of her mouth. *Aramis thought that he could just walk back into my life after what he did? I would never let a man do me wrong and get away with it.*

Chapter 3

Sybil unlocked the door to her room. She spied the tumbled mess of clothing on Peyton's bed and stared at it. *Is she back? I can't remember if she took any of those clothes with her and her side of the room is always a disaster so I can't tell from that either.*

She heard the door being opened behind her and Peyton bounded inside, her blonde hair flying as she pushed her bangs out of her face.

She and Peyton screamed, ran to each other and hugged. "I missed you so much, Sybil. I didn't have any female with an ounce of intelligence to talk to while I was at home."

Sybil grinned. "I had someone to talk to but I still missed you."

"Mmm," Peyton sniffed appreciatively. "Did you get some new perfume?"

"Yes, Nanny bought it for me. First I opened a box of socks and old lady underwear." Sybil rolled her eyes. "But then," she pointed to the small box that lay on her bed, "she handed me that bottle of perfume."

"What kind did she buy?" Peyton asked as she sat on top of a pile of unfolded clothes.

"It's called Chance and I absolutely love it. But I wish she wouldn't buy me things because I know that she doesn't have a lot of money and she sends me an allowance." Sybil heaved a sigh. "I can't wait until I graduate and get a good job. I'm moving her up here so I can take care of her. I want her to be closer to me."

"She might not want to come," Peyton said with uncharacteristic insight. "You know old people don't like change."

"She won't have a choice," Sybil said firmly. "Besides, Nanny's not that old. She had my dad real young and he followed suit with me. She'll have to come. I'm all she has left."

The telephone interrupted their conversation. Peyton grabbed the phone and as she listened her face got a look of frustration on it. But she calmly said, "Of course I understand. Well then, tomorrow evening will be good." She whispered, "I love you."

Sybil got up and pretended to busy herself by unpacking. She'd left a lot of her clothes on hangers and she pulled them out one by one and started putting them away.

"Sybil."

At the soft call Sybil turned around.

Peyton had hung up the phone. She unsuccessfully tried to blink away the tears glistening in her eyes. "What were we talking about?" Peyton said, "Oh, did Nanny like the gold earrings you bought her?"

Sybil rolled her eyes again. "She loved them but told me that they were too fancy for her and she fussed at me for spending my allowance on her."

"Those were hard for you to get," Peyton affirmed. "You ate oatmeal for two weeks and for dinner made do with that slop in the school cafeteria. But at least you accomplished what you wanted."

"Now I have to start all over again."

"Why?" Peyton asked.

Sybil raised an eyebrow and said firmly, "Christmas is right around the corner and I want her to have the matching bracelet." Trying to pretend that nothing was wrong, she asked Peyton, "Did you buy anything when you we were home?"

"Conrad took me downtown and bought me a couple of dresses. I also bought a pair of cowboy boots so when I go to Kane's ranch during spring break they'll already be broken in when we go horseback riding."

"Oh that was a smart thing to do. The worse thing in the world is to try and break in a new pair of anything on your feet when you need them to feel comfortable."

"Yeah," Peyton replied in a distant voice. She turned and stared vacantly out the window.

Sybil walked up behind her and touched her on the shoulder. "Are you okay?"

"I'm sure that you figured out that was Kane on the phone." Peyton mumbled, "He said that he was tired after his trip and he can't see me until tomorrow."

"I think that's reasonable, Peyton," Sybil acknowledged in a soothing voice. "Why are you so upset?"

"Because the whole weekend we were gone, I didn't hear from Kane. Then he left a message at the desk to be given to me when I got here that he'd be over around six o'clock. Now he just up and cancels." Peyton's face was full of anger and pain. "Doesn't he want to see me? I did nothing but think about him the whole time I was gone."

"Then why didn't you call him and make it plain to him how much you were missing him?"

"He went hunting in Maine with some of his friends and I didn't have the number to the lodge where they were staying. And he never answered his cell. Then my cell was cut off for nonpayment."

"Peyton," Sybil said exasperatedly, "if you're angry with Kane about his behavior, tell him."

"No man likes a nagging woman. My daddy is always complainin' to Ma that she nags too much."

"But they're married and you and Kane aren't. Make him respect you from the get go. Otherwise, further on down the road you're always going to have to fight to get treated that way you want."

Steel showed in Peyton's eyes. She stated with a hard edge to her voice, "I know what I'm doing."

Later that night, Sybil was awakened to the sound of her dormitory room closing. *She's making a mistake by running after him. Men like a challenge.*

Less than an hour later she was awakened again by the room door opening and being shut.

Peyton crept into the room without turning on a light, and slid into bed.

Sybil listened to sobs of anguish Peyton tried to muffle by burying her face deep into her pillow. A fiery wrath filled Sybil when she thought of Kane Hamilton.

*****

A couple of days later, Sybil was sitting in the stacks with her head buried in her adolescent psychology book when she heard her name being called.

"Sybil Masterson. Sybil where are you?"

She screwed her face up, and whispered loudly, "I'm over here in the corner. Who is it and what do you want?"

Dane Hamilton rounded the corner and when he did he was grinning widely. "Why in the hell are you all the way back here? This could be dangerous. Unless you're back here for what everyone else does."

"Meaning?" Sybil said, leaning back in her chair with her arms folded across her breasts.

"Girl," he drawled, "don't you know people screw up here in these stacks?"

Sybil's mouth fell open in surprise. "No, I didn't, but obviously you know from experience."

"Maybe." Dane sat in the booth next to her and said with a wicked grin, "I'm the kind of guy that when the mood hits, I go for the gusto."

"Don't forget to stop by the clinic tomorrow and get an AIDS test," Sybil muttered sarcastically.

Now when Dane spoke his Texas accent seemed heavier than ever. "Now that's a real mean thing for you to say, Sybil. I always keep at least two condoms on me. Wanna see?" He began to reach into his pocket to pull his wallet out.

"No thank you, Dane," she responded hastily. "By the way, why are you here bothering me when I'm trying to study for Friday's test?"

Dane returned his wallet to his back pocket. He said with a cocky smile, "This is how you greet me when I been all over this damn place looking for you? I find you northern women to be some cold heifers."

"And I find you men from Texas to be full of shit." Sybil flipped one hand outwards. "My question is why are you looking for me?"

"I need a study partner for the next test. I thought that you might be willing to help me."

"Now why would you think that?" She pointed at herself with her index finger and said, "*I* don't need a study partner."

He gave her an engaging smile that revealed a row of pearly white teeth. "Well then, how about you being my tutor? I'll pay you."

"Your tutor?" Sybil asked suspiciously.

"Hell yeah. As a matter of fact since we've got some classes together it would be easy for us to be study partners. You can make some money on the side," he wheedled. Dane pushed his cowboy hat back with the tip of his finger. He leaned the chair against the back of the booth and it lifted his feet off the floor.

"I'm surprised you care about your grades so much." Sybil couldn't help sounding a little snide. "All you need to do is graduate. You've already been accepted into med school down there in Texas and a job is waiting for you in your daddy's practice."

Dane gave her a serious look. "I may not want to go back Texas after I graduate from school so I need to have other options. How much would it cost for you to help me get through the rest of the term?"

I sure can use the money. I could also keep an eye on Kane through Dane to see what he's really up to with Peyton. "I've got the highest G.P.A. in our class. It would cost you fifty dollars an hour."

"Whew," Dane whistled. "You are an expensive filly."

She shrugged. "If you think that's too much money, at the Challenger Building there's a list of tutors. Go and find somebody else." She began packing up her things and putting her books and papers away.

"You sure are frisky," Dane sputtered.

"Also, if you're going to be around me I would appreciate it if you stopped being so Texan."

"What the hell do you mean by that?" Dane said, lowering his chair to the floor.

"The hat and boots." She pointed at his attire. "Have you not noticed that no one else on campus dresses that way?"

"I don't care about that." Dane looked at her with narrowed eyes. "I'm my own person."

"Even Kane doesn't dress like that every day." She looked at him intuitively. "I think that you do that just so people don't confuse the two of you."

An unfathomable look crossed Dane's face. He said through gritted teeth, "The only person who would confuse me with my twin is someone who doesn't know either of us."

She gave him an unyielding look. "I have another request."

"You've got an awful lot of demands for me to be the one paying you," Dane stated tersely.

"Stop missing so many classes. I didn't even know we had the some of the same until you told me. All the tutoring in the world won't help you if you skip lectures, and I'm not going to let you copy off me," she said firmly.

Dane digested Sybil's words as he studied the look of gravity on her face for what felt like a full minute. "All right, Sybil." He stood and held out his hand. "By the way, I'll get rid of my hat, but not my boots."

"That's better than nothing." She grinned and held her hand out. When Dane shook her hand she felt a curling sensation in her abdomen that she couldn't define.

*****

The next morning in their Adolescent Psychology class Dane plopped down in the empty desk next to her and handed her a steaming cup of coffee.

She looked at him in surprise.

He scribbled something down on a piece of paper and handed it to her. She read the words. *It's hot, black and sweet. Just like you.*

Sybil felt herself blush. *Is he flirting with me?* She slid him a sidelong look, and when she did he winked at her.

An hour later when Professor Devine was in the middle of closing his lecture she felt Dane's eyes once again on her.

Professor Devine said, "Remember the famous line from *Candide*, 'This is the best of all possible worlds...'

From somewhere in the back of the auditorium she heard someone shout, "Pangloss from *Candide* didn't know what the hell he was talking about. This can't be the best of all possible worlds because this class *is* hell on earth. I can't wait until it's over."

Laughter erupted from the students as they tried to quickly leave so they could talk outside. It was all Sybil could do not to burst into laughter but she saw by the glowering look on the professor's face that he was not amused.

Professor Devine directed his booming voice to the back of the auditorium." Mr. Charles Rothchild, please stay after class. I'd like to have a word with you."

"Uh oh," she whispered. "He's going to get in trouble."

"Naw," Dane replied. "Rothchild is a frat guy. We're expected to act silly. It's not that serious. He'll just get yelled at."

Sybil stood and packed her backpack. She turned her back to the front of the room because Professor Devine was glaring at everyone and she didn't want him able to read her lips. "Everyone knows that Devine isn't someone to be fooled with."

"Then he needs to lighten up." Dane ambled to his feet. "Life's too short."

She gave him a look of appreciation. "Thanks for the coffee, Dane. But you shouldn't have."

"It's the least that I can do. You stayed up until after eleven o'clock last night quizzing me for our test this afternoon."

"But you pay me to do that," Sybil said softly.

"It's worth the money. I really feel ready to take the test." Dane took the palm of his hand and rubbed his stomach. "That coffee wasn't enough. Did you eat breakfast?"

"No," she said, feeling the pangs of hunger she'd ignored during Professor Devine's lecture.

"I've got the Mercedes. Let's go down to The Cracker Barrel and have something to eat before the next class."

"I don't like that place," she demurred. "Can't we go somewhere else? I'll treat."

"You're the only person I ever heard say that they don't like their food. I want some fried catfish and they make it the way I like it."

54

"I've never eaten there," she said truthfully. "I just don't like the looks of it with those big, white chairs or the name for that matter."

"What's the matter, girl?" Dane threw his head back and guffawed. "Do you think that there's a bunch of white people in a barrel or something down there?"

Dane's laughter attracted the notice of a few remaining students as they passed them.

Sybil joined Dane's laughter before playfully punching him in the arm. Brushing past him Sybil flung her next words over her shoulder. "Oh all right," she said strutting up the aisle. "But the food better be excellent."

Once seated inside the restaurant Dane told the waitress, "I'll have the catfish." He leaned back and said suggestively staring into Sybil's eyes, "I love to eat fish."

Their eyes remained locked. Sybil felt as if she were drowning in a pool of pure green water.

The small cough from the waitress broke their trance.

"I think that I'll have the smothered biscuits and gravy with sausage," she said hastily handing her the menu.

Once they were alone Dane said, "That's a good Texas dish."

"Do you miss Texas much?" Sybil stammered, still flustered from Dane's innuendo.

"Yeah, I do," he said. "I always feel like a fish out of water anywhere else."

The waitress reappeared at their table with their food and once she left, Sybil attacked hers with relish. Then stunned, she stopped.

Dane had his hands clasped and his head was bent. He was obviously saying grace. Once he lifted his head he broke into a grin at the look on Sybil's face. "I can't break the habit, no matter how far away from home I am."

She felt like a heathen because she hadn't attended church while living in New London.

She stuttered, "I don't know why I'm so shocked, but I am."

"We Texans take our religion and traditions very seriously," Dane said with an enigmatic look on his face. He spoke now almost as if he thought he was talking to himself. "Prayer is a good thing but there are other traditions we should break. Instead, we follow them no matter how ridiculous they may be."

"But you didn't pray the time we all ate at The Outback."

"You and Peyton were strangers to me then. I don't show my true colors until I feel comfortable with someone. Now eat your food."

Sybil picked her fork up and while she ate she surreptitiously studied Dane. His fingernails were clean, he didn't lean his elbows on the table, and he'd opened his napkin and put in his lap. *Humph*!

After their meal, instead of driving back to campus, Dane headed in the opposite direction.

"Where are you going?" Sybil asked as she viewed the unfamiliar terrain.

"Another *Transformers* movie is out. I thought that you'd like to go and see it."

"Excuse me," she said huffily. "I don't have time for this and I don't appreciate you hijacking me somewhere that I didn't agree to go."

"I knew that if I asked you that you'd say no you because you needed to work on a paper or something."

"Maybe I'd say no because I don't want to go to the movies with you," she retorted swiftly.

Dane grinned. "Then if that's the case, once we get to the theatre you can go and sit somewhere else."

"Dane," she exclaimed, "I don't have time for this."

"Why not?" he said. He parked the Mercedes in front of the theatre. "What do you have to do this afternoon that's so important you can't take a little time out to enjoy yourself?" He got out of the car and walked around to open her car door.

Sybil sat in the seat with her arms folded. Then she said with meaning, "No wonder your grades are crap. You do whatever you want to and don't think about the consequences."

Dane's hearty laugh was his only response as they walked up to join the line of people at the ticket booth.

Once inside he pointed to the concession stand. "I'm going to go and get us some snacks."

"We just ate," she protested. "I'm not hungry."

"Me either," he said. "But you have to buy popcorn. It's tradition."

They sat in the middle of the dark theatre. *Transformers* in 3D was better than any other movie she'd seen at the theatre. Sybil enjoyed every scene of the huge machines that dominated the screen.

Dane had one arm casually around the back of her chair.

Sybil was acutely conscious of his body as he leaned in close to her. They shared popcorn from an oversized bucket and each sipped on a large soda. Once the credits rolled at the end of the film, Sybil was sorry that it was time to leave.

On the drive back to campus, she broached a topic that had been on her mind for days. Lying, she said, "I don't get to see much of Peyton lately. She and Kane must be getting on like a house afire."

Dane took his eyes off the road for a second and studied Sybil. Yet no reply from him was forthcoming.

Frustrated, Sybil sank back into the plush leather interior. *Good going, Einstein. Now he knows that you're fishing for information about his brother.*

Once they got back to campus, Dane pulled into a parking space in front of the student union. Turning to her he asked, "Are you interested in Kane?"

"Hell no," she gasped with a look of extreme displeasure on her face.

The way Dane watched her was so concentrated she stammered, "I don't like him."

"You wouldn't be the first woman to claim that you don't like him when in fact you do," he stated curtly.

Revolted by Dane's insinuation she protested hotly, "He's going with my roommate who also happens to be my best friend at this school."

"He *is*?" Dane said enigmatically and then opened his car door and got out. He quickly walked around to where she still sat trying to process his remark and opened her car door.

Feeling dismissed, she quickly got out.

Dane activated his car alarm with his remote. Not looking at her he said, "See you in class."

Sybil watched Dane's six foot frame as he towered over others as he made his way across campus. *What the hell just happened?*

*****

Sybil sat in the stacks of the library and with her laptop and researched the information for her sociology class. "Is the World a Better Place Because of Technology?" She typed two columns and headed them Pros and Cons.

Dane grunted as he settled into the chair next to her.

There was tangible tension in the air. He hadn't come around since they'd gone to lunch and the movies. He'd been sitting in the back of the room during class instead of the seat next to her.

Leaning over he read the screen on her laptop. Once finished, he eased himself back and stretched his long legs out in front of him. "I think that the world is a worse place because of computers. There's no anonymity."

"Who wants to be anonymous besides criminals?" She smiled at Dane, wanting to erase the displeasure of their last encounter.

"Do you know how many crimes are committed because people can access anything they want to know about you?"

"That's true. But look how much progress we've made because of them."

"Such as?"

She thought for a minute. "Those *Transformers* movies wouldn't be possible without computers."

"That's true, Sybil. But you can't miss what you never had so I don't think that it would matter that much."

"There's a world of information at your fingertips if you go on the Internet."

He shrugged indifferently. "But who needs it?"

"It levels the playing field between the rich and the poor. As a child when I had a paper due I'd have to go to the town library in order to get the information to write it. Sometimes Nanny got home from work real late. The other students whose mothers didn't have to work had an advantage over me. Their papers outshone mine that were thrown together at the last minute."

"You sound like you had a rough time growing up." Dane searched her face.

"It could have been rougher," she said. "We were dirt poor. But still I didn't feel as if other kids had a life so much better than mine because Nanny showered me with so much love."

"That must be nice," Dane said with a wistful look on his face.

For hours they worked side by side in the stacks each immersed in gathering information for their research paper. Finally exhausted, Sybil shut down her laptop. Stretching her hands high above her head she groaned.

Dane was staring at her stomach because her shirt had ridden up and a large part of her flesh was exposed, showing off a gold belly button ring. His eyes darted away. When he looked back at her he said drolly, "I wondered how long I was going to have to pretend to work."

Sybil chuckled at the look of aggravation on his face.

"This paper is due right before spring break and we also have that one in Professor Devine's class."

"Yeah, and he's nobody to be played with," Dane said in a displeased voice. "Did you know that he kicked my frat brother out of class?"

"Who?" Sybil asked surprised.

"Charles Rothchild."

"Are you serious?" Sybil exclaimed. "Devine really took it that far because of what Charles said? He was just fooling around."

"Charles told us at the last frat meeting that Devine tried to get him kicked out of school but the chancellor wouldn't let him. Instead, he made his counselor change his class to a different instructor."

Aghast Sybil said, "Good grief. Whose class did he end up going to?"

"That teacher they call Killer Steinhold."

"Oh my God. No one passes her class." Then Sybil added, feeling sorry for her classmate, "Damn! Sixty percent of her students have to take her class twice in order to pass."

"They say that the first day of class she tells her students to look to the left and then the right. Then after they do that she says," 'Half of the people you just looked at won't pass the course.' "

Appalled Sybil asked, "How can she get away with that?"

"This is a private institution. The faculty makes the decisions as to what the rules are."

"I feel sorry for Charles."

"You better. He said that Killer Steinhold is making him do all the assignments that he missed while he was in Devine's class. Charles said that he doesn't have the time to attend frat meetings anymore."

"Do you think that Charles can do it?"

"I don't know," Dane said in a worried tone. "He'd better try because he has a job on Wall Street hinging on his G.P.A. His dad is some hot shot financier down there."

"Well," Sybil said as she stood, "I hope for his sake that he takes care of business. The way I see it, to have come so far and not graduate is worse than never going to college at all. If I were Charles I'd work doubly hard just in order to laugh at the professors as my degree was handed to me on stage."

*****

Dane and Sybil walked the almost deserted campus. The street lights illuminated their path. They were each quiet, lost in their own thoughts. Once they got outside Sybil's dormitory, Dane turned to her with an intense look. "Sybil, I enjoy spending time with you."

Then he took his hand and pulled her towards him. He lifted her chin.

Sybil closed her eyes.

Dane's lips were frigidly cold from the weather but when they touched hers she felt heat invade her lower extremities.

Dane enfolded her into his embrace, and she melted. Their lips remained locked. The kiss got deeper as she felt Dane's tongue leisurely explore her mouth.

Somewhere from out of the deep recesses of her subconscious she heard laughter and their spell was broken.

Bemusedly, Sybil looked around to see who had ruined their moment, but she couldn't discern anyone in their vicinity.

Feeling self-conscious she looked at Dane who looked as if he were unsure of what to do next.

"It's getting late. I'll see you in class tomorrow," he said abruptly.

Still Sybil stood there watching him, waiting.

"Go inside," he said gruffly. "It's too late at night for you to be out here alone."

Dutifully, she turned and walked up the steps. Once she got to the glass doors, she rang the bell and identified herself by giving her name and secret code number that allowed students entrance into the building at night. Once inside, she turned and her eyes followed Dane as with head bent he trekked the route back to his car.

As Sybil rode the elevator to her room, she didn't realize it but she held her forefinger to her lips that still felt warm from his kiss. The minute she entered the room her happiness dissipated.

Peyton lay face down on her bed sobbing.

Damn! What a way to ruin my mood, Peyton. But instead of voicing her displeasure she walked over to her and sat down on the bed. Sybil touched her shoulder. "Peyton, what's wrong?"

Peyton sat up and turning to Sybil threw her arms around her neck. She said tearfully, "I saw Kane in his car and he had Penelope with him."

Sybil patted her soothingly on her back. "So what? That doesn't really mean anything."

"They were laughing," Peyton wailed. "Oh my God, what am I going to do?"

"Stop being so dramatic," Sybil said sharply. "So what if you saw Kane with Penelope. So what if he even screws her tonight. I don't think Kane Hamilton will be turned out by a little pussy. I mean he hasn't so far, has he?" The minute Sybil uttered those words she wished she hadn't because of the stricken look on Peyton's face.

Sybil amended her words saying, "Look, Peyton. Kane is young and I think that he's going to date a lot of women before he settles down."

"But I'm in love with him," Peyton sobbed.

"Why?" Sybil looked her straight in the eye and gave her a severe look. "He hardly spends any time with you, and he makes you cry more than laugh. There's no reason for you to love him or put up with his shit."

"But you don't know how he is one on one with me." Peyton took the back of her hand and wiped the tears that had fallen. "When I'm with him it feels as if we're the only two people in the world."

Sybil gave her a look full of doubt and pity. "Well, if you really want him you're going about it all wrong."

"What do you mean?" Peyton looked at her pleadingly for advice.

"You need to play hard to get. Don't be so available. He knows that he totally controls you and I think that Kane Hamilton is all about the thrill of the chase. Let him know that he's not the only male on campus who wants Peyton Monroe."

There was a long silence in the room as Peyton digested what Sybil said. "Okay, Sybil. I'll try and be more offhand with him." She said gratefully, "You're such a good friend."

"Try and get some rest, Peyton. It's late and you look like hell."

Peyton lay back down on the bed.

Sybil smoothed Peyton's long blond tresses. They looked as if Peyton had been raking her hands through them.

"Where have you been all night?" Peyton asked in a drowsy voice.

Sybil hesitated. She didn't think that it was a good idea to tell Peyton that it seemed as if her lover's brother was interested in her. After all, it was just a kiss and might have been one of many that Dane doled out.

"I was in the library working on my research paper."

"You're so smart, Sybil. I wish that I was more like you," Peyton murmured.

Later that night, as Sybil listened to the light snores of her roommate, she felt warm from Dane and his kiss.

Chapter 4

Sybil was awakened by the sound of something hard hitting her window. She looked over at Peyton's bed to find it empty. Walking over to the window, she pulled back the drapes.

Dane was standing outside.

During the night a fresh blanket of snow had fallen making the campus look like a winter wonderland. Bracing herself against the cold she opened her window, and hollered down, "What on earth are you doing?"

Dane was dressed in a parka, hat and gloves. "Classes are cancelled because the professors can't get here. Come on down."

Sybil's heart skipped a beat. "For what?"

"I've got a surprise for you."

"I'm not even dressed yet."

"Go on and get dressed. I'll wait."

Sybil felt a shiver of anticipation. "Okay," she yelled. "I'll be down as soon as I can." She shut the window and went to the bathroom. After all the morning rituals, she brushed her short black hair. Then she reached into the vanity drawer and pulled out a lipstick and eyebrow pencil. She applied each and stepped back to examine her reflection. *Not too bad considering I was up half the night thinking about Dane's kiss.* Sybil decided to opt out of her usual thong underwear and instead don the old lady underwear that her grandmother bought her for Christmas. *Nanny, you always did know what was best for me.* After she was dressed in warm

67

corduroy pants, leather boots, turtleneck sweater, parka, mittens and a hat she dashed out the door to meet Dane.

Once outside she looked around and saw several people trudging in the snow but no Dane was in sight. Standing with her hands on her hips, she suddenly felt a ball of snow hit her in the middle of her back. She turned around and saw Dane grinning. Then he bent to gather up another handful of snow.

"Dane, don't!" she shrieked. She began to run to distance herself from him. Right when she thought that she was safe she was hit in the middle of her back with another snowball. "Dane, stop hitting me," she screamed.

"Stop being such a girly girl," he laughed.

Sybil dodged behind a tree and scooped up some snow, formed it into a good-sized ball and peeked around. Taking careful aim, she threw, but it fell short of where Dane stood poised and ready with another snowball.

When she saw that she'd missed her mark she turned she broke into a run. Sybil huffed and puffed as she ploughed through the snow her chest heaving from exertion. *I'm out of shape. I really need to go on a diet and get some exercise.*

Behind her Sybil heard Dane's footsteps crunching in the snow and decided to give up. She turned and he was abreast of her.

He menacingly held a snowball in his hand. Chuckling he said, "I won't pulverize you if you say Dane Hamilton you're the king."

Sybil covered her face with her hands for protection and yelled, "No."

"Sybil," he said in a threatening tone.

"Dane Hamilton, you're the king," she gurgled.

Dane dropped the snowball onto the snow and said clapping the residue of snow off of his hands, "And you're the queen."

Sybil flushed with pleasure at his words.

Dane leaned over and kissed her lightly on the cheek. "For being such a sport I'll buy you some hot chocolate from the coffee shop around the corner."

"Okay."

They were quiet on the short walk to Mom's Coffee Shop. Once they got there, they saw that the restaurant was filled with other students. Everyone seemed to be celebrating the fact that there were no classes that day. Dane got a number from the ticket machine and then came back to where Sybil stood.

Charles was sitting in a booth and when he saw Dane, he waved him over.

"Come on," Dane said to Sybil and strode over to where Charles sat. Stepping aside he let Sybil slide into the booth first.

Charles smiled acknowledging Sybil's presence, but quickly switched his attention to Dane. "Hey, man. I was going to call you." He pushed his now empty breakfast plate away from him. "When I leave here I'm going snowboarding with some of the other frat guys."

"Really?" Dane said. "That sounds like fun. Where are you guys heading to?"

"We're going to take a quick trip to a lodge in Maine. Do you want to go with us?"

"How are you going to get there and back by class tomorrow?" Dane asked doubtfully. "You know that lightning doesn't strike twice. We're sure to have class tomorrow."

"We're coming back tonight," Charles said. "Three hours up, four or five hours of snowboarding and then three hours back. I'll be back at the frat house by eleven."

"I wish I could but Lehman's paper is due tomorrow. I have to finish it up."

"I hear you. I just finished Killer Steinhold's paper."

"Good job," Dane said. "Did you get caught up on everything else that you needed for her?"

"Pretty much. I completed everything except one paper. But I calculated my grade and even with a zero I'll be okay. The one due today is done, but now that classes are cancelled I'll turn it in tomorrow."

The waitress appeared, smiling at Sybil and Dane. "Are you ready to order?"

"I want a cup of hot chocolate," Dane said. "How about you, Sybil?"

"I'll have the same."

The restaurant door opened and everyone turned as Peyton strolled in arm and arm with Tristan. He had his head bent listening to something she said and suddenly he threw his head back and laughed.

There were now empty booths and Peyton began to saunter to one in the back of the small restaurant. When she came abreast of the booth where Sybil was seated, she stopped and posed in front. "Hey, Roomie," she said.

"Hey, Peyton," Sybil answered.

Then Peyton turned and smiled at Dane and Charles. "Long time no see," she said coyly to Dane.

"It hasn't been that long, Peyton," he replied shortly.

Sybil studied Tristan as he stood behind Peyton. He had a triumphant look on his face. But more importantly to Sybil was the fact that when he looked at Peyton his face was full of joy. *He really cares about her.*

Peyton looked at Sybil and said breezily, "I'll see you back at the ranch," and she sashayed away, swinging her hips as she walked.

Dane spoke to Charles as if none of Peyton's obvious ploy for attention had occurred. "I think that I'll have to pass on the road trip."

The waitress returned with their mugs of cocoa, tore the bill off a pad, and placed it face down on the table.

The restaurant door opened again. This time it was Kane and Penelope who entered holding hands. Sybil took a huge gulp of her drink which was so hot it burned her throat. Her eyes automatically went to where Peyton sat.

Peyton was staring trance-like at the couple. Her face was ashen.

Kane was dressed in all black and Penelope was dressed in a hot pink, ski jacket and cap and she looked like a Penthouse Bunny. Sybil knew that Kane hadn't seen any of them because he only had eyes for Penelope.

They strolled over to sit on the other side of the restaurant in an intimate booth for two. Once they sat down Penelope started talking to Kane who listened raptly.

"Damn! It seems as if this place is the hot spot for all the drama around school. If I didn't have plans I'd hang out and see what was going to happen next," Charles said.

Sybil looked at Dane. His expression said that he wished that he was anywhere but there. Abruptly he looked at her. "Are you done?"

"Yes," she replied, quite tired of the antics of her classmates.

He took a bill from his wallet, placed it on the table and stood. "Then let's get out of here," Dane said.

Outside, Sybil stood off to the side and waited as Dane talked to Charles by his car. *Why was Dane in a hurry to leave once Kane walked in? Is he ashamed for his brother to see us together?*

*****

A couple of evenings later, Sybil was in her usual spot in the empty library, and as usual her thoughts were of Dane. She hadn't seen him since class that afternoon, when he'd seemed distracted.

When he suddenly sat across from her she looked up but didn't speak. Instead she looked back at the book in front of her.

Dane coughed.

She ignored him.

He coughed again.

"So now you want to speak." She tried to sound dispassionate but failed miserably. "You've had little to say."

"I've had a lot on my mind."

"Such as? You turned in all your work on time and from what I saw you did a pretty good job on it."

Dane said nothing for a moment and then with a voice charged with emotion said, "My brother is in trouble," he said.

Sybil immediately stiffened at the mention of Kane. She made no reply because she didn't care.

"He's going to get an 'F' in Steinhold's class so he can't graduate with us."

Surprised, she said, "I didn't know that Kane even had Steinhold."

"I'm talking about Charles, my frat brother," Dane explained brusquely.

"Charles? But why?" she said. "He said at the coffee shop that he had everything done that he needed to pass."

"He did. His Range Rover broke down on the way back from Maine and he didn't make it to class on time. Professor Steinhold wouldn't take his paper late."

"That's a tough break, but you pretty much warned him not to go," Sybil replied, though she was troubled by the news.

"That teacher doesn't have to be such a hard ass," Dane said angrily. "We're talking about people's futures."

Sybil said quietly, "Charles had a choice and he made the wrong one. People have to suffer the consequences of their actions."

"No one is perfect, Sybil. People don't always do the right thing. Sometimes you can be caught up in things. You know the right thing to do but you don't." He added in a voice full of pity, "Charles's father came up from New York and tried to talk to Chancellor Roberts but he said that he couldn't overrule a teacher's decision.

"Then afterwards his dad came over to the frat house. You could hear him screaming at Charles calling him stupid." Agitatedly, Dane took his hand and raked it thorough his hair. "After his dad left I've never seen Charles look so destroyed. He looked like he'd lost all hope."

"It's a horrible situation but not the end of the world. He can retake the class." She slid her hand up and down his thigh soothingly.

Dane looked at her hand, lifted it, and kissed it.

Hours later, as they were descending the stairwell, they heard what sounded like rapid gunfire. Sybil and Dane stopped and looked at each other questioningly. Then they heard shouts and screams and sounds of people running. Sybil heard someone scream, 'Look out! He has a rifle.'

Dane grabbed Sybil's hand and turned, dragged her back up the stairwell. They got to the top of the stairs and opened the door to the deserted library. Large windows lined the wall and it was easy to get a view of the campus. They ran over to the window.

Sybil's heart palpitated wildly as she saw her fellow students running wildly in all directions. "What's going on?" She turned terrified eyes to Dane.

"I haven't got a clue. But I sure as hell ain't gonna go out there and find out. Come on," he ordered.

Still holding tightly to her hand, he ran towards the area they'd just come from and then stopped. "It's too wide open," he muttered.

Off to the right was the door to the room where DVD's and media equipment were stored. Dane tried the lock and it opened. He dragged her inside and locked the door.

Sybil sagged to the floor in relief.

Pulling her into a corner he motioned for her to sit down, and then turned away.

Is he leaving me here? "Don't leave me here!" she shrieked.

"Be quiet," he ordered sharply. "I'm not leaving you. I'm looking for a blanket." Then he disappeared around one of the storage cabinets.

Shortly Dane returned with a blanket he spread on the floor.

Sybil crawled onto the blanket feeling overwhelmed with thankfulness that Dane was with her. "What do you think is going on?" Her voice shook.

"I'm thinking it's some kind of school shooting," Dane said, his tone was clipped. "We're not going anywhere until I know it's safe."

"What are we going to do if they find us?" Sybil whimpered anxiously.

"I don't know," Dane replied. Raw emotion was etched in his voice, "I just don't know." He got up and switched off the lights. Lit only by the light from the street lamps, the room was bathed in semi-darkness. "We have to be very quiet. Our lives may depend on it."

"I'm scared to death," she said.

Dane settled on the blanket next to her.

Then she whispered, "I hope Peyton's okay."

"I hope everyone's okay," Dane said.

All of a sudden, their dilemma got to Sybil. She began to tremble and her teeth chattered.

Seeing this, Dane's hand snaked out and pulled her to him. She continued to shake and he eased her into a reclining position and lay behind her, cradling her to him. His breath fanned her cheek. "You've got to keep it together, Sybil. We're in for a long night."

Hours later, Sybil was awakened by Dane gingerly moving his hand across her face as if he using Braille to read her expression. Groggily, she scooted closer into the folds of his body.

He ran his hand across her abdomen and whispered into her hair, "Your skin is so soft. It's just like velvet." Then he began to nibble her neck. As he did so his hands moved across her breasts, kneading them until they ached. Then he unclipped her bra.

She sat up on her knees and pulled her shirt over her head. She turned to him. Her breasts popped free of her undone bra that fell to the floor.

Dane took off his shirt and she saw that his chest was matted with black hair. A line of it ran down disappearing beneath where its sight was blocked by his trousers.

She ran the palms of her hands across his chest and then down loving the feel of his taut stomach.

Holding her gaze in the semi-darkness, Dane very deliberately undid his belt and unbuckled his trousers. Then he stood and pulled down his jeans and stepped out of them.

Sybil stared at his rock hard shaft pointed towards her. Taking him in her hand, she slid her fingers up and down it careful not to scratch him with her long fingernails. Then she took her forefinger and rubbed it against the tip.

Dane gasped with pleasure and almost lost his balance.

Sybil smiled loving the moistness on the head of his penis. Then she took him into her mouth. As she circled his pink tip with the tip of her tongue, she felt a slick moistness seep into her mouth. Sybil gripped her lips around him and applied pleasure. Then she drew him as much of him into her mouth as she could handle.

"Sybil!" Dane screamed.

She slapped him firmly on the buttocks, as a reminder that there might be danger lurking outside and he needed to be quiet.

She sucked him, increasing and decreasing her tempo at intervals.

Dane moaned and moaned and moaned, having a hard time stifling the desire to scream his pleasure for any person within a six mile radius.

Suddenly Dane grabbed Sybil's head and stopped her.

As she looked up at him questioningly, he dropped to the floor and pushed her on her back. Then he yanked off her tights and underwear. He spread her legs, put his head between them and took a big whiff.

"Ummm," he whispered.

Parting the lips of her vagina he began to lick her with long even strokes from top to bottom. Then he stuck his tongue in her center and held it there for what seemed to be an eternity.

When Sybil felt it snaking up to her clitoris, she writhed in pleasure. Then threw her hands up in the air and planted them against the wall behind her.

Suddenly she climaxed. Her hands fell to her sides as she felt her draining into Dane's mouth. She felt Dane's tongue leave her, but before she could protest he was inside her.

"Sybil, Sybil," Dane groaned as he thrust inside her.

She clung to him and met him stoke for stroke. "Harder, harder, harder," she demanded hoarsely.

Dane obliged and beads of perspiration dropped from his face onto her face. She licked her lips and cherished the salty taste.

Dane cupped his hands under her hips and lifted her as he pummeled her body with his.

She groaned her pleasure. Sybil lost track of time but finally she and Dane exploded at the same time.

Instead of moving from on top of her, he remained still. The rapid beat of his heart, along with hers, made Sybil feel as if they were truly in sync.

After his labored breathing subsided, Dane moved off her and once again pulled her close.

Satiated, the two fell asleep.

*****

When light began to sleep through the windows, Sybil woke. Turning, she saw the Dane was still asleep. She sat up, trying not to disturb him.

Nevertheless, his eyes opened, and he stared at her naked breasts. A strange look crossed his face. Then as he came fully awake, he said flatly, "I'm going to go and see if we can get out of here, and maybe find out what the hell happened."

When Dane stood she got a full frontal view of his body. He had the physique of a basketball player with his long arms and legs.

She looked at the black hair that curled around his manhood. *He's so hairy!*

Hurriedly he got dressed and with a last look of assurance, he unlocked the door and left the room.

After he left, Sybil pulled on her clothes. She waited a few minutes then cracked open the door, only to see an empty library. *Why isn't Dane back?* She was on the verge of venturing outside to see what was going on when Dane returned.

He wore a gloomy look on his face. "It looks like a ghost town out there. But I think it's safe for us to leave."

Sybil chewed her bottom lip nervously. "Okay," she said weakly.

"I'll make sure you get to your dorm safely and then I need to go and find Kane."

Once outside, Dane practically ran, pulling Sybil along with him as they fled to what they hoped was safety.

Once they reached her dormitory, Sybil found the door locked. She gave Dane an apprehensive look as she rang the buzzer.

A voice bellowed through the intercom, "State your name and code, please."

Sybil quickly complied. She heard the sound of the door lock being released and grabbed the handle. As she turned to say something to Dane, he gave her a quick wave, then took off.

With a sense of foreboding, Sybil crossed the deserted lobby and took the stairs to her room. She opened her room door with caution.

Peyton was lying on her back with her hand rubbing her stomach. She stopped when she saw Sybil and sat bolt upright in the bed. "I was worried to death about you all night! Where have you been?"

"I was leaving the library and heard gunfire so I ran into a storage room and hid. What the hell happened?"

"Charles Rothchild shot and killed Professor Devine when he was going to his car. Then he started running through campus waving a semiautomatic."

"Charles?" she exclaimed. Sybil sank onto her bed in shock. "You've got to be kidding me."

Peyton's face was pale. "They say he went berserk," she said.

"Was anyone else hurt?"

"The security guards killed Charles." Peyton shook her head in despair. "They said that he pointed his rifle at them and they felt threatened not knowing if he was going to shoot." Peyton said in a confused voice, "I don't know why Charles did what he did."

"It was probably the first major disappointment in his life." Sybil made no effort to wipe away the tears that cascaded down her face. She said glumly, "The shock of not graduating after four years of college was too much for him to bear."

"It's so sad," Peyton murmured.

"It's more than sad." Sybil lay face down on her bed and muttered into the mattress, "It's a tragedy."

"I'm sick to death of this place," Peyton said in a strained voice.

*****

That night Sybil was awakened by the sound of Peyton vomiting in the bathroom. She raised her eyes heavenward. *I'm exhausted from all this drama around me.*

She closed her eyes when she heard Peyton come back into the room and get back into bed. Soon she heard the soft snores of her roommate.

In the darkness she thought about Dane. *I need to check on Dane and see how he's doing.*

Stealthily, she quickly dressed in the darkness. She glanced at Peyton's sleeping form as she crept out of the room. She walked the short way to Independent Row where Dane lived gazing wistfully at the neatly manicured lawns of the apartment homes that housed the majority of the rich students. She had never been there before but had heard tales of the exorbitant rent. She knew which apartment Dane lived in because she'd seen the address on letters in his book bag when he'd fished around for a pen or pencil.

As she stood on his front porch, a feeling of trepidation arose in her. *What am I doing here? I don't know that Dane would want to see me or even if he's alone.* She hesitated, wondering what she should do, then suddenly she said to herself, *We're friends. Friends can check on friends if they're worried about them. If he doesn't want to be bothered I'll just leave and there'll be no hard feelings.*

She rang the bell but hearing no chime, pressed the buzzer again several times. Sybil was turning to leave when the door suddenly opened.

Dane stood there. His hair was sticking up all over his head and his eyes looked red from crying. He wore only a navy blue pair of gym shorts with white piping down the sides. He stared at her with an impenetrable expression.

"Dane." Her voice croaked from nervousness as she stared at the black hair on his chest. "I just came by to check on you. I'm sorry about Charles."

Dane quickly ran his eyes up and down the length of her body.

Sybil had dressed in the first thing she could put her hands on. Her curves stood out in the leggings and knee length black boots. Over the leggings she wore a gold mid-length sweater. Large hoop earrings were her only jewelry. She didn't know it but she look like an African queen.

Without speaking, Dane stepped back and opened the door wider.

Sybil walked past him and found herself in a large den in complete disarray. The couch was covered with clothes and she couldn't count how many pairs of sneakers were spread out on the floor. The kitchen wasn't much better because dishes were piled high in the sink. When she turned to face Dane his face was beet red from embarrassment.

"I'm sorry this place is such a mess," he said sheepishly. "I wasn't expecting company."

"I should've called. But I've been having problems with my cell and I couldn't get a dial tone. Are you okay?"

"Let's go in here," Dane said and walked to the left.

Next she found herself in what was obviously his bedroom. The sheets were rumpled but otherwise it was the cleanest room she'd seen so far. Dane sat on the bed and she sat in the chair across from him.

"My frat brothers and I are obviously upset," he said in a passionate voice. "Those guards lost their cool. They didn't have to shoot him."

Sybil remained silent because she knew that Dane felt the need to blame someone. It wouldn't do any good for her to point out the fact that Charles took a man's life. "When is the funeral?" she asked gently.

"His father is having the body sent to him. It's a private family ceremony. His fraternity brothers aren't invited."

"I'm sorry, Dane. That must be another blow." Then she asked hesitantly, "Have you heard about arrangements for Professor Devine?"

Dane ran his hand distractedly through his hair. "Devine's wife and kids want to have the funeral in Kentucky where he was raised." Then abruptly he asked, "Have you seen the news?"

"No," she said slowly. "I didn't want to hear their spin on what happened here."

"They're trying to paint Charles as some spoiled, rich psycho." His voice was ragged from pain.

"Don't pay any attention to that," she said soothingly. Sybil got up and walked over to Dane and softly touched his cheek. "You know the real Charles."

"They don't realize the pressure rich kids face from their families."

Sybil whispered, "Obviously he snapped from the pressure."

Suddenly Dane grabbed her hand and pulled her to him. His eyes never wavering from hers, he placed it on his rock, hard penis.

She felt an intense heat invade her lower extremities.

"What are you really doing here?" he murmured looking deeply into her eyes.

"I don't know," she said her voice unsteady.

Dane released her and stood to smooth the sheets on his bed so it looked inviting. Then he turned toward her and quickly divested himself of his clothes.

Sybil stared at his manhood. Unable to stop herself she grabbed it and pulled it towards her.

The grimace of pain that crossed Dane's face made her release him.

Dane impatiently stripped her of her clothes dropping them in the chair she'd vacated.

When she stood before him naked, he took one nipple in his mouth and sucked it as he gently pushed her down on the bed.

Dane covered her body with his and didn't bother pulling the sheet over them. As his mouth devoured hers he took his finger and inserted it. When he found that she was already wet he entered her in one fluid movement. No words were spoken. There were only the moans of ecstasy in the room that let each of them know that they were sopping wet from desire. This time when he came, Dane was free to scream her name.

She took her hands and rubbed the mounds of his hips and whispered in his ear, "What are we doing?"

"I don't know," he murmured before he fell into a deep sleep.

Later that night, Sybil opened her eyes and surveyed the man sleeping next to her.

Dane slept on his back. His legs were spread and his manhood hung limply to one side from their second bout of lovemaking. A small smile was plastered on his lips as he slept.

Chapter 5

Sybil and Dane held each other's gaze in the early morning sun. Suddenly feeling self-conscious, Sybil reached for the sheet to pull over them and cover their nakedness.

"Don't," Dane ordered sleepily.

Sybil slowly let her hand drop to her side.

"You are absolutely beautiful."

"No, I'm not," Sybil demurred. "I'm too fat."

"No way," Dane whispered. "I like a woman with some junk in the trunk." He looked deeply into her eyes. "One hazel and the other one honey. It's uncanny."

"Blame it on my dad," she whispered.

"So I take it that you're daddy's little girl."

"Not at all," she replied with a hard edge in her voice. "My father abandoned me when I was a toddler and he died without me ever really knowing him."

"Did he really?" Dane raised his eyebrows in surprise. "I don't understand how a man could walk off from his kid." He said, "So then it was just you and your mother? That must have been tough."

"My mother died when I was a baby. My paternal grandmother raised me."

"That's a sad story, Sybil."

"Don't feel sorry for me!" she said, stung at of the note of pity in Dane's voice. "At least I had someone who wanted me. Some people have no one."

"You're right," Dane said quietly. "Some people have no one." Then suddenly he said in a quivering voice, "Stay with me."

"What?" Confused, she looked at him.

"I want you to stay with me," Dane whispered.

"Here?" The mere thought sent trickles of excitement down her spine. "What would Kane think of that?"

"It doesn't matter," Dane said dismissively. "Besides, Kane's never here. He spends his nights at Penelope's apartment. Please stay, Sybil. I don't want to be alone," he said in a pleading voice.

Sybil studied the vulnerable expression on Dane's face. "I don't know about that Dane," she said suppressing her excitement at the prospect.

"Because of the shooting, classes have been cancelled for a week. A lot of people are leaving campus. I know that you don't want to spend the time in a deserted campus; stay with me unless you plan on going home."

"I didn't know that the school was closing, but I won't be going home."

"I got a text. The administration decided that everyone needs time to grieve." Dane's eyes filled with tears. "And don't forget they have to find someone to take over Devine's classes." He blinked and turned his head away from her stare.

She reached up and gently touched his wet face with her index finger. Once she wiped away his tears away she whispered, "I'll stay with you, Dane, but I need to go to the dorm and get some things."

Dane laid his head on her breast. Sleepily he said, "When you're ready, take the car keys off my dresser and drive the Mercedes."

After she felt Dane's breathing deepen into a heavy snore she edged her body from under his.

As Sybil stood by the bed and looked at Dane's inert form, a feeling of hope flooded her body.

When Sybil opened her dorm room, she was surprised by the neatness on Peyton's side of the deserted room. Then she spied a note taped to the mirror. As she scanned its contents she felt a sigh of relief.

Sybil: I want to get away from campus so I'm going stay at Tristan's until classes start up again. If you need to reach me call me on my cell. Take care and be safe.

Love Peyton.

*****

Following Sybil, Dane dutifully pushed the grocery cart from aisle to aisle.

"We also need washing powder, fabric softener, and dishwashing liquid," Sybil said as she read the list she'd drawn up at Dane's apartment.

"I didn't bring you to my house in order to clean it up," he protested.

"I know you don't think that I'm staying in it the way it is, do you?" she asked in a teasing voice.

"No," Dane said. "Let me call Merry Maids. Once I make the call they usually show up the next morning."

"Not soon enough for me," she said. "What would we do about tonight?"

Dane shot her a look full of lust. "I can think of a lot of things that we can do tonight instead of cleaning up."

"So can I." She made sure that no one in the aisle was eavesdropping on their conversation and asked, "But I'd like a set of clean sheets on the bed first."

Once the cart was loaded with the staples on their list they got in line. Sybil reached for her pocketbook in the small compartment by the handle.

Dane's eyebrows drew together. He said in a voice that brooked no argument, "Don't even think about paying for this stuff."

Sybil acquiesced, knowing from the look on his face that it was pointless to argue.

Once the bill was tallied, Dane said to Sybil, "Thanks, Daddy."

He gave her a sly wink and put his credit card away.

Sybil smothered a laugh as she followed Dane out to the car.

*****

Sybil stood at the sink washing dishes. After her third sink of dishes was disposed of she felt satisfied that she could now begin to prepare dinner. She looked into the den and saw Dane as he propelled the vacuum cleaner across the floor. His arms flexed as he purposefully went over each trail on the rug several times.

She hid a smile at his look of concentration. Yelling over the din she asked, "Do you want spaghetti or pork chops for dinner?"

"Pork chops," he grinned, he turned off the vacuum cleaner.

"Why am I not surprised?" she drawled.

"I'm going to be a fat old man," Dane kidded, "but if the woman I marry really loves me she won't care."

"Not really," Sybil said. She opened the refrigerator and withdrew a package of pork chops that she hadn't put in the freezer because she had foreseen that was going to be Dane's choice for dinner. "Fried foods are very unhealthy. If your wife is really looking out for you she won't fry food for you."

Dane came into the kitchen and stood in front of her. "Does that mean that you don't care what happens to me because you're letting me have my way?"

There was a small silence and then Sybil looked up at him.

Dane towered over her in height and it made her feel small and feminine.

"I think that you already know that you matter very much to me, Dane Hamilton."

A flush of pleasure came over his face. He kissed her upturned nose. "I know that now, Sybil."

Sybil slid her arms around his middle.

Dane drew her closer and laid his head on top of hers. Then he nuzzled the side of her neck with his mouth.

Every time he did that, Sybil turned into a pile of goo in his arms.

Dane cupped her breasts and then found her nipples. Then he dropped his hands to her waist and held her so tight that she could hardly breathe.

The only sound in the room was their breathing.

Sybil reluctantly pried herself out of his arms. "Go into the den, or I'll never get dinner cooked."

"Don't you need me to do anything?" Dane offered.

"No," she said. "You'll just get in the way."

"Good," Dane responded gleefully. "There's a game on."

With an indulgent look on her face, Sybil watched Dane speedily put the vacuum cleaner in the closet before lying down on the sofa.

Once the pork chops were simmering in gravy, she took out a novel. Sybil kept one eye on the stove as she read, and before she knew it dinner was done. Putting the novel aside, she went into the den and slid next to Dane. "Dinner's done. Are you ready?"

Dane picked up the remote and hit the pause button. "What do you think?" He grinned.

Once they were seated at the table, Dane bent his head and silently blessed his food.

Sybil respectfully kept quiet until he was finished. "If you don't mind, I'd like to be included next time."

"Give me your hand," Dane said in his slow, southern drawl.

Sybil held her hand out to Dane him.

He clasped hers and bowed his head.

Once Sybil saw that, she in turn bowed hers.

"Lord, thank you for this food Sybil has lovingly prepared for us. I also want to thank you for bringing her into my life." He hesitated then said in a thick voice, "I pray that my brother Charles Rothchild rests in peace. Amen."

"Amen," Sybil echoed.

When she looked up her eyes met Dane's and she knew. The revelation struck her like a thunderbolt. She had fallen head over heels for Dane Hamilton. In a sort of bemused state she stared at him. She was shaken from her reverie when she saw Dane pick up his fork and begin to eat the rice, mixed vegetables, and gravy she'd prepared to complement the pork chops.

Nervously she waited for his verdict.

When Dane was able to cut his meat without using a knife, she relaxed and tackled her own plate of food.

Swallowing a mouthful of food, Dane nodded at her. "This is as delicious as I knew it would be, Sybil. Thank you."

Pleased, she responded, "You're welcome."

In between swallows of food he nodded at her romance novel. "What are you reading?"

"Hope," she laughed.

"You're reading a book called *Hope*?" he said, slightly confused.

"No," she laughed. "I'm reading *Not His Type*. It gives women hope that Mr. Right is somewhere out there. It's a good form of escape."

"So you feel the need to escape from the daily humdrum of life?" Dane eyed her questioningly.

After wiping her mouth she grinned. "After all the heavy social work texts that I have to read, I like to read stuff on the lighter side in my free time."

Dane's eyes focused on the book's cover. *Not His Type*. That doesn't sound like hope. It says it all right there. She's not the woman for him. It sounds like a nay instead of a yea." Now he grinned at his play on words.

"I read this kind of novel because it's a catharsis. The bad people get their comeuppance and good people end up together." Peyton's face rose to the surface but she pushed the image away. "In real life things don't always work out the way people want them to."

Dane's narrowed eyes as he listened intently to every word she uttered.

After a long hesitation, Sybil felt compelled to ask, "Do you think that I'm your type?"

"Yes," he answered without hesitation.

"Without stating the obvious, many people would beg to differ."

"Why," Dane said bluntly, "because you're African-American and I'm Caucasian?"

"That's an old fashioned way of putting it," Sybil said with a grimace.

"That's an old fashioned way you're thinking," Dane countered.

"It's not just that," she said slowly. "Our backgrounds are very different."

"Yet we like the same things. We enjoy the same movies, sports, and don't forget food." Dane leaned back and patted his full stomach. "Day to day living and getting along is what really matters in a relationship."

Sybil looked at Dane's sincere expression and her heart did a somersault. "Dane Hamilton, where did you come from?" she whispered.

"I don't know," he said with a twinkle in his eye. "You just got lucky, I guess."

As they finished cleaning up the dinner dishes, Sybil handed Dane the wet frying pan and let the dirty sink water drain out. "I'm kind of tired," she said. "And I don't know why. It's not as if I did that much today."

"I think that you did a lot. We went to the grocery store, Wal-Mart, and cleaned up around here."

"I know," she said. "But that was kind of fun doing it with you."

"I feel the same." Dane reached over and planted a kiss on her mouth. "Go sit down and rest. I'll be in shortly."

When Sybil turned to leave the room, Dane twisted his drying towel into a whip and flicked it across her on her bottom.

She gave a yelp of surprise but not pain.

She heard Dane's throaty laugh behind her.

When he sat on the couch next to her, she automatically handed him the remote control.

He gave her a questioning look.

"I want to read anyhow," she said agreeably. "I rarely get to in my dorm room."

"Why?" Dane asked as he turned back to his game and set it in motion on the plasma TV.

"Peyton chatters all of the time. Don't get me wrong. I love her to death, but sometimes I could strangle her."

"That's how I feel about Kane."

Sybil instinctively stiffened at the mention of his twin's name.

Dane gave her a look that begged for understanding. "I know that you don't like my brother and I understand why. But we've very close; we've been through a lot together."

"Really?" she exclaimed. "I thought that you had a kind of charmed childhood living the dream in Dallas society. Sort of like the cast in *Dallas*."

"Notice how complicated their lives are. It gives an accurate depiction how rich people are always in each other's business. I used to hate suppertime at my house."

"Why?"

"Because that's when we all sat down together and talked about our day. If my father felt we hadn't accomplished anything worthwhile, he'd make sarcastic remarks. After a while I got used to tuning him out."

"Did Kane grow a tough hide too?" she asked.

"Not really. He'd embellish on whatever his story of the evening was going to be. So he always was the center of attention at supper."

"So he lied," Sybil said sarcastically. "Why doesn't that surprise me?"

"He felt he had to," Dane countered defensively. "He was put on the spot every evening. The pressure of trying to be more important than you are is dreadful."

"Yet you didn't lie," Sybil said softly.

"But I had an easier time in school than Kane did. He always struggled and because of that he gave himself props in areas that couldn't be checked out easily."

"I believe you should tell the truth at all costs and in the end everything will be all right."

"That's a naïve way of looking at things, Sybil." Dane shook his head in disagreement. "You don't know how intimidating it is to try to live up to the expectations of one of the most prominent physicians in Dallas. Father expects us to be not just as good as he is but us to surpass him."

"You're right. I don't know how that is. Nanny accepted me for what I was. All of my successes she magnified and my mistakes she minimized."

"You're blessed," he said with an obvious note of jealousy.

"I know that," she acknowledged.

"Kane is the only sibling that I have," Dane said quietly. "Hate him if you want, Sybil, but I love him."

"You should love your brother." Her next words seemed to have been wrenched out of her. "I don't hate Kane. I just don't like what he's done to Peyton. She's a different person since she got involved with him. She seems to have lost all of her self-confidence. I dislike Kane for the part that he's played in that."

Dane shook his head pessimistically. "I wish that I could tell you that in the end things are going to work out for them like it does for the characters in your romance novels, but I can't." His eyes slid away from hers and then back. "What did Peyton say when you told her that you'd be staying with me for a couple of days?"

"Nothing," Sybil said, "because I didn't tell her."

"Why so secretive?" Dane asked. His piercing green eyes watched her closely.

"There wasn't any secret," she explained hesitantly. "I haven't talked to Peyton. She wanted to get away from campus also so she's staying at Tristan's. She left me a note."

"Oh," Dane said with an inscrutable look on his face.

"How come Kane never comes and gets the car?"

"Penelope's father bought her a Jeep for her birthday. They've been riding around in that."

"Oh, I guess wanting to ride in the newest car is understandable."

"Fine by me," he said. "It works out better not having to share. That means that I can take you places."

"Like where?" she said eagerly.

"I don't know," he mused as he scratched his head. "But we better go while we can. We're sure to have a tough time for the rest of the year because when classes resume our professors are sure to make up for lost time."

"You're probably right," Sybil said apprehensively.

An eerie feeling filtered through her body and she couldn't shrug it off.

*****

She buried her face in his chest when she found him watching her.

"Morning, sleepyhead," he whispered.

"Good morning," she whispered shyly.

Noting her discomfiture, Dane chuckled. "How many times do I have to make love to you before you get used to not being shy around me the first thing in the morning?"

"I don't know," she muttered, "I just feel so vulnerable when I wake up and find you staring at me."

"I don't want you to feel vulnerable to me, Sybil. I would never purposefully hurt you," he said with conviction.

Sybil lay on her back and stared at him. She slid the sheet that covered them off exposing their bodies in the morning sun. "I believe you, Dane," she said softly.

"Are you ready?" he said, staring at her naked frame.

"I'm ready," she responded dutifully.

Dane slid out of bed and held his hand out to her. She put hers in his and allowed him to half drag her out of bed and lead her to the bathroom for their morning ritual.

Once inside, Dane turned the faucets on. Then he gave her a sardonic smile before he lifted the toilet seat.

Knowing that he would join her shortly, Sybil grabbed her shower cap, stuffed her hair underneath it, pulled back the curtain and once inside, immersed her body in the stinging spray.

Steam rose from the shower awakening every fiber of her being.

She felt a rush of cold air and knew without looking that Dane was joining her. Over her shoulder, she handed Dane a loofah sponge soaked with shower gel.

Obligingly he began to wash her back with small circular movements. Applying light pressure, he scrubbed her from head to toe.

Sybil had planted her hands on the tiles in front of her steadying herself so that she could withstand the force of the slippery shower and Dane's overpowering sensuality. When she felt a sharp slap on her buttocks she knew to turn around.

Dane's black hair was slicked back from his face and he looked like a villain in an old movie. A tremulous feeling shot through her at the feel of the sexual power he had over her. His penis instead of pointing down bridged the distance between their bodies as he began to soap her breasts.

Dane methodically washed every bit of her skin, taking care to be extra gentle on her face and around her eyes. She smiled in ecstasy when he swirled his index finger around her belly ring and then stuck it inside her navel. Slowly he pushed her backwards completely immersing her in the water and rinsed her. Then he handed her the sponge.

With painstaking concentration, Sybil mimicked Dane's every movement that he'd subjected her body to but when she was done she dropped to her knees.

Dane joined her on the shower floor. She put her arms around his waist and held him tight.

They remained motionless, letting the hot water gush over them.

After she'd dressed she found Dane in front of the television eating a bowl of cereal.

"We'll go out for lunch today."

"That works for me," she said as she headed towards the kitchen. Once she got to the coffee pot she stopped. In front of it was a check made out to her for three hundred dollars.

Staring at it Sybil unsuccessfully forced back angry tears. Then she grabbed the check and stormed into the den, planting her rigid body in front of Dane.

Shocked, Dane stared at her.

Her face was mottled with rage.

"What's wrong?" he said.

"How could you?" she choked out.

"What? Pay you the money that you earned?" he said, flummoxed by her wrath.

"I'm not a fuckin' prostitute," she screamed, waving the check angrily in the air.

"No kidding," he said dryly. "You're so damn good in bed, honey; I couldn't afford you if you were selling it. That's the money I owe you for tutoring me this week."

"Our time together is different." Her eyes filled with ears and droplets hung on her heavy lashes. "Or at least I thought it was."

"You thought right." Dane put his cereal bowl on the coffee table and reached up, dragging Sybil down next to him. "We do have something special. But the tutoring is another matter. We have an agreement. You've kept your part of the bargain. I need you to let me keep my mine," he said soothingly.

"The money ruins things for us."

"It does not," he said patiently. "You need to learn how to separate things. The money doesn't diminish the fun we had on our cold as hell picnic in the park. It doesn't change the good time the day we spent hanging out in Boston. And it sure as hell doesn't denigrate the nights you spent in my arms. But as for the tutoring, you earned that money and it's rightfully yours."

Sybil looked away.

Dane knew that meant she was doing some hard thinking. "Think of it as sticking it to the man," he teased.

"Who?" she said.

"My father. He wants me to graduate with honors. And he's willing to pay whatever it takes to help me get there. Quite frankly, you could have asked for double what you're getting and he wouldn't have questioned it."

Sybil looked doubtfully at Dane.

"Haven't you been sending the money that I pay you to Nanny?"

Her eyes opened wide in surprise. "How would you know that?"

"You always look good to me, Sybil, but I know women. I haven't seen you sportin' a whole lot of new clothes. I have a sneaking suspicion that's where your earnings are going."

Sybil shook her head, marveling at how astute Dane was about things.

"Even if you don't want the money, Sybil, send it to your grandmother. She's certainly owed it for raising such a beautiful, independent, smart granddaughter."

*****

After lunch, Sybil said as Dane closed her car door, "I need to go by the post office to send this letter to Nanny."

"Yes, Miss Daisy," Dane teased.

Once Dane pulled up in front of the post office and parked, Sybil unclipped her seat belt. "This should only take a minute," she said. "I'm going to get a book of stamps out of the machine. Do you need any?"

"No," he said. "I'm a phone person. I write as little as possible."

"Me too," she agreed. "Nanny is my exception. Sometimes she can't hear me on my cell phone and it frustrates her. The only other time I write letters is when I have to deliver some bad news and I'm too much of a coward to do it in person."

"So a letter is your way of dealing with sticky situations?" Dane scoffed in a playful voice.

"It sure is…" Then after giving Dane a quick look, she opened her car door. Immediately, she felt a blast of cold air hit her face and she scurried with head bent into the post office.

Once inside, she inserted a ten dollar bill into the stamp machine and then quickly plastered a stamp on Nanny's letter. After mailing it, she hunched her shoulders and braced herself to go out into the strong December wind.

Sybil was so intent on climbing back into the Mercedes, she didn't notice her every move being watched by a couple in a red Mustang.

*****

Dane slapped a card on the table and said, "Gin."

"Dammit," Sybil declared vehemently. "I hate this game."

"You don't hate it when you're the one winning," Dane laughed.

Sybil defended herself, "That's everyone."

"Now that I've won the last five games I think that I ought to let you in on a secret."

"A secret?" she asked suspiciously. "I knew it. I knew your ass was cheating."

"I have not been cheating," Dane said mimicking her. "You have a tell."

"A tell? What the hell's that?"

"I can tell when you're bluffing about your cards."

"How?" Sybil placed her hands on her hips enquiringly.

"When you're really nervous you drum your fingers."

"What! I do not!"

"Yes you do. Every time I picked up a lot of cards I did it because I knew that you needed something. So I took it. That meant that I got to add up a whole lot of points and you couldn't go out and leave me holding the bag."

"Dane, I ought to spank you," she exclaimed, astounded by his revelation.

"If you wish, you can later tonight." He chuckled agreeably.

"Speaking of what I need to be doing tonight," she said with resignation, "I need to go and fold my laundry since I'm going back to the dorm in the morning."

"You don't have to," Dane said. "You know that you can stay here."

"Indefinitely?" she said. "I think not. We have class Monday and I have some work that I need to do."

"You can do it here," Dane countered with a pout on his face.

"We do work well together but I need total concentration, and sir, you are a distraction."

"Is that a bad thing?" Dane asked.

"Not at all." She grabbed his hand. "It's just that we have only a week before we break for Christmas. I don't want to take any work home with me during the holidays."

"I understand," he acquiesced grudgingly. "I know what an early riser you are so wake me when you want me to take you back to campus."

"Okay," Sybil said.

Chapter 6

The next morning, not being able to bear saying goodbye to Dane, she crept out of the bedroom and closed the door gently. As she walked down the street she didn't see Kane glaring at her as he watched her out the window.

When she let herself in her room, Peyton was reclining on her bed flipping through the pages of a fashion magazine.

"Hey girl, long time no see," Sybil exclaimed. She bent down to hug Peyton but the hug she received was not the effusive one she was used to getting from her.

"I've missed you too," Peyton answered. Closing the magazine and putting it aside she asked, "Where have you been?"

"I stayed off campus for a couple of days. This place is kind of morose because of, well, you know."

"I do know," Peyton said. She folded her arms across her breasts and looked at Sybil. "Where did you stay?"

"With a friend," Sybil hedged. She placed her suitcase on the bed and began unpacking her clothes. She felt Peyton's eyes boring holes in her back as she put them away in her dresser drawers. "Did you enjoy your stay at Tristan's?"

"Tristan and I are only friends," Peyton said firmly. "What friend did you stay with?"

Sybil turned around and faced Peyton. Watching her closely for her reaction she said slowly, "Dane."

"At least you didn't lie," Peyton said with obvious attitude. "Tristan and I saw you at the post office yesterday."

"Why didn't you say anything?" Sybil demanded.

"I just thought that he was giving you a ride because you don't have a decent car," Peyton said jealously, "So you are trying to tell me all this time you've been staying with Dane at his apartment?"

"Yes," she said quietly.

"When did you two start seeing each other?"

"We were just friends at first. After the shooting we got closer and then he asked me to stay with him at his place while the campus was closed."

Peyton squealed, "You got to stay at Kane's apartment for days? Was Kane there too?"

"No," she said slowly. "I think that he stayed at Penelope's place."

There was a long, uncomfortable silence in the room.

Peyton's eyes mirrored her hurt. Heatedly she asked, "Why did hide your relationship with Dane from me?"

Sybil stiffened at Peyton's hostile demeanor. "I don't have to tell you my comings and goings, Peyton."

"Why not?" she retorted. "You're always sticking your nose in my business."

Sybil drew herself up short. "You ask me for my opinion, Peyton. I don't ask for yours."

"Well, I certainly hope that you don't think anything is going to come from your affair with Dane." Peyton's lips pursed in anger. "I think that he's like his twin brother."

"Dane is nothing like Kane," Sybil retorted emphatically. "I knew that from the first moment I met them."

"I thought that Kane was a nice guy too, but he showed his true colors."

Sybil stared at her roommate then decided to be frank. She sat down on the bed next to her. In a crystal clear voice she said, "Kane treats Penelope better than he ever treated you. I'm sorry if it hurts you to hear that but it's the truth. I was with Dane for five days and I never saw hide nor hair of Kane. He's content with Penelope.

"And as for Dane, he pursues me. He looks for me. He takes me places other than bed." Then she said very deliberately, "He not only let me stay the night, he let me stay the week. You need to move on from this infatuation that you have for Kane because he's not the man for you."

Peyton burst into tears and buried her head into her pillow. Huge sobs made her sound as if she was choking.

Feeling like a monster, Sybil patted her consolingly on her back.

Peyton pushed her hand and continued to weep.

After a moment, Sybil grabbed *Not His Type* and went downstairs so she could read in peace.

A couple of hours later she was curled up on the loveseat in the lobby. A shadow fell across her, blocking out some of the light. She looked up and saw Kane standing over her.

Sybil scowled at him.

Ignoring the ferocious look on her face, Kane sat down on the couch next to her and put his arm around her shoulders. "How are you doing, Sybil?" he asked with a smirk.

Sybil recoiled and dropped her novel.

Before she could answer him with a scathing remark the hairs on the back of her neck stood up.

She felt him before she saw him.

Dane had noiselessly walked up behind them. "What do you think that you're doing?" he asked his brother. There was a flinty look in his eye.

"Nothing much." Kane's eyes didn't flinch as he met his brother's. "I just wanted to see if Sybil is as much fun as her roommate."

"She isn't," Dane replied shortly.

Sybil gasped in indignation.

The two men stared each other down in the chilly atmosphere.

Kane got up. "I believe you, brother," he said with a snicker. Then he left without a backward look and entered the stairwell that led to the rooms upstairs.

"What did Kane mean that he wanted to see if I'm as much fun as Peyton?" Her lips were pursed irritably.

"Nothing," Dane snapped in a sour tone. "He's just being a prick."

"What do you mean by telling him that I'm not?" she asked crossly.

Dane scowled at her. "Do you want to go and see what fun Kane means?"

"Hell no!" she sputtered.

"Then I did you a favor."

Huffily Sybil picked up her novel and resumed reading it.

Dane sat in a chair across from her.

From the corner of her eye she saw him reach for a magazine on the coffee table.

He became engrossed in it.

"What are you reading *Cosmopolitan* for?" she demanded tartly as she put her finished novel aside.

"I want you to take the questionnaire they have in it. I'd like you to rate the sexual position that you like the most. I can't answer that for you because you're so flexible."

Against her will, Sybil felt her lips twitch in amusement. "What made you come over here tonight?"

"I came over to ask you if you wanted to go and get some ice cream with me."

"In this weather?" she gasped. "It's freezing outside."

"'It's freezing outside,'" he mimicked. "Stop being such a girl."

"But I am a girl!" She acquiesced, "Okay, I'll go."

"We have to walk. Kane's staying back at the apartment and he's making up for lost time by monopolizing the car."

"I don't mind," she said. "Let me just go upstairs and get my coat and things."

"I'll wait here." Dane picked the magazine up and started reading it again.

When Sybil opened her room, Peyton met her with a brilliant smile.

"Guess what?"

"Oh," she grimaced. "So you're speaking to me again? Lucky me."

Peyton chose to ignore that. "Kane came over and asked me to go to the movies with him tonight."

"You're so lucky, Peyton." Sybil took her right thumb and held it up in the air. In a high pitched voice she said sarcastically, "It's your turn tonight to go out with Kane Hamilton."

"Stop being so mean about him, Sybil." Peyton gave her a quelling look. "He's never asked me to go to the movies with him before. Maybe some of Dane's ways have rubbed off on him."

"I doubt it," Sybil replied cynically. "If it's not in him to be a good man nothing in this world will change that." She gave Peyton a searching look. "What about Penelope? Remember her? The girl he's been seeing exclusively for months."

"They broke up," Peyton said smugly. "I knew that he'd tire of her."

Sybil threw her hands up in despair. She grabbed her coat and hat out of the closet. "I'll see you later, Peyton."

"Maybe yes, maybe no." An enigmatic smile played on Peyton's lips.

Feeling really sorry for her, Sybil practically ran out of the room.

*****

She and Dane held hands as they walked from the neighborhood ice cream shop.

"I can't believe we're eating ice cream in thirty degree weather," Sybil said. Then she took a huge lick of her cone.

"Ice cream is my weakness. I should have bought a bigger cone," he said. Dane finished his cone and threw his napkin in a garbage can they passed. "Back home I eat it all the time. My mom makes homemade ice cream."

"You and your mother are very close, aren't you?"

"Yeah, we are," Dane replied. "It's always been like that." With a pensive look on his face he said, "She and I are close and Dane and Father are close." He leaned over and licked some of her ice cream.

"You really have a sweet tooth, Dane. When you get older you're going to have to watch out that you don't get diabetes or something."

"I hope by then that they'll have a cure for it." He sounded contemplative. "One day I'd like to do something great in medicine."

Sybil gave him a nudge. "Of course you will."

"I don't know," he said. "Research takes money and people aren't giving to charities the way they used to. They're holding on to every penny they have."

"I think that within the next few years the economy will get better. You know that it's always darkest before the dawn."

"You're such a breath of fresh air, Sybil. You're different from the girls I usually go out with."

She cast him a sexy look from under her long eyelashes. "How is that?"

"Well, we both know that you're a very beautiful woman. But you're not high maintenance. You don't whine and moan about things. And you also have a soul and a heart as big as Texas."

"You've never seen my bad side, Dane." She gave a small laugh. "I can be a real bitch."

"I think that someone would have to do something real mean to you or someone you loved in order to bring that out."

They reached the stairs in front of her dormitory. He reached in his pocket and when he withdrew his hand it held a gold chain with a locket. "This is for you."

With trembling hands Sybil took it out of his hand. Inside the locket was a picture of him. "I don't know what to say," she managed.

"If you wear it, I'll always know that I'm close to your heart."

Without speaking she turned around.

Dane took it and fastened it around her neck.

The locket fell perfectly between the mounds of her full breasts.

Dane nuzzled her from behind, "I love you, Sybil Masterson."

Sybil felt as if the wind had been knocked out of her.

He turned her to face him.

She barely managed to whisper, "I love you too, Dane," before his mouth closed on hers. After an eternity, he lifted his mouth from hers. "You better go in. It's late and you have a lot to do before class."

Sybil stood there not wanting to let him go.

"Go ahead," Dane said. Now he gave her a nudge.

Obediently Sybil walked up the steps and when she reached the top, she turned and blew him a kiss before disappearing inside.

*****

Now that classes had resumed there was an air of solemnity on campus. As Sybil walked to class she noticed that her fellow students kept their eyes downcast, as if fearful to trust anyone or afraid for others to recognize how traumatized they were by the recent events.

Sybil went to a memorial in front of Vincent Hall where Professor Devine had taught. The steps were covered with bouquets of flowers, cards, stuffed animals and pictures of students who had loved him and his class. Students stood around in clusters talking quietly.

Gulping at the sight she swallowed hard. When she felt the sensation of being watched she turned around.

Dane leaned on a tree a distance away studying the scene. Then he gave her a curt nod, strode quickly to his car, and drove off.

Sybil felt rejection flood every fiber of her being. Then she shook her head distractedly trying to clear her thoughts. *Don't take it personal that he didn't want to talk. This is his first time on campus since the shooting. He's lost someone who was like a brother to him and he's still trying to make sense of it all.*

When she got back to the room, Peyton was in the adjoining bathroom. Hearing her familiar morning ritual, Sybil knocked sharply on the door and without waiting for permission to enter pushed it open.

Peyton was on her knees with her head bent over the commode.

Exasperated, Sybil stood with her hands planted on her hips and glared at her.

Peyton struggled to get up and Sybil handed her a damp washcloth to cleanse her face.

Peyton took it with a chagrined look on her face and said, "Thanks."

Sybil said in a strict voice, "You need to get healthy. Eating and then vomiting it up to stay skinny is an eating disorder and I'm tired of watching you do this to yourself. You need to take control of your life and stop letting your life take control of you." She turned on her heels and stomped back into the bedroom.

Wearily, Peyton followed her and eased herself on the bed. "I'm not vomiting on purpose. I'm vomiting because I'm pregnant."

The air hung heavy around them. Sybil's eyes went automatically to Peyton's stomach. A small bump seemed visible under her wrinkled nightgown.

Peyton's face was flushed and sweaty from her bout of morning sickness and she moved her foot in agitation.

Sybil said with a horrified expression, "Peyton, how could you let this happen?"

"It's not the end of the world." Peyton hung her head. "Women have babies all the time."

Hesitantly Sybil asked, "Are you going to tell me who the father is?"

"The baby is Kane's of course," Peyton answered stridently.

Sybil looked at her. "I don't mean to be crude, Peyton," she said carefully, "but you've been hanging out lately with Tristan."

"I'm not a whore," Peyton declared vehemently. "Tristan and I aren't having sex. I keep telling you that we're just friends hangin'."

Her eyes shifted away from Sybil's before she added, "Besides, I'm four months along and Kane and I were going hot and heavy then. He can't deny that the baby is his."

Appalled Sybil said, "Do you mean to tell me that you haven't told him yet?" Her eyes rested on Peyton's stomach, "What on earth are you waiting for?"

Peyton got an uncomfortable look and glanced away from Sybil's disapproving countenance. "The first trimester is the hardest. I wanted to wait until I was feeling stronger."

Sybil sat down next to her Peyton picked up her hand. She scrutinized her face and asked softly, "Peyton, are you sure the baby is Kane's? You have to be certain when you tell a man like Kane that you're carrying his baby. He'll do anything to duck out of his responsibility to you and if there is any chance that it actually belongs to someone else..."

"I was only hanging out with Tristan to make Kane jealous just like you told me to." Peyton's sky blue eyes met Sybil's.

"I did not tell you to start staying the night at his place," Sybil protested harshly.

"But it worked. Kane came to me a couple of weeks ago and said that he wanted for us to work things out. I went over there and we hung out and talked. For the second time he let me stay the whole night. Not long after that he broke up with Penelope and took me to the movies. I must mean something to him."

"Do you hear what you're saying? You act like it's a big deal that he didn't kick you out of bed right after he finished screwing you. It should be a given that you stay." She bit her lip but felt the need to knock some sense into Peyton's head. "Kane Hamilton is not daddy material."

"He'll come around once he gets used to it," Peyton said with a stubborn look. She stood and walked over to the mirror and stared at her reflection. "Look at me and think about how Kane looks. The baby is bound to be beautiful."

To this Sybil rolled her eyes from sheer annoyance.

"I'm going to be the mother of his parents' first grandchild. That ought to mean something."

"You haven't even met them," Sybil said in a disparaging tone. "Kane doesn't think that you're worthy."

Peyton's eyes clouded with tears and she began to sob, burying her face in her hands.

"I'm sorry, Peyton. I didn't mean that the way it came out." Sybil felt awful and went and gathered her close.

"Maybe you could tell Dane what's going on and get him to talk to Kane for me."

"It is not my place to tell Dane that he's going to be an uncle," she said sharply.

Peyton began a fresh torrent of tears.

Sybil patiently waited for the deluge to stop.

Once Peyton got control, Sybil got some tissues and handed them to her.

Peyton wiped her face, then blew her nose. Then noise in the room was deafening. Then she looked at Sybil expectantly.

Intuitively Sybil said, "Of course I'll stand by you. But you need to tell Kane." She added thoughtfully, "The sooner the better."

"I will," Peyton whispered quietly.

*****

Sybil entered her room, and Peyton lay on the bed staring vacantly up at the ceiling.

Sybil gave her a quick look of assessment. Taking a deep breath she asked, "What now?"

"Kane doesn't want the baby."

Duh!

"He gave me money for an abortion," she whispered so softly that Peyton could barely hear her.

"You're almost too far along for that."

"I'm not having one," Sybil said, her voice suddenly stronger.

Sybil decided to keep her personal thoughts to herself. No matter what she said it would be the wrong thing.

"That's entirely up to you but you need to realize that you'll probably be raising this baby alone," Sybil said grimly.

"He said that he doesn't think that the baby is his."

"I figured he'd say that," Sybil uttered in a thoroughly disgusted voice.

"Once I have the baby and if it has his eyes he'll be convinced."

"Peyton," Sybil said forcefully, "if you're having this baby in order to hold on to him you're living in a fool's paradise. Men don't usually like being tricked into getting married or being a father."

"Will you go and talk to Kane for me?" Peyton whined. "Tell him that you know that he's the father of my baby."

"Me go and talk to Kane?" she spat out. "I can't stand him. Besides, how could I tell him that I know for sure that the baby is his? I wasn't standing next to the bed watching the two of you do it."

"He needs to take responsibility for some of this," Peyton snapped.

"You can't make people be responsible," Sybil said resentfully. "If that was the case my daddy wouldn't have dumped me on my grandmother and taken off never to be heard from again until it was time to bury him."

"Kane said that Dane told him that I've been sleeping with Tristan." She shot an accusatory look at Sybil. "Dane told Kane that you said I was staying with Tristan during our school hiatus so he doubts that the baby is his," she whispered in a forlorn voice. "Why would you tell Dane that?"

"It just sort of came up," Sybil stammered in a guilty voice. "I didn't mean to discuss your personal business like that."

"I know you didn't, Sybil." Her face full of dejection, Peyton said, "I know that you're a loyal friend." She passed a weary hand over her eyes. "I'm exhausted, and it's only five o'clock." Peyton turned on her side to face the wall and soon Sybil heard her light snore.

Feeling like a wind-up toy, Sybil crossed over to the small refrigerator that they had in the room and mixed a drink of double rum and pineapple juice; then quaffed it. Then she made another. She turned the television on and began surfing the channels. *I Love Lucy* was playing and it was the episode in which Lucy told Ricky that she was pregnant. He was so happy and joyous that he sang a song to her in front of a nightclub of people. *Yeah right!*

She looked at Peyton as she fidgeted in her sleep. Her hand lay in a protective gesture on her stomach.

Loathing for Kane gurgled in her stomach as she watched Peyton and thought about what she was up against in the future. *I wonder if Dane knows. If he did he might try and talk some sense into Kane.* She knew that Kane wouldn't marry Peyton but if their father knew he might make Kane financially support Peyton in order to help the baby at least have a decent start in life.

I'll go to Independent Row and find out what the hell Kane is going to do.

As she walked it began to drizzle but she barely felt it. Her stomach was on fire from all the alcohol that she'd consumed and it gave her the impetus to demand some answers from Kane. Once she got to the sidewalk in front of their house she saw that their storm door wasn't completely shut. She could see that Dane and Kane were having heated words.

Dane stood in a confrontational stance glaring at Kane and he was gesticulating wildly. *It must be about Peyton. I want to know what they're saying and you always hear the truth when people don't know that they're being overheard.* She sidled up onto the porch unnoticed and leaned in to hear.

"I don't know if that's my baby," Kane argued furiously.

"You don't know that it isn't," Dane screamed.

"And you don't know that it isn't yours," Kane sniped back.

Sybil's jaw dropped and she felt her heart plummet. *What?* She took her hand and placed it over her heart to see if it was still beating.

"I'm not marrying no damn Peyton," Kane yelled in a disgruntled voice. "And I'm not claiming that damn baby. I'm giving Whitney an engagement ring on her next birthday."

Who the hell is Whitney?

"If Whitney hears about this she might not marry you." Dane's words sounded like ice breaking.

"Dude, you better not breathe a word of this to her," Kane warned.

Dane's voice sounded raw. "I'm not going to say anything to her."

"And you better not tell Tara because they're sisters and that's the same thing as telling Whitney," he added menacingly.

"I'm not going to say anything to Tara."

Who's Tara?

"But this kid has a right to know who his father is."

"Are you serious?" Kane answered in an exasperated voice. "I gave Peyton five hundred dollars and told her that she should get an abortion. Can you imagine me trying to introduce her to Father? He'd have a coronary and disown me. How would I look introducing her to Dallas society?" He added disparagingly, "Peyton doesn't even know which fork to use during a meal."

"What if Peyton doesn't agree? We might not have to tell father. You know he has spies all over the place."

Sybil could visualize Kane shrugging his shoulders nonchalantly.

"That whore's been hanging out with Tristan. For all we know it could be his." Kane added derogatorily, "You know she fucks any dude who gives her a compliment."

"God! I feel so sorry for this kid," Dane said.

"I know that you're fucking Sybil," Kane said with a hard edge in his voice. "Tomorrow morning, go tell her to make sure that Peyton knows that I'm not going to change my mind. Peyton needs to get rid of that baby because I don't want her or it."

"I'm not fucking Sybil," Dane denied sharply.

Sybil's heart constricted when she heard Dane denying that they slept together.

"Don't lie," Kane sneered. "I saw you kissing her outside her dormitory. That scenario was really funny," he said in a contemptuous voice. "*And* I saw her leaving your room one morning. Be careful before she tries to put a baby on *you*." Kane paused and when Dane didn't say anything he asked with laughter in his voice, "What are you thinking, anyhow? Everybody knows. It's the talk of campus." He added in a challenging voice, "I bet you won't take her home to meet Father." Then he drawled, "But how could you do that when you're engaged to Tara."

Sybil's mouth dropped in horror. *Fiancée? Dane's engaged? That bastard!*

"If Father hears about your antics," Kane continued in a smug voice, "he might disown *you* so maybe you should worry about your own damn business."

"Sybil and I are friends," Dane said defensively.

"She and Peyton are just alike, you know," Kane said dryly.

Dane denied strongly, "Peyton and Sybil are as different as night and day."

"I'm not talking about skin color, asshole. Even though Obama won the presidency people in our world aren't down with that mixed kid shit. The world ain't changed that damn much. They still look at zip codes."

"What do you mean?"

"Peyton and Sybil have no breeding whatsoever," Kane said contemptuously. "That's why the administration put them in the same room freshman year and they've been together ever since. Peyton's here on a fucking cheerleading scholarship and Sybil's on an academic one. Hell, they don't belong here. They just got lucky."

Sybil had heard more than enough. She crept off the stairs. The skies had opened and rain poured from the heavens as if trying to cleanse the world of all its sins.

Adrenalin pumped through her veins as she ran back to her dorm. Her brain was scrambled with what she'd overheard and now a deep, dark hatred for both Kane and Dane flooded her body from head to toe.

When she got to her room, Peyton was leaving the bathroom.

She gave Sybil a weak smile and climbed back into bed.

Ignoring the fact that she was completely drenched from the torrential rain, Sybil stomped over to Peyton and loomed over her. "Have you been sleeping with Dane?"

A look of discomfort sent a flurry of emotions across her face. "No, I have not been sleeping with Dane."

Sybil's fists were balled at her sides. "Then why did Kane tell Dane that he could be the father of your baby as well as him?" she yelled.

Peyton sat up and pulled her legs up to her chest. She dropped her arms around them and whispered, "It only happened once."

"So you did," Sybil said in a sickened voice. "And you wanted me to go and tell Kane that I knew that he's the father. Peyton, how could you?"

"Because it was only one time," she stammered. "Dane wasn't even into it."

Sybil glared at her. "What do you mean?"

"It was when I first hooked up with Kane." Peyton's eyes slid away from hers. "I told him that I was too tired to get up and Kane said that I could stay if I let Dane join us."

"So you let the two of them totally use you like that?" Sybil asked with revulsion.

"We went and got into bed with Dane. When he woke up and found us there he got a real funny look on his face. I could smell liquor on his breath. Then Kane told him that it was what I wanted."

"Why didn't you tell Dane that Kane was lying?" Sybil's voice was high with fury.

"I didn't want to piss Kane off. And Dane does anything that Kane tells him to anyhow."

Sybil offered in a horror-struck voice, "So that's why you said that once the baby was born and if it had Kane's eyes he'd be convinced that it was his?"

"It is Kane's baby," Peyton said firmly. "It took Dane awhile to get hard and then he was so quick it was over in a second. He didn't even come. The minute it was over he got dressed and slammed out of the apartment."

Sybil sank to the floor and cradled her head in her hands. She moaned, "Peyton, what is the matter with you?"

"I will do anything to keep Kane in my life." Peyton wore a stubborn look and her jaw was hard. "I love him."

"Kane doesn't give a shit about you," Sybil stated emphatically. "He thinks you're beneath him. Having this baby will not keep you in his life."

She stalked into the bathroom and grabbed a towel. She stripped and threw the sopping wet clothes in the bathtub. Then she briskly dried her body and hair before rejoining Peyton.

Peyton stared at her with a remorseful look on her face.

"You let people use you. And anyone who's a part of your life gets dragged into your chaotic drama."

Ignoring the grief-stricken look on Peyton's face, she stalked back into the bathroom. Sybil dropped to her knees and with wrenching sounds emptied her guts of the alcohol and turkey pot pie she'd had earlier.

Once her body was purged, she turned both knobs on the faucet full blast. The loud noise was a muffler and allowed her to once again drop to her knees. She closed the lid of the toilet and laid her head on the cold seat, then let a flood of tears rack her body.

*****

Sybil was putting her luggage in her car when she heard someone cough behind her. She turned and found Dane staring at her with a quizzical expression on his face.

"So you're on your way to Nanny's house?"

Sybil insolently looked him up and down. "I don't want you to speak to me or ever come near me again," she spat out venomously. "You user," she sneered. Then she very deliberately drew her arm back and slapped him with all the force that she could muster.

The blow made a crackling sound that reverberated through the crisp air around them.

With a flabbergasted look on his face, Dane stumbled backwards from the blow.

"Never speak to me again," she screamed before she got in the car and locked it. Almost blinded by the hot tears falling on her knuckles Sybil gripped the steering wheel and drove down the street tires squealing. She looked in her rear view mirror.

Dane stood there, nursing his cheek with his hand, as he watched her departure.

That night she tore off her pendant, put it in a wooden box and stuffed it in the side of her suitcase out of sight.

*****

As she lay with her head on her grandmother's lap, Sybil cast her eyes through the doorway that led into the living room.

Nanny smoothed her hair lovingly. "Why don't you go out or something? You don't have to spend all of your Christmas holiday babysitting this old woman."

"I don't want to go anywhere." Sybil buried her head deeper into Nanny's lap. "I'm quite content to stay here with you."

"But it's the holidays. I'm sure that some people you went to high school with are out at those speakeasies you young people seem to enjoy so much."

"Naw," Sybil said. "There's no fun in that without Chloe."

"But you have to be bored," Nanny protested. "After all, it's your vacation."

"I'm not bored," Sybil denied. "As a matter of fact I'm really enjoying the solitude. You don't know what a relief it is to be somewhere that's so calming. Lately school has been nothing but a mess that I can do without."

"Young people have a tendency to be mess cats. Back in my day..." Nanny's voice tailed off. The gold bracelet that Sybil had given her for Christmas jingled with every movement her arm made.

Sybil sat up. "Are you trying to tell me that you were a drama queen when you were younger?"

"I don't quite know what that means. All I do know is that I always had a quick temper and did things impulsively. Sometimes that got me in trouble."

"I find that hard to believe, Nanny. You've always been someone so calm about things."

"Maybe now," Nanny said. "But I had to mature." Nanny gave her a painful stare. "When I had your father I was so young. My mother took care of him the first couple of years of his life. By the time I was ready to take him it took a lot for him and me to develop a relationship. Things got better between us, yet I was never able to be the person that he ran to with his problems.

"Only after my mother passed did he come to me. I was angry with him because he wanted me to take you so he could duck his responsibilities. But I was mostly mad at myself. It was like looking in a mirror at my own history. But there was another part of me that was overjoyed. I felt that I was being given a second chance at being a mother."

"And you have been, Nanny," Sybil said with deep respect. "I couldn't have asked for a better mother."

"You'll break the dysfunctional cycle of our family history. You've already done that because you're the first person in our family to graduate from college. I think that you're also going to be the first black person from Scranton to graduate with a master's degree from Harvard."

"That's not true, Nanny," Sybil exhaled shyly.

"Well," she admitted grudgingly, "you'll be the only person I know."

"I haven't gotten in yet."

"But you will, Sybil." The look on her face suggested that her thoughts were light years away. "Don't ask me how I know. Just believe what I tell you. The road is not always easy to travel. Sometimes things happen that are out of our control. What you have to do is deal with whatever is thrown at you, study the situation, and make the best decisions possible."

Chapter 7

Sybil slowly cracked open the door to her grandmother's room.

Nanny sensed that she was being watched and turned over on the bed and looked at Sybil. "I'm awake, honey."

"I was just checking to see if you were still asleep. Do you want me to fix you some soup or something?"

"I can't have it," she mumbled unhappily.

"You can't have soup either?" Sybil asked as walked into the room.

"Not the good kind," she grumbled. "This diet Doctor Caldwell has me on is horrible. I cheated Christmas Day and ate what I wanted, but I guess I need to do better." Frustrated she exclaimed, "Who in the world wants chicken soup with no noodles? I'd rather have nothing."

Sybil sat down on the bed and patted her consolingly. "I'll make you a nice broiled steak."

Continuing to speak in a petulant voice Nanny said, "I'd like fried steak and onions."

Sybil gave her an uncompromising look. "But you're going to make do with broiled steak and a baked potato."

"A baked potato?" Nanny's facial expression perked up. Then she asked hopefully, "With cheese and sour cream and butter?"

"With butter-lite spread, chives, and fat free sour cream."

"I'd rather do without." Nanny lay back down on the bed.

Sybil chuckled at the indignant look on Nanny's face. "I'll call you when dinner is ready."

Sybil listened to the radio as she busied herself in the kitchen. Whistling as she washed two porterhouse steaks and seasoned them with Lawry's Seasoning salt, broiled steak seasoning and garlic powder, she placed them on a broiling pan, turned the oven on broil and put them in the oven.

Then she got two huge potatoes and vigorously scrubbed them. Once they were squeaky clean she rubbed them lightly with no trans-fat oil, put them each in a brown paper bag and placed them in the microwave.

The telephone rang and after wiping her hands on a wet dishcloth she picked up the receiver. "Hello," she said into the mouthpiece.

"Is that you, Sybil?"

It was a bad connection but Sybil knew that it was Peyton.

"Yes, it's me, Peyton. How are you doing?"

"Okay, I guess," she said in a voice of resignation. "My ma figured out that I was pregnant the minute she saw me."

"I'm not surprised. You seemed to bulge out all of a sudden," Sybil said dryly. "What did she say about it?"

"Ma cried and told me that they didn't let me go up there so I could get knocked up," Peyton whispered a hurt voice. "Daddy yelled at me and threatened to call Kane's father, but I talked him out of that."

Thinking about the conversation she'd snooped on she said, "I don't think that talking to Kane's father would make a world of difference."

"I know. Also Kane would get mad and we'd never work things out."

Is she still praying for that pipe dream?

"But I wanted to let you know that I'm not coming back after Christmas break."

"What?" Sybil protested. "You can't give up when you're this close to graduating."

"Ma took me to the doctor and he said that the baby will be born in May. I need to stay here and get ready for it. We took the money that Kane gave me and bought a second hand washing machine and dryer."

"So you're not going to finish school?" Sybil said regretfully.

"I'm going to take my last semester somewhere down here after the baby is born. Ma's going to keep it for me so I can finish."

"Are you sure that's a good plan?" Sybil said doubtfully. "Most of the time people never go back to school once they quit."

"I can't walk around school with a big stomach, Sybil," Peyton said, obviously mortified, "People were already staring and snickering at me before I left."

"I understand that you'd feel embarrassed," Sybil agreed sympathetically.

"If Kane was acting right instead of prancing around with that stuck up ass Penelope it would be different," Peyton said in a pitiful voice.

Thinking once again back to the conversation she'd eavesdropped on, Sybil said without thinking what the impact of her words would have on Peyton, "Penelope's not going to be the one to end up with Kane," she said firmly.

"So you think that she's just a passing thing, too?" Peyton said hopefully.

"Yes, just like the others," Sybil replied with quiet deliberation.

A long silence ensued.

"Kane is going to marry Whitney." Sybil felt compelled to tell her.

"Who the hell is Whitney?" Peyton's squeaky voice shook through the bad connection.

"She's the family choice and Dane is going to marry her sister Tara."

"How do you know that?" Peyton made a gulping sound. "Did Kane tell you that?"

"No," she said. "I went to talk to him the night you told me you were pregnant and I heard Kane and Dane talking about it."

"Why didn't you tell me?" Peyton asked caustically. "Maybe I could have done something about it."

"You couldn't have done anything then and you can't do anything now. Besides," Sybil added resentfully, "I meant to tell you but I got sidetracked with the information that you did *ménage e trios* with a set of twin brothers."

"I told you how that happened," Peyton stammered. "Anyways, it was before you and Dane had anything to do with each other." There was a long silence on the telephone. "Are you in love with Dane, Sybil?"

"I can't stand to even look at Dane or Kane Hamilton," Sybil replied truthfully. "They're not fit to lick my boots."

After she hung up the telephone she turned around to see Nanny standing in the doorway. She wore a perplexed look on her face and her eyes were narrowed as she assessed Sybil's stormy countenance.

"Was that Chloe?" she asked.

"No, Chloe's still out of town visiting relatives. That was my roommate Peyton or maybe I should say ex-roommate."

"Why is she your ex? Did you two fall out?"

"Yes and no," Sybil said cynically. "She's pregnant by some guy who thinks that he's too good for her, and she's too embarrassed to come back."

"That's a shame," Nanny said as she settled herself in a chair at the table.

Sybil turned the steak over in the oven and pressed the dial on the microwave that held the potatoes. "Dinner will be done in twelve minutes."

"I can't believe how fast that microwave you bought me works." Nanny chuckled. "Where did you get the money for that thing?"

"I did some tutoring," she replied shortly. An image of Dane Hamilton's face appeared in front of her and the hatred that she now felt for him ignited.

"You must be making a lot of money doing that. Those are some hefty checks you've been sending me."

"The tutoring job is over. I won't be doing it anymore."

"That's okay, dear. Even though I appreciated it I wished you wouldn't." Nanny gave her a look.

"I enjoy doing things for you." Sybil patted her on the head as if she were a small child. "It makes me feel good."

"I also noticed you have some new clothes. They look good on you."

"I wish that I hadn't bought them. I thought that I was going to start going out on dates more, but," she shrugged her shoulders in an attempt to appear nonchalant, "now I think not."

"Why not?" Nanny looked at her perceptively. "What's changed?"

"It's no big deal. I just thought that someone I knew was special and now I know that he's a fraud. In fact, he's lower than the low," she ended on a bitter note.

Nanny studied the pain in her granddaughter's eyes that she tried to hide. She said perceptively, "He hurt you and I'm sorry."

"Don't be. I won't be hurt again," Sybil stated with authority.

Nanny squeezed Sybil's hand comfortingly. She said tenderly, "If you keep living in this world you're bound to be hurt at one time or another."

"That's true but you need to take something away from each episode. I've learned that like hangs with like and blood is thicker than water no matter how murky it is."

*****

Sybil sat patiently flipping through pages of a magazine at Doctor Caldwell's examination room.

Nanny sat on the table in a blue gown. Her brow was furrowed with annoyance as she impatiently waited for her results.

"I don't know why you insisted on me coming in here again," she wailed plaintively. "I was just in here not too long ago."

Sybil gave her grandmother a piercing stare. "I want to know why you keep having diabetic episodes," she said. "The doctor may need to change your dosage."

"Humph," she muttered in a grumbling voice, "all you're doing is giving him a reason to put me on more medicine. I have to pay for this visit."

"I'll pay for it," Sybil said. "So stop complaining and let me look out for you."

"But I'm supposed to be looking out for you, not the other way around," Nanny whined.

"And you do take care of me," Sybil said gently. Placing the magazine in the rack on the wall she said, "You have been the rock of my life." Sybil's voice broke. "If something was to happen to you..."

"Nothing's going to happen to me, Sybil. I'm as strong as a horse."

Doctor Caldwell entered the office and his smile broke into a grin when he saw Sybil. "How are you doing, young lady?"

"I'm fine but I'm worried about Nanny," she said. "Since I've been home she's had two episodes where her eyes glazed over and she couldn't hear me talking to her. After I gave her some orange juice she responded." Sybil's voice trembled, "But what would have happened if I wasn't here?"

Doctor Caldwell nodded his head in understanding. "I do realize how upsetting that can be to see." He stared at Nanny with censure. "Are you taking your medication the way you're supposed to?"

"Yes," she answered roughly.

"Are you sure? I don't need to up your medication if you're not following directions." He glared at Nanny.

"I get tired of timing that mess. Thirty minutes before every meal I have to stop and do that. It's annoying," she muttered.

"And it's keeping you alive," Doctor Caldwell said seriously.

"Well, it's killing my social security check," Nanny replied caustically. "My insurance knows that I need it to live. Why won't they work with me on the price? Or how a about generic insulin? They could come up with it if they wanted to."

With an astonished look on his face Doctor Caldwell asked, "Are you sitting here telling me that you're not following the instructions that I gave you three months ago?"

"I'm doing the best I can," Nanny said defensively. She admitted in a sour voice, "It's so expensive that sometimes I cut my dosage in half."

"Nanny!" Sybil exclaimed in horror. "How could you?"

"I'm just trying to hang in there until Congress gets this universal healthcare mess straightened out."

"Don't hold your breath on that," Doctor Caldwell said grimly. "You're playing Russian Roulette with your life by cutting your medicine. I'll give you a month's supply of syringes and insulin. That should help."

"What about after that? I'm in the donut hole and I have to pay for all of it until January fifteenth," Nanny said grumpily.

"You can't cut your medication, Nanny." Doctor Caldwell gave her a scolding look. "You could go into a diabetic shock that you can't recover from."

"She won't cut it anymore," Sybil promised with fervor. "I'll make sure of that."

As Sybil helped Nanny get situated in the car she said decisively, "I'm going to come here this summer to work so I can keep an eye on you."

*****

Sybil sat in the front row of Professor Lehman's class and scribbled into her notebook the material on the board. Someone suddenly sat down in the vacant seat next to her. She looked up and when her eyes met those of Dane, hot white anger flooded her entire being. Her eyes bored holes through him.

Dane's emerald eyes stared back at her. Then suddenly he dropped his eyes and without uttering a sound, slid out of the chair and with shoulders hunched over, walked to the back of the auditorium and sat in an empty desk on the aisle.

At the end of class Professor Lehman stood at the podium and said in a clear no nonsense voice, "Your last paper is due the first Monday after Easter. No late papers will be accepted. Class is dismissed."

There was no grumbling or complaining as students filed out.

Sybil put her backpack on and walked up the aisle. She came abreast of Dane who was still sitting with an uneasy look on his face.

Sybil gave him a haughty look and stalked by with head held high.

When she got back to her empty dormitory room, a feeling of loneliness consumed her. She missed Peyton's ceaseless chattering and for the first time since she'd been at college felt really alone.

The ringing of her cell phone startled her. "Hello," she said into the receiver.

"Hey, Sybil."

The weak voice of Peyton shook her. "Peyton, I was just thinking how much I miss you."

"Do you miss me enough to come and see me?" Peyton asked in a small voice.

Sybil's heart pounded from fear. "Come and see you? There's nothing wrong, is there?"

"They're going to take the baby soon," she said in a voice that bordered on hysteria.

"They who? The Hamiltons?"

"No," she said and her tone expressed her embarrassment. "I haven't been able to talk to Kane since I left school. Have you seen him?"

"From afar," Sybil answered truthfully. "He looked the other way and so did I." Sybil asked in a frightened voice, "Who's going to take your baby?"

"The doctor," she said.

"But why so early? You're only seven months," Sybil asked anxiously.

"They say that I can't take it to term because I didn't get the right prenatal care while I was in school. The umbilical cord is wrapped around his neck. The doctors have just been waiting for him to get a little bit stronger."

"So it's a boy," Sybil said, trying to sound of cheerful. "Congratulations."

"Yeah, I got what I wanted."

Sybil wanted to say, "You did?" But instead she said, "When are they going to take the baby?"

"Next Sunday."

"That's right before spring break," Sybil mused.

"I hope that you'll come down. I want you to be Kane's godmother."

"I would love being the baby's godmother." Then Sybil asked in a disapproving voice, "You're going to name the baby after Kane? Have you asked him for permission to do that?'

"It's impossible for me to ask him since he hasn't returned any of my phone calls," Peyton retorted in a strained voice. "But I can name my son whatever I want. He deserves to know where he came from."

Sybil held her tongue, not wanting to upset Peyton while she was in her precarious state.

"Will you come?" Peyton asked. Sybil could hear the strain in her voice. "My ma and I... We ain't, I mean, aren't getting along."

"Peyton, why don't I come after graduation?"

Peyton whimpered, "If I just saw your face when I opened my eyes... Sybil, I just miss you so much. And this place..."

"I'd have to drive and that means I'd barely have any time to spend with you," Sybil said doubtfully. "I think that they keep you for days in the hospital if they do a C section."

"But I'd feel better just knowing that you were here." Peyton's voice dropped even lower, "Please."

After a long hesitation Sybil promised, "I'll be there."

"Thank you, Sybil," Peyton said and for the first time since they began their conversation there was an upbeat note in her voice.

After Sybil finished talking to Peyton she went to her computer and Googled MapQuest. "Twelve hours," she groaned. *If I leave before daylight Saturday, I'll get there before Peyton's surgery Sunday morning.* After mentally making her plans and ticking off things that she needed to take care of, Sybil sat down and began writing Professor Lehman's paper.

*****

Sybil rolled over and looked at the clock on her nightstand. Groggily, she stood up and her eyes settled on a white envelope. With a harsh sigh of irritation, she padded over and picked it up. She glared at Dane's familiar scrawl. *Sybil, please read.*

Sybil did what she'd done with the last ten letters she'd found slid under her door. Without opening it, she walked over to her paper shredder, inserted the letter, and punched the start button. She unblinkingly watched it shred into miniscule slivers of ribbon.

*****

146

In the dusky light, Sybil took her hand and wiped the frosty windshield until she could see the sign that pointed east. She read silently, "Boone, North Carolina, three hundred and twenty miles."

She pulled her cell phone out of her purse. *I need to call Nanny and let her know that I'm going to see Peyton.* She turned it on and waited for it to light up. When there was no response, she pushed the power button off, waited a minute, and then turned it on again. Still there was no response. *Damn it! It's finally done. I'll have to purchase another when I get to the next town.* Sybil took the SIM card out of the back and put it in the dash of her car. Then out of sheer frustration, she rolled down her window and chucked the phone out. It bounced off a tree and fell into the lake that had flanked the road for the last few miles she'd driven.

Sybil slowly stepped on the gas and her slick tires slid on the ice. *It's a hell of a lot colder here than I thought. These mountains must insulate everything from the sun.*

Shivering in her coat, she mentally calculated that at the rate she was going it was going to take her four hours more than she'd anticipated when mapping out her route.

Her car suddenly fishtailed and apprehension gripped her. She slowed down even more on the winding road. *My nerves are on edge and I'm too sleepy to keep driving. I should stop at the next rest stop and catch a nap. That coffee that I had at the last gas station didn't do me any good at all.*

The next intersection was a four-way stop. Sybil looked to the left and then the right. Seeing that it was clear, she stepped on

147

the gas and pulled out. From behind Sybil heard a screeching of tires just before the back of her car was hit with such force that it spun around in a complete circle and stalled in the opposite lane. BAM! Sybil's head hit the steering wheel and bounced back. The contact set off her horn. Feeling dizzy and reeling from the impact, Sybil painfully lifted her head just enough to see a semi-tractor trailer careening towards her.

The high whistle sound of brakes filled the air as the driver applied brakes in a futile effort to break its speed. Sybil covered her face with her hands.

The eighteen-wheeler slammed into the passenger side of her car. It crashed through the steel rail that separated the road and headed towards the water. As her car tumbled down towards the dark, gloomy lake, Sybil managed to unbuckle her seatbelt, open her car door, and throw all of her weight to the left out of the car. Sybil lost count of how many times her body rolled over. Just before she succumbed to unconsciousness she saw her car tumble into the water and disappear from sight.

*****

Sybil tried to pry her eyes open but couldn't. She heard distant voices in the background.

A male voice with a heavy twang said, "Nurse Greer, do we have any information on this Jane Doe yet?"

"No, Doctor Weiss," a female voice said.

"Two weeks is too long for someone not to have notified missing persons that a member of their family disappeared."

There was a clucking sound of disapproval. "It just doesn't make any sense."

"The officer working the case said that he can't identify her because her car and all of her belongs are still submerged into the lake."

"Can't they bring it to the surface?"

"No," he said. "The mudslide has made it impossible to find a steady place along the embankment for a crane to lift her car out of the water."

Inside her head, Sybil was screaming. She inwardly moaned, *Why can't they hear me?* Before she lapsed back into unconsciousness.

*****

Sybil lay flat on her back and stared at the ceiling. Her face was in excruciating pain. Her mouth was dry and her lower extremities ached. When she gingerly opened her mouth, electric currents shot through bones in her face. She closed her eyes in an effort the block the pain.

"I think she fell back asleep, Doctor Weiss," the nurse said in an agitated voice.

"Well she needs to wake up again," he replied resolutely. "Three weeks is far too long for anyone to be in a coma. I'm going to check her vitals."

Sybil's eyes fluttered open when she heard the familiar voice that she recognized from the deep recesses of her mind. *Three weeks? What in the world is he talking about?*

149

She opened her eyes and fixed them on the man in the white coat. He had white bushy hair and brown eyes. He stared at her with a serious yet warm expression.

She swallowed and her throat felt scratchy and hurt. Her tongue felt leaden when she tried to move it. Her eyes spied the liquid on the side of her bed. It was connected to a tube that was inserted into her vein in her left arm.

The doctor took a small flashlight and leaned over. He lifted one eyelid and shone the light in it. Then he lifted the other and did the same. The doctor looked at the nurse that stood hovering behind him. "Have you checked her blood pressure?" he asked abruptly.

"Yes, Doctor Weiss. It's a bit low, but that's bound to be due to her inactivity."

The doctor focused his attention on Sybil. "My name is Doctor Weiss. Do you understand what I'm saying?"

Sybil stared at him and slowly nodded her head.

"Good," he said.

"Can you speak?"

When Sybil opened her mouth, she felt as if her muscles were moving in slow motion.

The doctor turned to the nurse. He ordered in an authoritative tone, "Give her some water."

Immediately Nurse Greer poured water from a plastic pitcher into a cup and put a straw in it. She pressed the button on the side of the bed and it slowly moved to an upright position.

Every movement of the bed painfully tore at her insides.

Once the straw was placed gently between Sybil's lips she drank deeply. Then closed her eyes and turned her head to show that she'd had enough.

"Do you know where you are?" Doctor Weiss asked.

Sybil slowly shook her head no. A sharp pain shot from the back of her neck to her forehead and she winced. She slowly moved her hand to her head and felt a heavy bandage. She immediately became alarmed and her eyes relayed her fear.

"Don't make any unnecessary movement," Doctor Weiss cautioned. "You have a lot of bumps and bruises, but you're still all in one piece. Just blink twice for yes and once for no. We have morphine being delivered to you through this drip. Do you need more?"

Sybil blinked twice.

Immediately the doctor turned to the nurse and nodded.

Nurse Greer took a packet off a small cart at the side of the room and changed the clear plastic bag that was connected to the IV drip.

Sybil tried futilely to crane her neck to see what she was doing.

"Do you remember your car accident?"

She blinked once and tears began to cascade down her cheeks their progress hindered by the bandages on her face.

"Don't fret," the doctor said. His brow furrowed as he studied her. "I'm sure that it'll come back to you soon enough."

Sybil finally spoke and when she did her voice was a mere whisper. "I have something to ask you, Doctor."

"What is it?"

"What's my name?" she asked before she fell into a sedated sleep.

*****

She sat in a wheelchair and stared out the window. Sybil turned her head to glance at Doctor Weiss when he entered the room then looked away.

"I take it by the look on your face that you don't want to see me today."

Sybil continued to look out the window ignoring him.

He sat down in the chair in front of her. "I know that it was a shock to call home and find out that your grandmother passed away while you were in a coma," he said in a pained voice.

Still she didn't answer.

"It's not your fault," he said quietly.

"Yes it is," she denied in a soft whisper.

"Sybil, I'm sure that you feel that you've lost everything but…"

She broke in harshly, saying, "I *have* lost everything. My grandmother *was* everything, and I wasn't there for her. She died alone."

"Everyone dies alone, Sybil," he said gently.

Sybil passed that off. She reiterated, "She had always been here for me and I let her down."

"I doubt if this will make you feel any better, Sybil, but when people go into a diabetic coma and die they don't suffer." Doctor Weiss spoke soothingly, "They don't even know what's going on. She died with dignity."

"But I wasn't there." Sybil stared at some unseen object somewhere behind Doctor Weiss.

"Because you were going to see about a friend in need." He sat down in the visitor chair that had only been used by him. "What's wrong with that, Sybil? Do you wish that you hadn't put someone else's feelings in front of yours and not gone?"

"Yes. No. I don't know. It seems as if I lost everything while I was unaware of what was going on around me."

"And that couldn't be helped. Even after you regained consciousness it took a while for your memory to work its way back in."

"I should have been more careful," she said morosely.

"There was nothing that you could do," Doctor Weiss gently scolded. "The car that hit you was driving carelessly. And the truck driver was also speeding. Being struck like that one right after the other... it was one of the worse freak accidents that I've ever heard of."

"And now I'm the freak." Sybil turned and looked in the mirror. She touched her new cheekbones that gave her a slightly hollow look.

Her face was angular from all the weight she'd lost but whenever she looked at her reflection it was her nose that caught her attention. Doctor Weiss doctor had reconstructed it during the operation in order for her to be able to breathe freely. Now it was straight as an arrow. Her cheekbones had been broken in the accident and she now had cheekbones models would pay thousands of dollars to have. But to Sybil the changes represented more pieces of her that were gone. "I don't even recognize my own face," her voice broke in the unusual bout of self-pity.

"The surgeries did make quite a difference," Doctor Weiss admitted. "I'm sorry if you're displeased with the changes, but I had to do something and I had to do it quickly."

Sybil looked at the doctor who had become her confidant and a shoulder to lean on for the last couple of months. "I'm not blaming you."

"Then don't blame yourself either. Have you decided when you're going to call Peyton?"

"Why would I call her?" Sybil asked coldly. "If she hadn't pressured me into making that trip none of this would have happened."

"You have a point," Dr. Weiss said quietly. "But if you cared enough about her to put her feelings in front of yours, you might want to let her know why you didn't show for the birth of her child."

"How about her?" Tears formed in Sybil's eyes. "Why didn't she try to find me? I laid here for weeks like some homeless woman. Nanny I can forgive because she didn't even know that I was traveling and where to look for me, and Chloe was in London on an education exchange program. But Peyton is so self-absorbed she probably didn't even try."

"Maybe," Doctor Weiss agreed. "Or maybe she thought that you were tired of her antics and that's why you didn't show up when her son was being born. That makes sense as to why you haven't heard from her. I'd at least hear her out."

"I don't have the strength to deal with her right now." With a bleak expression Sybil turned and looked out the window.

"How did physical therapy go today?"

"It sucked." Sybil glared at him. "I'm not going tomorrow."

Doctor Weiss decided to let that matter drop for the moment. "Why did you refuse to let Chloe visit you?"

She turned her face away from his. "I wasn't ready to face her shock of seeing me look so different."

"I understand," Doctor Weiss said. "This morning your lawyer called me and asked if it was okay for him to come to see you this afternoon."

"I don't have a lawyer," she replied in a frigid tone.

"You don't have to hire who I recommended but you need someone. The people that hit you are trying to settle way too fast for my liking."

"I don't care about money," she said listlessly.

"You may not care right now but you will when you start thinking clearly." Doctor Weiss pinned Sybil's eyes with his. "You need to take care of business," he stated forcefully. "You lost the joy of graduating on time. And you have a huge hospital bill that you need to make sure that they pay." He hesitated before he said softly, "Sybil, there is nothing in this world that can bring your grandmother back."

She stoically continued to look out the window avoiding his eyes.

Doctor Weiss zeroed in on her making sure his words hit home. "But you can certainly use the money to go to Scranton and put a beautiful headstone on that grave of hers."

*****

Sybil was sitting up in her bed using a laptop that Doctor Weiss lent her. She Googled Harvard University. Once the webpage opened she narrowed her search to online courses. *They offer everything that I need to finish my degree. If I can get accepted, I'll finish my classes online. I'll e-mail the Dean of the Department of Social Work and ask him if can have my credits transferred.*

Later that afternoon, Sybil sat staring sullenly out the window. The day was sunny and the birds were chirping but the happy sounds didn't lighten her mood. *Dane and Kane Hamilton.* The thought of them made her blood boil. *They use people and then don't care what happens to them. If there is ever a way that I can pay them back, I will.*

Her dark thoughts of revenge were interrupted when she saw Doctor Weiss enter her room with a tall, blonde man in a navy suit who was carrying a briefcase. Sybil looked at him with a

156

cynical twist on her mouth. *This must be my lawyer. Why is he in such a hurry to have me become his client?*

"Sybil, this is attorney Thomas Vanguard," Dr. Weiss said. "He represented my mother-in law in a car accident a couple of years ago and we were quite pleased with the results."

Sybil glared at Thomas Vanguard.

His eyes met her hostile ones and he didn't flinch.

That made her feel that she could trust him, and her eyes softened.

Seeing this Dr. Weiss said, "I'm going to leave the two of you alone to talk business." He patted her shoulder and left the room.

"May I sit down?" her lawyer said.

Sybil nodded.

He pulled up a chair opposite her. Placing his briefcase on the floor next to him he said with a sympathetic look on his face, "How are you doing?"

Sybil shrugged.

"Obviously Dr. Weiss has filled me in as much as he could without breaking his Hippocratic Oath. But he sent for me because he felt that you needed someone to look out for your interests."

"I do since now I'm all alone," Sybil said in a monotone.

"I know that you lost someone very dear to you while you were in a coma," he said gently.

Tears threatened to fall and Sybil furiously blinked them away because she never felt comfortable showing vulnerability in front of strangers.

"There's nothing that any person on this earth can do to fix that, but I can make sure that the people that were so careless pay for what has happened to you. If they do, maybe in the future they'll think twice about what impact their actions have on others. You've had multiple surgeries and been through a lot of trauma. I can make sure that you never suffer financially or have to work another day in your life."

Sybil gave a start of surprise. "You think that I could get that much?" she stammered.

"I know that you can get that much." He opened his briefcase and pulled out some papers, handing them to Sybil. "I took the liberty of doing some digging before I came to see you. The person in the sports car that hit you is the grandson of Eli Smith."

"Who's Eli Smith?" Sybil asked in confusion.

"Since you're not from this part of North Carolina you don't recognize the name. Eli Smith owns the textile industry in most of the state. That's who we're going sue."

"But he wasn't driving the car. His grandson was."

"But he bought him the car for him as a sixteenth birthday present. The car is in the grandfather's name and that makes him liable. Whoever owns the title of the car is as responsible as the driver of the car in a court of law."

"That doesn't seem fair," Sybil protested. "He was trying to be nice to his grandson by purchasing him a car."

"People know their family. Eli knows that his grandson is spoiled and immature. He shouldn't have bought him that car in the first place. Kyle has a history of getting into trouble and his grandfather always gets him out of it."

"I heard that Kyle suffered very few injuries from the accident."

"He certainly fared a lot better than you did. That boy has nine lives."

"I still don't see why Kyle Smith isn't the one I'm suing."

"Kyle doesn't have anything or we'd sue him too. Eli wants to keep this as quiet as possible. His grandson was speeding and had alcohol in his system. This could keep him out of Princeton, the family university. All that matters to Eli is his family lineage and how it goes down in history."

Kane and Dane's faces suddenly appeared before her. "So the Smiths are supposed to be a big deal around here?"

"Yes, and they think they own the town. People are usually afraid of them. They walk all over people thinking that they're better than they are. They're a very vengeful family if you get in the way of something that they want. But you don't live here so you don't have to worry about any repercussions being taken out on you. You can take your money and run," Thomas Vanguard added smugly.

"Obviously you don't like them."

"No, I don't," he answered bluntly. "In the beginning there were quite a few families involved in running the mills around here and little by little Eli Smith bought them out, giving them only a fraction of what they should have been paid. He had friends in the banks that wouldn't give the families loans to keep going so they had to sell or go under. Then he raised prices on everything the mills produced yet hasn't given the workers a decent raise in years."

"So he's a bully on top of everything else," Sybil stated in disgust.

"Yes. He's totally uncaring about the lives of others. To top it off, the truck that hit you is owned by his company so we can also sue his precious industry."

Another vision of the Hamilton twins surfaced. "Get as much out of them as you can," she said in a stony voice.

"I will," he promised.

Chapter 8

From under her long eyelashes, Sybil watched the hospital psychologist as she scribbled notes on a pad.

"We're releasing you tomorrow, but I'm worried about whether or not you're ready."

"I'm ready," Sybil responded quietly.

"I know from your physical therapist that physically you're ready, but I have great concern as to whether you're ready emotionally. You've been in the hospital for over six months. That's a traumatic experience in itself and after what you've been through, I would like you to stay in the area and have some counseling."

"I'm not a mental case and I sure as hell am not staying in North Carolina any longer than I have to," Sybil retorted.

Doctor Etheridge looked at Sybil over her bifocals. "You've never expressed how you feel about your new appearance."

"What do you want me to say?" Sybil gave her a hostile look. "When I look in the mirror I have to touch my face to make sure that it's my reflection that I'm looking at. There's not a damn thing that I can do to change it so why talk about it?"

"Do you hate the way you look?" Doctor Etheridge asked gently.

Sybil shrugged her shoulders.

"Have you not noticed the way the men on the hospital staff and any man that you encounter in the hall looks at you when you walk by?"

Again Sybil merely shrugged her shoulders for her answer.

"A lot of women would kill to look like you," she persisted, hoping to find out what Sybil was really thinking.

"Why? Because now I have a straight nose and high cheekbones?" Sybil's eyes were narrowed in self-derision.

"You do have a model's face," Doctor Etheridge agreed. "And with those beautiful eyes you are absolutely breathtaking."

"And don't forget the fact that I lost over thirty pounds and wear a size four." A memory of Peyton regurgitating her dinner flashed before her eyes. She said disdainfully, "I know how important it is for some people to look anorexic."

"You don't look anorexic," Doctor Etheridge denied. "You're still shapely."

For the first time since she sat down a half smile formed on Sybil's lips. "I'm a black girl. My butt will always be the biggest thing on me. But since the accident my breasts have lost something. I'm going to get them lifted once I get out of here."

Doctor Etheridge lifted her eyebrows. "I'm surprised. I thought that you said that you're sick of people poking at you."

"I am," Sybil said. "But I want to have my breasts feel like they used to."

"Sybil, you should do whatever makes you feel comfortable with yourself." Doctor Etheridge said carefully, "But you need to understand that no plastic surgery can make you be what you used to be."

A glint of steel radiated from Sybil's eyes. "I already know that I'll never be the person I used to be."

*****

The next morning Sybil sat on her bed waiting for the hospital orderly to come with a wheelchair and get her the hell out of there.

She looked up expectantly and when she saw it was Doctor Weiss she stood and held her arms out to hug the only father figure she'd ever known.

Sybil let herself be enveloped in his warm embrace.

Releasing her he said, "Doctor Etheridge informed me that you don't want any more counseling. I think that you're making a mistake."

Sybil brushed that aside. "I don't need it. I'm fine."

"You certainly look fine," he said, smiling at his play on words, "but emotionally you've been through so much."

"I'm capable of facing my demons on my own. Besides, my best friend got her degree in counseling. If I need to talk to someone I'll talk to her."

Doctor Weiss looked at the stubborn look on Sybil's face and knew that her mind was made up so he might as well let it go.

"I'm glad that things have worked out for you financially. I knew that Vanguard would take care of you."

163

"I hope that there aren't any repercussions to him from the Smith family because of what he did for me," she mused in a worried tone. "Wilmington is too small a town to have such powerful enemies."

"Don't worry about Vanguard. He's a big boy and can take care of himself. He's wanted to stick it to them for years."

"But to make the Smiths pay all of the hospital bills plus any plastic surgery that I wanted in addition to that massive settlement… I sort of feel guilty."

"You need to make a fresh start and they should help you get it."

"But I didn't expect millions," she murmured softly.

Doctor Weiss gave her a piercing stare. "You may have issues from your accident for the rest of your life and they know it. You've been quite generous to them because you could have gotten more, but you didn't want to go to court. In reality you could have pushed Smith near bankruptcy. The before and after pictures of you are worth a thousand words and if a jury had seen them…"

"But if I had done that the people that he does employ would be out of a job."

Doctor Weiss rubbed his chin thoughtfully. "I hadn't really thought about that. You have a good heart."

"I think you're the person in the room with the big heart." Sybil choked out, "I don't know how I can ever repay you for what you've done to help me."

"Just remember that life goes on," Doctor Weiss said in a sober tone. "You can't change the past, but you can help shape the present. So be healthy and happy. That's all the thanks I need."

*****

Sybil Masterson walked into the Jaguar dealership with a magazine tucked under her arm and stood there expectantly. She spied a cluster of salesmen in khaki pants and blue shirts.

They gave her a cursory look and then turned away resuming their conversation.

A receptionist glared at the group before turning to Sybil. She asked politely, "May I help you?"

"Yes, I'd like to take a look at the XJ model."

Now the receptionist looked at Sybil's appearance.

Sybil hadn't had time to clothes shop since she'd been released from the hospital that morning and she still wore the outfit that she'd gotten out of the hospital's donation pile for the needy. The yellow shorts and the lime green shirt she wore were too skimpy for the cool October air and she shivered. She'd refused to wear the shoes that had been the only item salvageable from the accident and had purchased a pair of flip flops from the hospital gift shop.

The receptionist smiled at her. She whispered conspiratorially, "We have a college student working here on an internship. He'd be more than happy to help you and he needs the practice."

165

"Does he get a commission for anything he sells?" Sybil asked.

"He sure does," she said. "But don't worry about that. He's such a nice boy he'd love to help you even if you don't buy."

A burst of laughter erupted from the group of salesman and one was clapping the other on the back as they guffawed at whatever joke had been told.

The receptionist picked up a phone and punched several buttons. She said into the receiver, "Swails, I have a customer who wants to look at a Jag." She said after she hung up, "He'll be right out."

Immediately a young man strode from the back. He too was dressed in khakis and a blue shirt but his demeanor was friendly as he held his hand out. He shook hers vigorously. "Ma'am. You're interested in test driving a Jaguar?"

"Yes," Sybil said demurely and opened the magazine under her arm. "I want one exactly like this."

"We just got two in yesterday. We have a black and a white."

"I'd like to drive the black."

"Of course, ma'am." He smiled engagingly. "Let me just get the keys that unlock the security bolt."

Minutes later Swails reappeared and gestured for Sybil to follow him.

166

Once in the parking lot, he quickly unlocked the car and opened the driver's side. When Sybil was seated he patiently explained the controls. Then he said, "Turn the engine on."

Sybil turned the key in the ignition but she didn't hear anything and leaned forward.

"It's on," Swails said, grinning. "The engine is so quiet you can barely hear it."

Not believing him, Sybil stepped on the gas and the roaring of the engine frightened her. She hurriedly lifted her foot off the gas and took her hands off the steering wheel.

"Ma'am, are you okay?" Swails looked at her expression.

"Yes," she stammered, wiping perspiration from her face with the back of her hand. "It's just that I was in an accident recently and haven't driven in a while."

"I'm sorry to hear that." Then his face brightened. "But then this is the car you want," he said with confidence. "The Jaguar is one of the safest cars out there."

"I know," Sybil said quietly. "That's why I chose it."

"Are you okay to drive now?" Swails watched her with narrowed eyes.

Sybil drew strength from her strong upbringing from Nanny and mustered up the will to continue. In her mind she knew that she had to pass the test and drive again because if she didn't, that would mean that she'd let her demons beat her.

"Yes," she answered softly and put the car in gear slowly pulling out.

Sybil and Swails drove back roads for about fifteen minutes not saying a word. As she got the feel of the car she picked up speed until she came to a four way stop and stomped on the brake pedal, making the car lurch to a standstill.

Her heart suddenly dropped. A flashback to the seconds before her accident surfaced and she sat there motionless as the car idled. Her heart felt constricted and beads of sweat broke out on her face. Her hands trembled on the steering wheel and she felt hot. Suddenly, Nanny's face popped into her mind. She wore an encouraging smile.

Feeling a surge of strength, she looked in her rear view mirror and saw nothing. Sybil looked to the left and then the right. Still feeling shaky, she looked to the left and the right again.

When she felt Swails' apprehensive eyes on her, she stepped on the gas pedal and slowly moved forward. Once she realized she wasn't going to be rammed into from behind, she made a U-turn and headed back towards the dealership. After she was safely parked she turned to Swails. "Let's go inside and write up the paperwork for purchase."

Swail's jaw dropped in surprise.

Sybil had to hand it to him because he quickly recovered.

He merely said, "Let's go to my cubicle located at the back of the showroom."

Sybil followed Swails past the receptionist where the other salesmen were still lounging around.

After pulling out a chair for her to sit down, he took out a sales ticket and started writing numbers down from the invoice he'd taken off the car window.

Curious, one of the salesmen broke away from the group and joined them. Leaning over the side of the cubicle he gave Sybil a charming smile. He asked Swails, "Do you need any help?"

"No, sir, I think I have it," Swails responded in a respectful tone.

"What's going on?" he persisted.

"I just had a wonderful ride in your XJ and would like to purchase it," Sybil explained.

The salesman's eyes narrowed in shock. He said in a deceptively smooth voice, "Well, Swails is on internship and hasn't ever had a sale so I think that I might need to help him."

The other salesmen that had been previously chatting with him ambled over. With keen interest they watched the exchange.

Hiding his expression, Swails looked down at the papers that he was shuffling around on his desk.

The salesman continued, "He would need one of the experienced salesmen who work here in order to access your credit report and things like that. It's just a safety precaution for you."

"He doesn't need any of that information since I'm paying by check." She looked at him dismissively. "If you call the bank they'll tell you it's good. So we'll be just fine."

Swails and the other salesmen's eyes opened wide in wonder.

Then the salesman drew himself up and without trying to mask his anger stomped off. The others glared at Swails and then followed suit.

Once they were alone again Sybil looked at Swails. "Do you really want to do this for a living?"

He nodded his head eagerly. "Yes, ma'am."

"Then make sure that you never judge a book by a cover because it might cost you a sale."

"I'll remember that," Swails promised gratefully. "Ma'am, thank you for what you did. The money that I'll make off the sale of this car will pay for all the books I have to buy for my last two years of college." Then a flustered look appeared on his face. "Oops. I don't think that I was supposed to say that."

"You weren't," Sybil said with a smile. "But don't worry about it. I'm happy to help."

"It'll take a while to get your car detailed. If you wish, you can wait in the lounge. We have Wi-Fi and coffee available for our customers."

"You know," she said musingly. "I think that I'm going to walk over to that mall across the street." She looked at her attire. "I need some new clothes."

"Let me drive you over," Swails offered.

"No thank you." Sybil smiled her refusal. "I need vitamin D from the sun."

Sybil walked past the salesmen whose heads were together whispering.

She strutted past them and avoided their eyes as they tried to make contact with hers.

Hours later after her black Jaguar with newly tinted windows was detailed, Sybil pulled out of the dealership. In her rear view mirror she saw the salesmen lined up shoulder to shoulder watching her as she drove off.

*****

With eyes open wide, Sybil stared in horror at her childhood home. The front windows were boarded up and trash was strewn all over the front yard. Gone were the rocking chairs where she and her grandmother had spent many quiet evenings sipping iced tea and eating graham crackers. She swallowed hard and opened her car door, then slammed it with a vengeance.

Stomping up the steps she tried to open the front door, but it wouldn't budge. She stormed back down the steps and started walking around the periphery of the building. Shattered glass from the broken windows crackled under her newly purchased sneakers. Quickly ascending the back steps she tried to open the screen door but it also was locked. Then she spied a broken window with a gaping hole large enough for her to reach through.

Sybil put one hand carefully through the hole and reached up to unlatch the lock. Then she opened the window and shimmied inside.

Once inside she surveyed the kitchen.   Anger filled her heart. The kitchen sink was filthy with empty Chinese food containers and the cupboards were bare.

A dank smell of mold permeated the air. Sybil held her finger to her nostrils as she walked from room to room. She was repulsed by the dirty linen on the unmade beds and the broken glass that was strewn from one end of the house to the other.   In the living room couch cushions were ripped and some lay scattered on the floor.

Sybil looked down carefully where she stepped and put her hand to her heart when she saw in a corner a pile of her family treasures. A photo album lay on top of Nanny's favorite red and white checkered housedress.   Sybil reached for the dress and buried her face into it. Not being able to hold it in any longer, she burst into tears.

She sat in the corner sobbing, not bothering to wipe the tears from her cheeks. After she was empty of tears she carefully folded the dress and placed it gently in her lap.   Then she reached for the water damaged family album and began to thumb through the pages.

Nanny had arranged photographs in chronological order showing Sybil's progression from toddler to a grown woman. After she looked at the last of Nanny's entries of their last Christmas together Sybil shut the book.

"Who the fuck are you and what are you doing in here?"

Startled, Sybil looked up and saw the stormy countenance of Chloe in a combative stance.

"It's me," she whispered. "Sybil."

Slowly Sybil stood and brushed the bits of broken glass from her knees. She stared at her childhood friend who now stared back at her with a mixture of confusion and dismay.

"Sybil," she croaked, staring at her eyes, "is that really you?"

Overwrought from the last hour's discovery, Sybil dumbly nodded her head in assent.

"Oh my God!" Chloe breathed as her eyes ran up and down the length of Sybil's thin frame. "If it wasn't for your eyes I would have never recognized you. Why the hell didn't you prepare me for the change in your appearance when we talked on the telephone?"

"A picture is worth a thousand words," she answered dully.

"What the hell happened?" Chloe exclaimed, "Did you have plastic surgery?"

"Not intentionally." Chloe's intense stare discomfited Sybil. She said defensively, "I told you that I was in a car accident."

"But I didn't expect this." Still trying to absorb the difference in Sybil's appearance, Chloe said, "You should have said something."

Sybil took her index finger and positioned it on her face. "All these changes fell to the wayside after you told me that Nanny was dead."

A long uncomfortable silence ensued.

Chloe placed her hands on her hips and couldn't stop herself from voicing her words. "If you had on sunglasses and walked past me on the street, I wouldn't have known you."

Abruptly Sybil asked, "Where is Nanny buried?"

In a distracted voice Chloe answered, "Mom and I put buried her in The Sanctuary Cemetery on Ribbon Street. I'm sorry, but we couldn't afford a headstone."

"I'm just thankful that you kept her from being buried like a pauper with no kin," Sybil said in despair. An image of the Hamilton twins surfaced and angrily she pushed it away. "Some people don't have enough and some people have too much. I'm going to buy her a headstone while I'm in town."

"How long are you staying?" Chloe asked softly, trying to gauge how Sybil was dealing with all the changes she'd been through.

"Just long enough to take care of some things." She looked around and spread her hands out at her sides. "What in God's name happened to my house?"

"Sybil, there was nothing that we could do." Anguish was etched on Chloe's face. "First some drug dealers were dealing out of here. Mom called and complained so the police ran them off. Later hobos camped out. We kept calling the police and finally they boarded up the windows, but there was rainy season and hobos broke in again."

"Oh."

Chloe stared at the dirty photo album Sybil clutched to her bosom. A sorrowful look was etched on her face. "Sybil, what are you going to do?" She put her arm around Sybil's shoulders and guided her out of the front door, away from the disturbing atmosphere of the house.

Sybil didn't answer until they stood next to her Jaguar and Chloe's dilapidated jalopy. "I'm going to finish my degree. Then I'm going to get my master's degree."

"When are you going back to New London?" Chloe asked.

"I'm not." Sybil's tone was adamant. "I'm enrolled at Harvard. Thank God all Ivy League schools are pretty much partners to each other so I didn't lose any credits."

"So your bachelor's degree will reflect that you're a Harvard graduate?" Chloe, trying to sound cheerful said, "You always wanted that."

"But I didn't want it like this," Sybil said bitterly. "I want my old life back with Nanny."

"Sybil," Chloe said delicately, "you can't bring her back. The only thing that you can do is to make her proud of you by being the person she raised you to be. Now let's go somewhere and have a cup of coffee."

*****

They sat in a corner booth and Sybil looked around at the yellow and green décor. "This is a nice place. Why is it so deserted?"

"It's the middle of the week, girl. People are at work so that they can afford to come here on the weekends."

"Yeah, in this economy small businesses are barely surviving," Sybil agreed.

Chloe eyed the expensive Abercrombie and Fitch shirt that Sybil was wearing. "You seem to be doing okay," she said. "That Jag you're driving is awesome."

"That's a payoff from an insurance company," Sybil said with a derogatory intonation in her voice.

"I'm glad that you made them pay through the nose." Then Chloe abruptly said, "I need a lawsuit." She looked out the window at her Chevy Malibu that was on its last leg. "I hope my car lasts me another year. I have school loans that I'm trying to get out of the way so I can't afford a car payment."

Sybil gave her a half smile. "Remember when we used to play the game we called that's my car?"

"I know." Chloe chuckled at the memory. "Every decent car that went down the street we'd point at it and say, "One day that's going to be my car. We'd sit on the curb for hours daydreaming."

"I can't remember what you said your favorite car was," Sybil said with a quizzical expression.

"It was a yellow Corvette." Chloe grinned. "Now I have more sense. I know a school counselor can never afford one of those."

"But you're making a difference in many people's lives. That's worth a million dollars."

"You're right," Chloe said contentedly. "I do love my job."

"Thank you for looking out for me and burying Nanny, Chloe," Sybil said with feeling. "You've always looked out for both of us."

"Nanny was a wonderful person. She treated me like I was her own so I felt that that was the least that I could do."

"What exactly happened to her?" Sybil asked in a grave voice. "The last time that I talked to her she said that she was doing fine."

"I think that most of the time she stuck to her diet. But Mother said that there was a huge church jamboree that week and there were all kinds of pies and cakes there," she said in a hesitant voice. "Nanny's system was probably unused to the sweets and went into shock. They took her to the hospital right away but by the time I got there it was too late."

Sybil covered her face with her hands and burst into tears.

Once the flood had subsided, she looked back at Chloe. She took the handful of tissues that she handed to her.

Sybil dried her face, but an air of despondency lingered.

"You can't possibly stay at your old house," Chloe said. "You're more than welcome to stay with me and Mom while you're in town."

"I'm already checked into the Marriott on the outskirts of town," she said. "I used a fake name," she added with a quirky tilt to her lips.

"What is it?" Chloe grinned.

"Eden Savoy."

"How'd you come up with that?" Chloe asked in a puzzled voice.

"Savoy was my mother's maiden name."

"And Eden?"

"Like the garden of Eden." Another image of Dane came to her mind. "I met one of the worse snakes in the world, and I need to remember that," she said bitterly.

Chloe stared at her childhood friend and when she saw the uncharacteristic coldness reflected in Sybil's eyes it distressed her. "What are you going to do with the house, Sybil? You can't leave it like that. The city has already condemned it and if you don't do something they will confiscate it for taxes."

"I'll go and pay the taxes tomorrow. But I can't go back there anymore. It's too hard."

"With your permission, I'll go over there and make sure there aren't any more items in the house. I thought that I'd already taken care of that but I guess I missed some things," Chloe said with a contrite look on her face. "If I find other things, I'll put them in my garage until you're ready to go through them."

"Thanks, Chloe," she said tremulously.

They sat quietly for a moment each lost their own thoughts.

Then Chloe persisted, "About the house? What are you going to do?"

"I just don't know," Sybil said and looked forlornly out the window.

"Whatever you decide to do about it, I'll handle it for you."

"Thank you," she said gratefully.

"When are you leaving?" Chloe asked solemnly.

"Once I get Nanny settled properly I'm out of here."

"Oh," Chloe said with regret. She said with some uneasiness, "Have you talked to Peyton yet?"

"No and I don't intend to," Sybil said with unforgiving edge to her voice.

"I still think that you should go and see her," Chloe persisted.

"No," Sybil said adamantly.

Chloe took her hand and covered Sybil's fist that lay clenched on the table. "I know you. You won't feel right until you settle things with her. Even if it's only to tell her how you feel about things."

"She could have tried to find me," Sybil said in obvious pain. "But I lay in that hospital bed for weeks and no one claimed me. She knew that I was on my way to see her that weekend. Why wouldn't I show up? I'd never let her down before."

"You don't know that she didn't try to find you. I called your university and they said that they didn't have any information on you."

"Yeah, and that's crazy. Why would a senior in college go away and just not return?" Sybil's eyes were bright with anger. "That's not normal behavior. Obviously I was just a number to them."

"Don't take it that way. I talked to the dormitory headmistress and she said that there were quite a few students who after the shooting just didn't come back because they were traumatized."

"Oh," Sybil said. "I didn't think about that."

"Your things were put in a storage unit with others who didn't return. You might want to go and get them."

"Maybe later," she said. "But right now that's the last thing on my mind."

"You say you want to move on and I think that it's the right thing to do. But if you don't settle your past in a way that sits well with you, the problems will only fester in your mind and in the end you're the one who will suffer."

There was a long heavy silence at the table. Finally Chloe said, "When you finish school, why don't we move to Atlanta? We could be roommates. We used to have so much fun there in the summers with my cousins." Chloe breathed a sigh of nostalgia. "Those were some good times."

"It sounds appetizing, but I'm heading to New York," Sybil said quietly.

"New York!" Chloe exclaimed.

"Yes," Sybil said. "I feel the need to live in a place with no memories. I think that's the only way that I can go on."

"You're not going to forget me, are you?" Tears brimmed in Chloe's eyes.

"Of course not," Sybil denied vehemently. "I just need you to promise me one thing."

"What is it?"

"Do not tell anyone what happened to me or where I am."

"Okay... I can do that." Chloe asked a little fearfully, "What are you planning to do?"

Sybil picked up her coffee cup and drained the contents. "Start over," she said quietly.

*****

That night Sybil tossed and turned in her hotel bed. As she lay in the darkness with her eyes wide open, the words *Habitat for Humanities* came to her. Calmed, she turned over and finally went to sleep.

In the late balmy evening, Sybil stared at the flowers that she'd placed on her grandmother's grave. Sybil made no effort to quell the tears that coursed down her cheeks. She bent her head and said a prayer. Once finished, she turned around and walked back to her car. After she buckled her seat belt, she turned on the ignition, gunned the engine, and tore out of the cemetery. She drove through the heart of town and when she eyed a Chevrolet dealership pulled into the parking lot.

She strutted into the dealership and stopped. Poised in a pair of designer jeans, she waited.

An elderly gentleman walked over to her, smiling and with his hand outstretched.

Sybil briefly shook it.

"May I help you?" he asked politely.

Sybil pointed at a shiny, yellow Corvette that was centered in the showroom. "I want that car," she said briefly.

The car salesman's eyes brightened. "Would you like me to get the keys so that you can take it for a test drive?"

"That's not necessary," Sybil said. "Draw up the paperwork. Deliver it to this address tomorrow morning." Sybil handed him a piece of paper with Chloe's address on it.

The salesman gasped in astonishment. "Yes, ma'am."

The transaction was completed in record time.

Once Sybil got back into her Jag she saw that her cell phone had a message on it. She hit redial because she knew that Chloe was the only person who had her new number.

"Hello, Sybil," Chloe said the minute she connected. "I just called to check on you. Have you left town yet?"

"Almost," Sybil said. "I was going to call you. I've decided what I want to do with the house."

"Already?"

"Yes. I want to donate the land to the Habitat for Humanity Foundation."

"I think that's a wonderful idea, Sybil," Chloe gushed.

"I'll get in touch with the organization and set everything up. But I'd like to establish you as my contact in Scranton in order to facilitate the process. Is that okay with you?"

"No problem whatsoever."

"And I picked out the headstone for Nanny's grave. I'll read to you what's going to be engraved on it. *With love everlasting, your granddaughter, Sybil.* I gave your telephone number. Once it's installed I'd appreciate it if you would check to make sure that its want I want it to be before I pay the balance. Do you think that you can do that for me?"

"Of course I can, Sybil."

"What's my name?" Sybil asked Chloe in an almost detached voice.

"Your name is Eden Savoy," Chloe said and now her voice was full of regret.

"Thank you, Chloe. I have to go now. I'll talk to you soon."

"Call me if you need anything else."

"I will, Chloe," she promised.

On the way out of town, Eden Savoy stopped at a Shell Oil station. As she filled her car she felt a pair of eyes appraising her and she swung her head around to find the source. Through her heavily tinted sunglasses, Sybil spied Aramis.

He nodded his head at her as a way of a greeting.

She did not return the nod.

Aramis strode towards her confidently. When he reached her he said with an engaging smile, "Hello, ma'am. That's one sweet ride you're sportin."

He doesn't recognize me because he can't see my eyes.

Her response was to give him a distant smile.

The pump signaled that her tank was full and she hastily hung up the nozzle.

"You're not from around here," Aramis cajoled, not at all put off by her standoffish demeanor. "Are you visiting relatives?"

Sybil was hesitant to speak, fearful that he would recognize her voice. She got in her car and said in a deliberately slow southern drawl, "No," and sped off in the direction of Boone, North Carolina.

In the rear view mirror, she saw Aramis watching her departure with a peculiar look on his face.

Chapter 9

As Sybil followed the road signs to Boone, North Carolina her limbs felt cramped from the grueling hours of driving twisting roads towards the mountains. She heard the impersonal GPS voice say, 'You have reached your destination.'

Sybil pulled into an empty parking lot beside a general store. She reached up to the navigation system and rekeyed in Peyton's family address.

'You have reached your destination,' the GPS voice announced.

Exhaling a sigh of irritation, she opened her car door and went inside the store.

"Hello there, young lady," a weathered-looking man said from behind the counter.

"Hello," Sybil replied. She headed to the back of the store and grabbed a can of Coca-Cola from the cooler and a bag of chips, before she made her way to the clerk. Placing them on the counter she looked enquiringly at him as he began to ring up her items. "Do you know how to get to Route 13 marker 707?" she said reciting the address of past letters she'd gotten from Peyton.

"Who ya lookin' for?" the clerk asked as he rubbed his goatee sprinkled with gray.

"The Monroe family," Sybil replied. "My GPS stated that this is the address, but I gather that it's wrong."

"That's because they got no satellite out there," he said. "But, they easy to find." The clerk shot an inquisitive look at her. He pointed out the window. "You take a left out the parking lot and drive a piece till you see a four way stop sign. Then you take that left and travel until you cross a brown wooden bridge goes over a small creek. Once you cross that creek you take a right onto a dirt road. Follow that road. You'll see a small white house on the left. That's them."

"Wow," Sybil said doubtfully as she handed him some money. "I hope that I don't get lost out there."

"You won't if you do as I tell you," he retorted gruffly. "It's a left, then another left and then a right. You can't miss the house because it's the only one out there."

"Okay," Sybil said taking her change. "Thank you very much."

"Anytime, miss."

Sybil painstakingly followed the clerk's directions and when she got to the four way intersection she stopped. Her hands shook on the steering wheel and she suddenly felt bile rise in her throat. Then out of the corner of her eye she saw a truck lumbering towards her. Sybil covered her face as she braced for the impact of the truck. Her trance was broken by the sound of a horn blaring and she looked up and saw the truck waiting for her to move because she had the right of way.

Gathering her wits, she looked in both side mirrors and then her rear-view mirror. Seeing that there were no other vehicles in the vicinity she took a left and soon found herself crossing a creek and driving on the dirt road that led to Peyton's house.

When she pulled up at the house, her eyes rested on two old trucks in the front. The back wheels were off the back of the blue one and the hood of the white one was held up by a heavy stick. Next, Sybil surveyed the house. The paint was peeling in several places and the front screened door hung lopsided on the hinge.

Suddenly a young man on crutches limped out. He had only one leg and the pants that he wore were cut off at the knees.

Staring at him Sybil felt a sense of dread. She recognized Conrad from the pictures that Peyton had had plastered on her walls at school but in all of the pictures he had legs. She sat immobile in the car unsure of what to do.

Conrad began to move towards the steps and that propelled her into action. She hastily exited the car. She bounded up the steps and held her hand out. "Hello. You must be Conrad. I'm Peyton's old college roommate, Sybil."

The suspicious eyes that glared at her caught her off guard.

"You ain't Sybil," Conrad said in a strong mountain accent. "I seen pictures of her and you don't look nothing like her."

Sybil took her designer sunglasses off her face. "I am Sybil," she quietly corrected him.

The look of doubt was replaced by one of astonishment as he stared at Sybil's eyes. "You her all right. But you sure look different."

Not wanting to explain to a stranger she inquired in a slightly uneven tone, "Is Peyton here? I'd like to talk to her."

"Peyton is dead," Conrad answered bluntly.

"Dead?" Sybil reeled from the shock and collapsed onto the front step with a force that seemed to rattle the boards.

"You're too late," Conrad said with a deliberate look of censure.

From out of nowhere a torrent of tears flowed down Sybil's cheeks. She wiped them away with the back of one hand. "What happened to her?"

"She gave up," Conrad answered in a hard tone.

"What do you mean?"

"What happened to you?" Conrad asked in an accusing voice. "Peyton tried to reach you, but she couldn't get a hold of you."

"I was in a car accident on my way here," Sybil explained in a strained voice. "I was in a hospital in Wilmington as a Jane Doe for months in a coma. Then they had to perform surgeries to repair my face."

"So that's why you look so different," Conrad said understanding dawning on his face.

"Yes."

"You're still as beautiful as you were in the pictures Peyton had of you," Conrad said. Now his gaze on her was sympathetic. "You're just different looking, that's all."

"What happened to Peyton?" Sybil said with a stricken look on her face.

"She died of a drug overdose," Conrad said sadly. "The doctors had her on antidepressants and she also was taking sleep medication. It was the combination of the two that killed her."

"Oh no," Sybil said with her hand to her mouth.

"And her son?"

"She didn't have a son."

"What happened to him? Did he die?"

"No, the doctor was wrong. Peyton had a girl not a boy."

"Is the baby okay?" Sybil attempted to swallow the pain that clouded her throat.

"Haley is okay." Then he said watching her, "Let's go into the house. You look a little faint."

Conrad turned on his crutches and led the way inside.

Sybil found herself in a small sitting room. Still slightly unbalanced from everything she'd learned, she sank weakly on the couch.

"Are you just getting out of the hospital today?" Conrad asked from his seat across from her.

"No, not really," she stammered guiltily. "I'm so sorry, Conrad. For months, I've been feeling sorry for myself," she averted her gaze, "and I'm ashamed to admit, blaming Peyton."

"But you also have been through a lot, and Peyton loved you to the very end," Conrad said softly. "Don't add any more burdens to yourself than you already have. Peyton wouldn't want that."

"You're so strong," she said and inadvertently looked down to where Conrad's leg should be. Immediately she wished that she hadn't alluded to his disability and felt even more ashamed.

"I have to be for Haley," Conrad replied with passion. "Don't you want to know what happened to me?"

Sybil mutely nodded her head yes.

"When I was on tour in Afghanistan, I got a letter from Peyton telling me that she was home and how that guy Kane did her. I told her that I'd come back at the end of my tour and help her raise the baby. A month before I was released," he looked down where his leg should be and said, "this happened. Haley has given me a reason to go on."

"Where is Peyton buried?" Sybil asked in a stricken voice.

Conrad looked shamefaced. "We don't have a lot of money so we had no choice but to cremate her."

Sybil drew in a deep breath. "Conrad, is there is anything I can do to help?"

"Peyton wanted you to be Haley's godmother. I would like to abide by her wishes."

"I would be honored," Sybil whispered.

"Peyton would be so pleased," he said fervently. "I used to hear her tell Haley that her godmother was coming to see her and how much she was going to love you."

Sybil had to ask. "Have you heard anything from Kane Hamilton? Is he now willing to accept Haley as his child and financially support her?"

"No, on all counts." Now Conrad's voice was as hard as nails. "After Peyton passed I was going through her things and ran across a letter that he sent her right after she had Haley. If I was the man I used to be I'd walk down to Texas and pistol whip his ass."

"You're more of a man than Kane Hamilton will ever be," Sybil declared heatedly. "But, Conrad," she vowed, "if I ever get a chance to punish him for what he did to Peyton, I will."

There was a profound silence in the room, each lost in their own thoughts.

Then Sybil looked at her watch. "I have to go. There's something that I need to do."

"Don't you want to see your goddaughter?" Conrad asked with a smile.

"Is she here?" Sybil asked with wide eyes.

"Sure she is," he said. "She's in the room pretending to take a nap. Usually my parents take her with them when they go to town, but today it's an all-day thing so they felt that she'd get too tired," Conrad said. "Come on."

Sybil followed him down a short hallway.

Conrad pushed open the door to the first bedroom he reached.

The minute he did a loud cackle of laughter filled the air and Sybil found herself gazing at a cherubic toddler.

191

Standing on her tiptoes in a crib she was the spitting image of Peyton, yet she had Kane Hamilton's big blue eyes.

Sybil swallowed hard and went to her.

Haley held out her arms and Sybil lifted her out of the crib, pulling her tight to her bosom. Sybil's heart beat rapidly and her breath blew the top of Haley's hair. "I'm your godmomma, Haley," she said. "I promise that I will protect you and try to keep you from all harm."

She heard a deep sigh of relief from Conrad who was standing behind them.

A couple of hours later, on her way out of town, Sybil pulled up to the Ally Bank. She signed in and asked to speak to a manager.

An hour later, Sybil left the bank satisfied with the savings account she'd opened for the Monroe family and the separate trust fund she'd set up for her goddaughter Haley.

Chapter 10

Thirty-two year old Eden Savoy sat in a soft, leather chair in her office. Her chin was propped on her hand as she absently stared at her office wall. Whenever she looked at her undergraduate and graduate degrees from Harvard she felt an immense feeling of satisfaction.

Three tentative knocks on her door made her look up.

"Come in," she called out.

Ryta Rogers, the floor's head nurse, pushed open the door and entered. "May I talk to you about something?" she asked.

"Of course, Ryta," Eden said with a beckoning smile waving her into a chair at the same time.

Ryta sat in the chair in front of Eden's desk. "I have a problem."

"What is it?" Eden asked.

"Doctor Fleischman wants to discharge Mr. Lewis in room 517."

"Again?" Eden said dryly.

"Yes," Ryta said with a sigh of irritation. "I get so tired of the battle, Eden. The minute a patient's benefits are cut off Doctor Fleischman wants them out the door. Mr. Lewis doesn't have anyone at home to look after him." Ryta held her hands out helplessly. "But I don't have the authority to override Doctor

Fleischman. If he says that a patient is ready to be discharged who am I to challenge him?"

"You can't," Eden acknowledged, "but I can. What is Mr. Lewis's diagnosis?"

"He has memory issues and shouldn't be left alone. He forgets what day it is and the medication that he's on should be taken religiously at the same time three times a day. Mr. Lewis has no family in the area and to my knowledge no one has ever come to visit him."

"That's really sad. I think to be old, sick, and alone must be one of the worse things to deal with," she said softly. "I can authorize Mr. Lewis to go into a treatment facility. I'll fill out the paperwork that shows he's destitute and have him placed on Medicaid. That should make everyone happy."

"Not Doctor Fleischman," Ryta said nervously. "He's going to know that I snitched. I've heard from other nurses that he gets angry if a nurse goes over his head."

Eden pointed to herself. "I'm the director of case management. It's my duty to question the decisions my staff has to make." Eden winked her eye conspiratorially at Ryta. "I'll just act as if it's my idea," she said.

"Thanks," Ryta said gratefully as she stood. "You have a heart of gold," Ryta said before she left.

*****

Eden stood at the nurses' station and pressed the numbers on the fax machine.

"Who told you to override my instructions and send my patient to Autumn View Health Care Facility?" Doctor Fleischman asked harshly as he walked up. His eyebrows were drawn together in a ferocious frown.

Eden bit back the retort, "I told myself." Instead, she replied in an expressionless voice, "I reviewed Mr. Lewis's chart and decided that he needed more care. However," she continued glibly, "I understand that the hospital cannot continue to incur the expenses for his care. I decided that instead of releasing him with the possibility of further complications that would put the hospital in jeopardy of being sued that the best course of action would be to put him in a nursing home for further treatment."

"Humph," Doctor Fleischman, said eyes narrowed in anger, "you picked one of the best facilities in the area. Who's footing that bill?"

"The system," Eden replied in a hard voice, "that Mr. Lewis worked his whole life and paid into it. I'm sure you feel as I do that he's not getting a tenth back of what he deserves."

Eden's eyes followed Doctor Fleischman's stiff back as he stalked down the hallway in a huff. She shook her head chidingly.

As she was putting the finishing touches on the paperwork to be sent to the Autumn View Nursing Facility, her attention was drawn to a group of doctors that stood with their backs to her, waiting for the elevator. Through a sea of white coats, Eden saw the vice president of the company with a clipboard in his hand pointing to a map.

Ryta sidled up next to her and whispered, "Check out the new doctor with the Suits."

"Vice President Lancaster must be really impressed by his credentials for him to take the time to show him around," Eden whispered back.

"Not really," Ryta said a little sarcastically. "I heard that he's his son-in-law."

"That figures," Eden said now openly sarcastic. "There are probably hundreds of more deserving doctors than him, but nepotism is alive and well at New York General."

Ryta stifled a snicker.

"Which one is he? I got a memo a month ago that the next recruit would be on the same team for our weekly meetings." She gave a grunt of dissatisfaction. "Now that I know his connections it's like having a spy in your midst."

"I think he's that tallest one. I heard him asking where the coffee machine was and he sounded like a Texan."

Eden focused on the doctor that Ryta had pointed out.

As she studied his back she saw him run his hand through his jet black hair.

An eerie feeling of *déjà vu* made the hairs on the back of her neck stand up.

The man turned to speak to another man standing next to him and Eden found herself studying the profile of Dane Hamilton.

Gasping for breath, she turned away, her back facing the group.

Noticing her agitation Ryta asked, "What's the matter? You act as if you've seen a ghost."

Eden didn't respond. Queasiness in her stomach made her almost topple over and her mouth was so dry she couldn't speak.

"Do you know him?"

Eden said nothing. Then in a voice that sounded faraway, "No."

"Then what's wrong?" Ryta's eyes were full of concern as she watched Eden.

Eden's eyes darted back and forth furtively. She finally managed to say, "I don't feel well." As she fabricated her lie she avoided Ryta's worried countenance. "I have a piercing headache."

Ryta observed the beads of sweat on Eden's forehead. "Why don't I go to the nurses' supply room and get something for it?"

"No thank you," Eden weakly replied. "I have stuff at home so I think that I'll just call it a day."

"Okay," Ryta said. "Do you think that you'll be in tomorrow for our team meeting?"

"I don't know," Eden said tersely. Then without looking over her shoulder to see if Dane was still in sight, she bolted to her office.

Less than twenty minutes later Eden was navigating her car through the New York City traffic. As she sat at a light waiting for it to turn green, she spied an optometrist's office and pulled into a parking spot in front.

Eden sat in the waiting room nervously chewing her bottom lip. She had one leg crossed over the other and her foot bobbed up and down in agitation.

After she heard her name called she grabbed a brochure on her way to the optometrist's examination room.

Once inside she was greeted by a bespectacled man with a warm smile.

"Hello, I'm Doctor Forsythe," he said, extending his hand. "I see from your paperwork that you're here to be fitted for some contacts."

"Yes I am," she said. "How soon can I get them?"

"That depends on what kind you want," he answered.

Eden handed him the brochure of the Fresh Look colored lenses. "I want a pair of the brown."

"That shouldn't be a problem. Do you have a current prescription for the contacts that you're wearing?"

"I'm not wearing contacts," Eden said. "And I have twenty-twenty vision."

"Then why in the world would you like to change your eye color?" Doctor Forsythe asked in bewilderment. "People pay to have eyes like yours."

"I want to blend in more with other people," she said as she avoided his stare.

Doctor Forsythe shook his head in confusion. Turning his back to her to pick up an instrument he muttered, "People always want what they don't have." Then in a more businesslike tone he instructed, "I need you to read the first row of letters on the wall so I can see if you indeed do have perfect vision."

Without squinting, Eden read every letter perfectly. Then she read all the other lines without a mistake.

"You were right," Doctor Forsythe said. "You do have perfect vision. Now I need to measure your eyes to see whether or not you need to be fitted for special lenses."

Once Eden was in the chair, she pressed her forehead to the scope as he measured her eyes.

Moving the machine away from her he said, "Your eyes are perfectly set into your sockets," he said admirably. "I'll give you a year's prescription and you can pick off the shelf any lenses that you want."

"I want the lenses that I only have to change every thirty days."

"Make sure that you do take them out and clean them periodically," Doctor Forsythe cautioned. "I don't want you going blind from an infection."

"I'll take care of my contacts," Eden promised. "My life depends on me being able to wear them."

Doctor Forsythe looked up from the prescription he was writing.

Seeing the interest she'd stirred up by her words, she pasted a blank look on her face and silently took the script.

Once Eden got home she stared at herself in the bathroom mirror. Even though the chocolate brown eyes complimented her ebony skin, seeing the last part of her old self disintegrate made her turn her away from her reflection. Burning anger churned in her stomach. *Dane Hamilton made me go through this today. I'll make him pay.*

*****

The next day Eden was the first person to enter the conference room for the weekly team meeting. As she shuffled through the stack of papers, she heard the door open and looked up.

Her heart constricted, making it difficult to breathe when she saw that Dane was the next person to arrive.

"We haven't had a chance to meet yet." He stuck his hand out. "My name is Doctor Hamilton."

Hesitantly, Eden held her hand out and allowed hers to be swallowed into his huge one.

His handshake was firm.

A fiery sensation made her quake at his touch.

Quickly she pulled her hand away and looked aside.

Dane sat in the chair next to hers. "I see that we have quite a caseload to deal with," he said.

"We always have a heavy caseload," she answered in an impassive voice. "It's because our hospital is known for having the most caring staff. At least it was," she added in a sharp tone.

Dane shot her an inquisitive look.

She continued, "Protocol dictates that the lead doctor sit on the opposite end of the table and the nurses, lead dietician, and chaplain fill in on the side chairs."

"Oh," Dane gave a slight smile. "I guess every hospital's different. At my last one, it didn't matter where one sat during meetings. It was first come, first served."

"Where was that?" The words spilled from Eden's mouth before she could still her words.

"Texas," Dane answered tersely.

"Well, we do things differently in the North." Eden retorted in a measured tone. "I hope that you don't have any difficulty adjusting because I know that Texans think of Texas as being their own little Utopia."

Upon hearing her words, Dane gave a start of surprise. Then he replied shortly, "It's a good place to live, but I thought that I'd like to return north."

"Humph." Eden uttered the word before she could stop herself.

Eden felt Dane's eyes studying her with obvious curiosity.

Pretending not to notice, she was thankful when the door opened. This time it was the other staff members who were required to attend the TMA meeting.

As they went through the cases, one by one, Eden pretended not to notice the thoughtful gaze of Dane.

*****

"What did you do?" Ryta asked.

201

Eden was gathering data together in order to get started on the list of things she needed to dispose of before she left for the day.

"My eyes were hurting me so I went to the optometrist. He said that I have a stigmatism and these are corrective lenses."

"It's a shame that you have to wear them," she said. "Couldn't you get clear contacts?"

"No."

Feeling nauseous from the ongoing lie her life had become Eden excused herself and fled the room. Walking with head bent she suddenly tripped over her own feet. Eden felt herself going down and reached for the wall, but missed it.

Before she hit the floor, a pair of arms grabbed her by the waist and kept her upright.

Eden's head was flung back and her upper torso rested on one strong arm. She gazed up into the eyes of Dane.

"Take your hands off of me," she demanded harshly.

She was immediately put in an upright position and released.

Eden's lips were pursed and her eyes flashed angrily.

Confused, Dane stared at her stormy countenance.

Without uttering another word she stalked off.

*****

As Eden let herself into her Manhattan loft, sheer exhaustion overcame her. Sinking into her plush cocoa sofa, she kicked off her shoes, closed her eyes and massaged her throbbing temples. The sound of her telephone ringing shattered her moment of solitude. She ignored the sound, instead preferring to let the machine answer.

Padding barefoot into the kitchen, Eden retrieved a glass from her cabinet and uncorking the bottle of wine she'd opened the night before poured herself a generous potion. The image of Dane Hamilton flashed before her eyes. She gulped it down and then refilled her glass.

The sound of her doorbell made her smile. She shouted, "Come in, Randall. It's unlocked."

Randall Swan followed Eden's voice and positioned himself at the door to her kitchen.

Eden was always in awe at the spectacular piece of man flesh. He had bronze skin, long limbs, and a bald head.

Leaning on the door jamb with his arms folded, he said in his low sensual voice, "How many times do I have to tell you to lock your door? We have security, but you never know. Some creep might find a way to sneak up here."

"I leave the door open because I know that within twenty minutes of my getting home you're going to be ringing my bell," she replied teasingly. "I'm tired of leaving my hot shower to let you in."

"How did it go today?" Randall watched her closely.

"Thank God I didn't see him," she said.

"The fact that after all of this time he can rattle you means that you need to settle your past once and for all."

Eden avoided his eyes. Instead she took an empty wine glass out of the cupboard and filled it. Then she handed it to Randall.

Eden left the kitchen to go into the den and Randall was right on her heels.

Once they sat down on the couch, Eden turned to him. "I think that I need to look for a position elsewhere."

"So you're going to let him run you off?" Randall asked quietly.

"I prefer to think it of as removing myself from a potentially catastrophic situation." She took another sip of her wine.

"You already tried to do that. You changed your whole life and you're still caught up in a history that you can't escape from." Randall pinned her eyes with his. "I can see the hurt in your eyes behind those lenses. You can't keep running, Eden."

"So you think that I should reveal to him who I am?" she exclaimed.

"Not if you don't want to," he answered quietly.

"I can't do it. You're the only person in New York who knows why I'm so scarred."

"You're not scarred," Randall said. "You're just trying to cope with losing so much."

"But it's been years," she muttered angry with herself. "You'd think by now that I'd have healed."

"You never got the chance to heal," Randall said quietly. "You've busied yourself with things, but you don't live your life. There's a reason why you spend all your free time with me."

"And I know what it is." Eden explained, "You let me try and find a straight man to go to all the museums and plays that we see without complaining," she laughed lightly.

Randall decided not to let her off so easily. "They're out there, but you don't even really try to find them."

"Relationships are too hard and rarely worth the effort," Eden whispered.

"Do you still have feelings for this Dane Hamilton?" he asked bluntly.

"No," Eden declared emphatically. "I can never forgive him for what he and his twin did to Peyton. Also, I lost all faith in him because I thought that we at least had a friendship and a mutual respect for each other. Then I found out that the Dane I cared about never existed."

"Then he can't hurt you," Randall said. "If I were you, I'd play with him," he said with a mischievous twinkle in his eyes.

"What do you mean?" Eden asked.

"Make him fall in love with you and then dump him. That might be what you need to come to terms with your past and get revenge on him for what he did to Peyton."

"I don't know about that," Eden said doubtfully. She took her hand and threaded it through her shoulder length hair. Then she gave a shudder of distaste. "I can't do that because he's married."

"That's better for you." With a smirk, Randall egged her on. "If he flirts with you and he's married, then you'll know that he hasn't changed and he deserves everything he gets."

*****

Everyone was present at the TMA meeting.

"We have a couple of patients that we need to decide what to do with. They can either stay here at the hospital in our rehab wing or find placement elsewhere. The first on the list is Zachary Fields."

"That's my patient," Doctor Fleischman said. "He's ready to be discharged."

"Okay, Doctor Fleischman," Eden said carefully. "The problem is that he needs dialysis once a week and where he lives there's not a facility within 100 miles."

Doctor Fleischman's frown was so ferocious it appeared as if he had a unibrow. "But he's not a resident of New York. I'm sorry, Ms. Savoy, but our system is stretched to its limits. Each state is responsible for its own citizens. I won't sign off for him to stay," he stated firmly.

Eden stared at the doctor and unsuccessfully tried to mask her disgust for him.

"Let's see if we can come up with a solution, Ms. Savoy." Dane interjected himself into the conversation and spoke in a concise manner. "Ms. Savoy, check and see if Mr. Fields has any children that live near a kidney treatment center. If he does maybe he can go and stay with them. It's quite common for centers to take patients that are in the area on vacation and we can document the paperwork that he's visiting for an extended time."

Everyone breathed a sigh of relief that it seemed as if there was not going to be another disagreement between Eden and Doctor Fleischman.

At the end of the meeting as everyone was gathering their things she felt Dane trying to catch her eye. When hers met his he gave her a smile of camaraderie. Ignoring it, she gathered her paperwork and stomped off.

*****

"We have an emergency," Ryta said with an anxious look on her face.

"What's the matter?" Eden stopped typing on her key pad and gave Ryta her full attention.

"Do you remember, Mr. Grimm?"

"Yes. We released him over a month ago. What's wrong?"

"His neighbor in his rooming house called. Apparently he's not taking his meds and is completely out of control."

"Oh, no! He's paranoid schizophrenic."

"He sure is. And with him not taking his medication he could really hurt himself."

"And others." Eden frowned.

"What are we going to do? This lady said that he'd been on a rampage for hours."

"Then why didn't she call the police?" Eden exclaimed.

"I think she's afraid that they'll hurt him or take him to jail."

"She's probably right," Eden said with a grimace. "How did she know to call us?"

"She found my card in his wallet." Ryta asked in an almost tearful voice, "What are we going to do?"

"Call the paramedics and tell them to bring him to the hospital. I'll admit him to the psychiatric ward and get him back on his medication."

"Okay, but what if he doesn't come? I'm afraid for him. Mr. Grimm is a really a nice man once you get over his gruffness, and the fact that he doesn't like to bathe."

"Tell them to make him come. He's in danger of losing his life or endangering others. If they can't get him to come in voluntarily, Baker Act him. I'm going to do the emergency paperwork right now."

After Ryta scurried out the room and slammed the door, Eden turned back to her computer and began filling out the forms.

Less than an hour later, Eden and Ryta stood at the ramp at the back of the hospital. Eden watched the ambulance back up and the doors open. The driver and passenger in the cab of the van got out and watched the attendants quickly wheel Mr. Grimm down the small ramp onto solid ground.

Mr. Grimm lay back on the rolling bed and glared at every one who looked at him. His arms were pinned to his sides in a straightjacket and he gritted his teeth ferociously.

Concerned, Eden went to him and searched his face. "Are you okay, Mr. Grimm?"

"Shut up," he said fiercely.

"What?" she said, appalled by the animosity on his face and in his voice.

"Get the hell away from me. You're that person that had them arrest me," he spat out.

Eden tried to reason with him. "Mr. Grimm, you haven't been arrested."

"The hell I wasn't. They handcuffed me and then put this damn thing on me. Who the hell are you to stick your fuckin' nose in my business?"

"Mr. Grimm," Eden said patiently. "Everyone here is just trying to keep you from hurting yourself and others."

"Fuck you!" Mr. Grimm shouted.

"Please take Mr. Grimm to the wing on the ninth floor," Eden instructed the paramedics. "The nurses are waiting for him."

"One day you'll get yours," Mr. Grimm said as he was wheeled away.

The ambulance driver gave Eden a consoling pat on the shoulder. "I've got another call. It must be the heat."

After he drove away, Eden looked at Ryta and said in a weary voice, "Come on. We're late for our TMA."

When they entered the conference room, everyone was already there.

"I'm sorry we're late, but Ryta and I had an emergency. If you look in the notes that I e-mailed you, we had to Baker Act Mr. Grimm and bring him in for treatment. To put it mildly, he was not happy."

"I heard that he's a pistol," the dietician said in a droll tone.

"That's putting it mildly." With a wry look she said, "He literally cursed me out."

Suddenly Dane began to whistle a tune from *The Grinch that Stole Christmas*. Everyone seated at the conference table started grinning. Then Dane bellowed out the words and sang the refrain, but changed the name. 'You're a mean one, Mr. Grimm,' over and over again."

Against her will Eden found herself laughing with the others as she listened to Dane's cocky rendition of the song.

Chapter 11

Saturday afternoon Eden was lazing on her sofa when the ringing of her doorbell roused her. She stumbled to the door and looked through the peephole.

After letting Randall in she gave a long whistle of appreciation. He was dressed in a pair of skinny jeans, crisp white shirt with a skinny tie, and black eel-skin shoes. He looked as if he'd just finished a photo shoot.

"Where are you going?" she asked.

"You mean where are we going?"

"I'm not going anywhere," Eden denied emphatically.

"I need a plus one for a wine tasting tonight," Randall said.

"No thanks," Eden declined.

"Come on, Eden. I'll owe you one," he promised.

"Why don't you take Colin?"

"We broke up." Randall swallowed the lump lodged in his throat.

"Oh," Eden said. "I'm sorry to hear that. What happened?"

"There were a few things." Randall shrugged his shoulders, trying to appear nonchalant but his gesture fell short. "Colin and I were never exclusive, but whenever I went out with anyone else his jealousy was over the top."

"Oh," Eden said.

"He was even jealous of you. I told him time and time again that lovers come and go, but the kind of friendship that we have isn't something to tamper with," Randall said.

"I agree," she softly acknowledged.

"The last straw is the competition we face in the modeling world. It's so cutthroat." Pain from the memories was etched on Randall's face. "Instead of being buddies we got pushed into the position of being adversaries."

"When did the two of you break up?" Eden asked in a sympathetic tone.

"Over three weeks ago," Randall replied with a downcast expression.

"Three weeks ago and you're just now telling me?" Eden gently scolded.

"Every time I started to tell you we got off on another subject. Besides," Randall explained, "I didn't want to bother you with my problems. You've got your own stuff going on."

Ashamed at herself for being so selfish, Eden slid off the couch. As she headed to the bedroom she pulled off her tee shirt. "I need thirty minutes to get ready. There's wine in the refrigerator."

Twenty-five minutes later, Eden stood in front of her dresser mirror. She'd donned a simple black silk dress with matching stilettos. She'd opted out of wearing a bra and her black lace thong was the only undergarment she wore.

As she applied bright red lipstick as the final touch of her makeup, she felt better than she'd had in a while.

Eden sauntered down the hall and she felt her confidence buoyed by his approving expression at the sight of her.

He gave a high pitched whistle.

Eden slowly turned around in a circle with her arms held out. "How do I look?" she asked. "I won't embarrass you as your plus one, will I?"

"You already know the answer to that so stop angling for compliments," Randall answered.

Eden's tinkling laughter was her response as she locked the door.

*****

"Where is this affair?" she asked as she sat in the bucket seat of Randall's Lexus sports coupe.

"It's at a new café not far from Times Square."

Once they arrived Randall handed the valet the keys and he and Eden strolled arm and arm up the short walk to the attendant at the door.

"There should be a reservation for two in the name of Randall Swan."

The twenty-something-old metro-sexual looking attendant quickly surveyed the list on his podium and made a check mark next to Randall's name. Then he nodded at the bouncer that stood by a red rope.

The bouncer unhooked it and allowed them entry through a set of maple doors.

Randall whispered to her, "The owner of the café also has a modeling agency so it's good for me to show my face. There's a new clothing line that he's showing during New York Fashion Week."

"There's the bar," Eden said

"Then let's go."

With her arm still looped inside his Eden and Randall made their way through the packed café. Before they could reach the bar, they were approached by a waitress with a tray of filled wine glasses.

"Would you like a glass of wine?" She smiled flirtatiously at Randall.

"What is it?"

"It is an exclusive wine from Italy. The owner, Mr. Dubonnet has given explicit instructions that we are not to say which winery produced it so that others cannot carry it."

Randall looked at Eden and winked. "That's no fun. That means that we can't stock up on it at home." He took two goblets off the tray and handed one to Eden. "Come and find us in about another fifteen minutes." He winked conspiratorially at the pretty waitress.

"It would be my pleasure," she said with a seemingly mesmerized look as she gazed into Randall's sparkling eyes.

Beaming from his attention she took off.

"See, that's why I prefer to go places with you." Randall said as he eyed her over the rim of his wine goblet. "After that,

Colin would have been so seething with jealousy it would ruin our night."

Eden's attention was drawn to someone behind Randall's back and he started to turn to see who had her attention.

"Don't turn around just yet," Eden said quietly. "Colin's here."

In a seemingly casual manner, Randall looked over his shoulder. He easily found his ex in the crowded room. Randall said, "I see that he's already found someone." The displeasure he tried to hide was betrayed by the curtness of his tone.

"We can go if you want," she said, now looping her arm protectively around his waist.

Randall placed his empty glass on the table and lifted Eden's chin. He lowered his mouth to hers and Eden stiffened in shock. The kiss was long, and firm.

Then he lifted his mouth and said quietly, "Randall runs from nothing."

Still in shock Eden didn't speak.

"By the way, you can slap my face later." The look on his face begged for forgiveness.

"Don't worry about it, Randall," Eden finally said. "That's what friends are for."

Randall breathed a deep sigh of relief that he hadn't ruined their friendship.

An hour later, Eden was almost tipsy from the amount of wine she'd consumed. Throughout their time there, she'd not left

Randall's side as he chatted to agents, designers, and other models in the industry.

The entire evening Colin hadn't acknowledged her or Randall.

With each passing minute, Eden became more livid about his behavior.

Colin had blatantly kept his arm around the tall, leggy blonde. They'd danced several times, and kissed passionately on the dance floor.

She'd not strayed from Randall because she felt the need to him to protect him.

Eventually, she broke away from him and sped towards the bathroom. Once finished, she smoothed her hair in the mirror and made her way back to rejoin Randall.

Eden stopped dead in her tracks.

Dane was leaning on the wall. His eyes were red rimmed from the effects of alcohol and he had an intense look on his face. His eyes quickly ran up and down the length of her in the clingy dress.

"What are you doing here?" she gasped.

"I saw you the minute you got here," he replied and his voice was slurred. "When I saw you head this way I followed you." Dane straightened his posture. "I want to ask you something."

Eden braced herself. "What is it?" she demanded in a haughty voice.

"Why do you dislike me?" He watched her face carefully.

She didn't know it, but a myriad of expressions rapidly crossed her face as she tried to mask what she was really thinking.

"I don't dislike you, Doctor Hamilton," she said coldly. "I don't even know you."

"At work I couldn't find the right time to ask you." He pinned her eyes with his. "I'd like us to get along; yet, every time I'm near you tense up and get a hostile look on your face. Have I done something to offend you?"

"I don't know," Eden countered swiftly. "Have you?"

All of a sudden, the men's bathroom door swung open and Kane Hamilton stumbled out.

At the sight of him, Eden shrank back against the wall.

Kane had put on a lot of weight since the last time she'd seen him, but she'd recognize Dane's twin anywhere.

"Whoa, brother! Introduce me to your friend," he said, surveying Eden's body. His face was blotchy from alcohol consumption and his eyes were watery. Kane looped his arm around Dane's shoulder. "I'm up visiting from Texas. I'd love it if you showed me everything your city has to offer," he said suggestively.

Eden clenched her fists at her sides to keep from delivering Kane a stinging slap to wipe the supercilious smirk off of his face.

It took every vestige of her will power not to tell them who she was but she held her temper in check. *I'll bide my time, and then I'll strike when its least expected.*

Obviously pissed, Dane shrugged off his brother's arm.

Kane looked at Dane. "Brother, you sure have lust for that dark meat. But I have to say, she is quite tasty looking. I'd like to do her my damn self."

A red flush ran from Dane's neck to his temple. He stammered apologetically, "I'm very sorry, Eden, but my brother's drunk."

"Clearly, you both are," she replied acidly. "And I never gave you permission to call me Eden. It's Ms. Savoy to you." She gave them a withering look before she stormed off in a huff.

Eden found Randall in the throng of people. She said with her chin quivering, "I have to get out of here." Then she took off and pushed her way through the crowd towards the exit.

Randall placed his glass on the bar and without looking in Colin's direction followed her.

*****

Eden sat curled up next to Randall on the couch. Her head lay on his shoulder.

Randall channel surfed with the remote until suddenly he cut the television off. He turned to Eden and searched her face. "What happened when you went to the ladies' room? You didn't say one word in the car and we've been home for over an hour and you still haven't talked."

"Dane was at the party," she answered in a monotone. "He waylaid me outside the bathroom."

"He was?" Randall said in astonishment. "Why didn't you point him out to me?" he asked with a hard edge. "I'd like to have seen the bastard that hurt you so much."

"I didn't see him when we were together," she explained.

"Oh."

"He said that he wanted us to be friends, blah, blah, blah, blah."

"So that made you bolt like that?" He gave her a quizzical look.

"It wasn't what he said," she answered slowly. "It's what Kane said."

"Kane!" Randall shouted. "He lives in New York too?"

"Evidently not," she said in a tired voice. "He said in his usual cocky manner that he was up for a visit and asked if I would show him around. Then he made a nasty remark about Dane having a thing for black women."

"He's got a damn nerve!" Randall exploded. "What did you say to that?"

"Nothing," she mumbled. "Before I could respond Dane apologized for him. I basically told the two of them to get lost and then I did."

There was a tense silence in the room. Then Eden in such a low voice that Randall barely heard her said, "After all this time, I still let the Hamilton twins unnerve me. Why can't I come to terms with my past?" Her countenance was marked by a mixture of frustration and disgust.

"Before I accepted my sexuality, I had a dysfunctional relationship." Randall spoke slowly, making sure that Eden digested what he was saying. "I hid it from everyone and it went sour in the worst way. Because I was in the closet, I had no one to confide in about how much I was hurting."

Eden gave him a sharp look.

"There were days that I didn't want to live. Then I got myself together." Randall gave her a look. "I ran into Ascott a few years later and he wanted to hook up. At first I said no because I was afraid of being hurt again, but he ruthlessly pursued me until I gave in. He always seemed to have a way of getting me to do what he wanted. Once I got back with him I realized that what I thought I'd been missing was nothing at all. The power that he'd had over me was gone so I broke it off. He was devastated. It was the most freeing thing for me to close the chapter of that book."

"So you think that I should go after Dane?"

"I don't think that you'll have to." Randall gave her a sardonic look. "I have a sixth sense about these things. I think that he's going to seek you out. Eden," Randall added forcefully, "you've changed your whole life. Even down to your hairstyle. Now it hangs past your shoulders."

"I did that because I don't have time to go to the beauty parlor every two weeks to have the back shaped," Eden protested.

"Maybe," Randall said. "But you've even affected a New York accent. But Dane still controls you. Take the power from him. Don't run anymore."

That night before she went to bed, Eden went into her office. She took out a writing pad. She headed the paper, Things That the Hamilton Twins Care About: What Daddy thinks. Prestige. Career. Money. After she finished her list, she tore the paper off the pad, folded it, and put it in her desk drawer.

*****

Monday afternoon Eden was putting the finishing touches on a client's file when her office door opened. When she looked up, Dane was standing in the doorway.

She was not at all surprised.

"I wanted to apologize for my brother's behavior." Dane looked at her for a minute before his eyes slid away from hers in awkwardness. "I have no excuse for him except that he drinks way too much."

"That is an excuse," she said. "Alcohol just makes people do what they want to do anyhow. Obviously he thinks that it's okay for him not to follow the rules of basic decency that the rest of us abide by."

"He's always been like that," Dane responded quietly. "Once again, I apologize."

Dane turned to leave.

"So you have a twin?" Eden said. "Which one of you is older?"

"He is by seven minutes," he said. "Because of that he's always trying to boss me around. That's why he was in town.

He's trying to change my mind about," Dane hesitated, "something."

Eden leaned back in her chair and gave Dane a measured look.

"I looked for you after you bolted and found that you'd left."

Eden leaned back in her chair and very slowly crossed her legs. Quite a bit of thigh was exposed during her maneuverings and she felt satisfaction at the look of interest on Dane's face as he watched her. Then she captured his eyes with hers. "Because of you and your brother, I missed out on the rest of an otherwise fun evening."

"Again, I apologize." Dane put his hands in his pockets and rocked back and forth on his heels. "What can I do to make it up to you?"

Eden leaned back and stretched her arms high above her head. The material on her shirt stretched across her full breasts.

Dane's eyes locked in on her movements. He swallowed hard.

She brought her arms down and placed her hands flat on the desk. Eden leaned towards him suggestively. "I don't know. What do you have in mind?"

Dane's body jerked in surprise. He stammered, "After work, how would you like to go to that same café on Madison? Maybe if we replace a not so good memory with a great one you'll forgive me. Besides, the food there is delicious."

She deliberately hesitated as if unsure whether to take him up on his offer. Then she said with a provocative smile, "I'll meet you there at six o'clock."

Eden picked up a folder and started reading its contents.

Dane knew that for the moment that conversation between them was over.

*****

When Eden arrived at the café she looked as if she'd just stepped out of a beauty salon. After raking a brush through her long tresses, she'd raided the emergency make-up kit that she kept at the office and reapplied foundation, and lipstick. She unbuttoned her ivory blouse a few more buttons at the top. Her black pencil skirt showed her legs off in her high heels. She sprayed a generous amount of perfume on her wrists and behind her ears, then sprayed it into the air and walked through it. She took a deep breath of nervousness and embarked on her journey to meet her nemesis.

Dane sat at a small table in the crowded restaurant. As he watched Eden saunter towards him he felt his temperature rise. For the second time that day, he swallowed hard as he noted how her slender frame was filled out in just the right places.

When she reached the table, he got up and pulled back a chair for her to sit down.

Oh, give me a break! But instead of giving him a mocking look she smiled at him with parted lips. "You're quite the gentlemen, I see," she acknowledged.

"I always try," Dane grinned.

Eden stared at him with a force that made him blink. Then suddenly her expression changed before he could decipher its meaning.

"I ordered a bottle of the white wine that you seemed to enjoy the other night."

"How do you know what I was drinking?" she asked sharply. Eden drummed her fingers on the table.

Dane gave a sort of embarrassed shrug. "I hate to admit it, but I asked the waitress," he said.

"Why did you do that?"

"Because I planned to ask you out on a date, and I wanted to know your tastes."

"We're not on a date," Eden said with a slightly hostile attitude. "We're simply two coworkers enjoying happy hour."

The waitress appeared with a bottle of wine in a bucket and two glasses. She filled each and then looked at Dane.

He simply waved her away.

Eden stared at her menu and felt Dane's eyes watching her.

She felt compelled to meet his gaze.

"Why did you agree to meet me?" he asked in his slow drawl.

Eden picked up her wine glass and drained it. Then she retorted, "Why did you ask me?"

"Because you're beautiful. Because you're smart. Because there's something about you that makes me want to get to know you."

"There are a lot of beautiful women in New York, Dane."

"But there's also something very familiar about you."

Eden's hand froze in midair.

"I love the way you tilt your head when you're listening. I was mesmerized by the way you just walked towards me. I find myself drawn to you, Eden. I feel as if I've known you forever, yet I know that's impossible because if we'd ever met, I wouldn't have forgotten," he said with a perplexed look on his face.

His words made her grasp for anything to get him off his train of thought. Eden's insides churned at the thought of her identity being discovered. "I think these are the sorts of things that you should be telling your wife."

"I have no wife," Dane said.

Eden knocked over her empty wine glass.

Dane calmly reached over and put it in the upright position.

"If I did have a wife, you're right, these are the sort of things that I should and would tell her," he said with a slight grimace.

"I heard that you were married." She looked at his left hand. "You wear a wedding band."

"Out of respect for my ex. My wife and I haven't been together for almost a year. She does her thing and I do mine."

"Give me a break." Eden rolled her eyes. "All married men say that. If you really didn't want her you'd get a divorce."

"We keep separate residences," Dane stated in a caustic voice.

Shocked by that revelation, Eden said, "Then why don't you get a divorce?"

"That's coming further on down the road." Dane spoke in an earnest voice. "She doesn't want her father to know. Whenever there's a family gathering I go to her place. I keep a few clothes there, but that's it."

"If that isn't dysfunctional I don't know what is," Eden said in a derogatory tone.

"She has a very weird relationship with her family and cares way too much about what her father thinks."

"And you don't?" The words shot out of her mouth before she could stop them.

"Not anymore," he said with emphasis. Then he picked up his wine glass and swallowed its contents.

"People get divorced all of the time," she scoffed. "You're just using her family as a smokescreen."

"I'm giving her time to tell him in her own way. It's not as if I was in a hurry. Our being married didn't interfere with anything that I had going on." He added almost as if an afterthought, "I've had nothing going on for a long time."

"Then why would you take a job working at the facility where he's vice president?" Eden asked with composure.

"It's an honor to work at New York General Hospital." His eyes hardened. "And because I feel as if I've earned the right to be there."

"So Tara is okay with you continuing to work for her father after the divorce?" Eden asked in a derisive tone.

There was heavy silence at the table. Dane stared penetratingly at her.

Eden had a sudden feeling of uneasiness that made her skin crawl.

Dane's next words shook her to the core. "Why would you think that my wife's name is Tara? My wife's name is Felicity."

The waitress appeared. "Are you ready to order?"

Not taking his eyes off Eden, Dane said, "I'll have the calamari and seafood trio."

The waitress jotted down Dane's order and then she turned to Eden.

"I'll have the same," she eked out.

After the waitress left, Dane sat watching Eden with an intent look waiting for her answer.

"You know how the nurses talk," she mumbled. "I think that I must have misunderstood what they said your wife's name was."

After another long silence Dane said, "So you were curious about me after all?"

"Just a little bit," she managed to say lightly.

"Was that your boyfriend that I saw you with the other night?" Dane asked in a slightly sullen tone.

"Maybe."

Eden saw a flare of jealousy in his green eyes and she felt a surge of power.

The waitress reappeared with their food.

As she nibbled on her meal she felt Dane's eyes on her breasts.

She picked up a piece of calamari and deliberately placed it on her thrust out tongue before swallowing it whole.

Dane licked his lips.

"What are you doing Friday night, Eden?"

"What did you have in mind?" she asked.

"I'd like to show you my loft in Tribeca."

"Why?"

"To prove to you that I'm not a liar."

Fear gnawed at her insides, but she brushed it aside. "What time?"

*****

Eden stood on the sidewalk and watched Dane try to hail her a cab.

"It's really not necessary for you to do this, Dane," she said. "I'm a big girl now. I can manage to get myself home."

"I wouldn't dare think of leaving you here standing on a sidewalk," he said curtly. "Why didn't you drive your car?"

"I drive only when it's absolutely necessary," she said equally curt.

"I don't know why you won't let me take you home." Dane gave her a look of candor. "I promise not to invite myself in."

"I don't let married men come to my house," she said firmly. "No matter how much they beg."

Now Dane shot her a dark look. "I've already explained my situation to you."

"Humph." Eden glared at him. "If a man is truly unhappy in his marriage he doesn't need another woman to get him out of it. The proper thing to do would be to leave his wife so she can move on and find someone else." Eden's stance was challenging. Her arms were folded in front of her and with a sense of intrigue she watched Dane wrestle for a response.

Suddenly a taxi pulled up to the curb next to them. The cabbie leaned over. "Ate you looking for a ride?"

Dane opened the taxi door for her to slide inside. He asked anxiously, "Saturday night at eight o'clock, right?"

With a curt nod Eden acquiesced.

That night she tossed and turned for hours, unable to sleep. Finally, out of frustration she sat up and turned on the lamp by her bed. She opened the drawer of her nightstand and withdrew the photo album she'd salvaged from Nanny's house.

Eden flipped through the pages until she found the picture she was looking for. It was of one of her and Peyton at college. They had their arms around each other's shoulder. With a set look of determination around her mouth, she gently closed the album and put it back in place. Finally she fell into a fitful sleep.

Chapter 12

Eden sat next to the window as she rode to the subway to Harlem. Even after a busy day at New York General Hospital, she enjoyed riding the rail to the clinic. Usually by the time she arrived she had unwound and looked forward to her three hour shift. Volunteering there once a week, she felt a sense of satisfaction every time she was able to help one of the patrons fill out paperwork to give to a health insurance company or guide them in the right direction when dealing with a health crisis.

When the train resumed its route, it was filled to capacity.

A group of teenagers chattered nonstop and mentally begging for relief Eden cast her eyes to the heavens.

Trying to distract herself, Eden surreptitiously cast looks at the people who sat across from her.

The man's pants were so baggy they gathered at his ankles and his three red tee shirts hung mid waist. Four gold chains with a huge medallion hung around his neck.

Sitting next to him was a young woman. With a worried look on her face she bounced a baby on her lap.

After the train stopped Eden walked the short five blocks to the clinic. Once she got to the clinic, she noted the large group of patients waiting for help. She went to her cubicle, locked her purse in her desk drawer, and then went in search of a cold drink from a vending machine.

In the small employee break room Eden stopped short when she found Dane sitting at a table reading notes.

"What are you doing here?" she blurted out.

"I'm going to be volunteering here on a weekly basis," he replied smoothly.

"Are you stalking me?" she demanded.

"Why would I need to stalk you when you've already gone out with me?" Dane settled back in his chair and looked at her enquiringly.

Walking farther into the room she said in a tart voice, "Maybe I should rethink my activities."

"Why are you always so nervous around me, Eden?" An ultra-sexy look shone from his eyes.

"Because everywhere I go you show up. It's too much of a coincidence for me," she said huffily. "I don't like being smothered."

"Let's dissect this conversation one piece at a time." He looked at her patiently. "First of all, we work at the same hospital so I can't help but bump into you. Also, you know that many of the doctors volunteer their time at clinics. This is one of the clinics associated with our hospital."

"But why did you pick this night?" she asked in a suspicious tone.

"Doctor Schaeffer asked me to take his place."

"Dr. Schaeffer left?" Eden asked, surprised.

"Yes. His wife is doing a lot more charity work so he has to take over her car pool duties."

"Oh," Eden said in a small voice.

"Where else have I happened to turn up where you were?" he watched her carefully.

"The wine tasting," she answered.

"That really was a fluke," he said. "Kane just got into town and he wanted to hang out in Times Square." There was a long silence in the room. "I knew that you volunteered here, Eden," he finally admitted. "But I didn't know which night. It seems as if I just got lucky." Dane got up from his chair, picked up a manila folder, and when he strode past gave her a wink.

After she'd seen over twenty patients and filled out too many forms to count, Eden went out to the waiting room. Her attention was immediately arrested by the couple she'd seen on the train. The baby's face was red from crying.

Once the father recognized her, he first looked surprised, then looked at her imploringly. Without looking at the sign in sheet to see who was next, Eden gave him a small distinct nod. Turning, he grabbed the baby off its mother's lap and hurried towards her with the mother following him.

When they were seated across from her Eden said. "What can I do to help?"

"We're Hector and Rosita Garcia," he said in broken English. "Our daughter's sick. I took her to the emergency room and we waited for over an hour and no one helped her."

"What's the matter with her?"

"She's had a fever for two days," the mother said in a frightened voice. "I can't get it to go down and she won't eat or drink anything."

Eden stood up. "Sit tight, I'll be right back."

She almost collided with Dane in the hallway. "I was looking for you," she said. "We have a really sick baby who needs medical care."

"Where is it?" he asked in a worried voice.

"In my office," she said.

"Have the baby brought to exam room three," he said. Without waiting for an answer, he took off in the direction that he'd been coming from.

Eden stood anxiously behind Dane as he examined the toddler. He didn't say anything as he went through a series of quick tests. After he shone a light in the baby's eyes he looked at the volunteer nurse who hovered.

"Call an ambulance, Linda," he said curtly. "She needs to be admitted to the hospital immediately."

The nurse rushed from the room.

The mother leaned on the father and buried her face in his chest.

"We should have never left the hospital, but we got tired of waiting," the father offered. "We figured we'd get seen quicker here."

"You probably made the right decision," Dane said. "I'm going to call ahead to the hospital so they're ready and waiting for you."

"Do you know what's wrong with her?" the mother asked.

"I can't say for sure but it looks like a case of meningitis," Dane said grimly.

"I knew that we should have had her get those shots," Rosita sobbed.

The screeching sound of an ambulance interrupted the rest of their conversation. Dane grabbed the toddler and rushed from the room with all of them following him.

After Eden watched the ambulance screech away with the Garcia family she turned and looked at Dane.

He too was following the vehicle's path with his eyes.

"I saw them on the train ride over here," she stammered.

"You did?" Dane looked at her surprised.

"Yeah." She looked down at her feet. "I'm ashamed to admit it but when he sat near me I looked at his clothes and automatically wrote him off as some kind of gang banger or something."

"The way he's dressed that's a logical conclusion."

"I know," she said. "But especially in my field of work I shouldn't make such snap judgments."

"Don't beat yourself up over that. Everyone knows that the first thing you notice about people is how they present themselves. If you want to be taken seriously you should dress the part."

"I agree," she said. "But he's not out applying for a job dressed like that. He's a loving father trying to care for his child."

"But I wouldn't be surprised if he did dress like that if he was to go to apply for a job. I have four wardrobes." He ticked each example off with his index finger. "There's my work wardrobe, my casual wardrobe, my hang out at home wardrobe and my dress to impress wardrobe."

"But maybe he can't afford all those changes of outfits."

"Why would you think that?" Dane asked in a teasing voice as he tried to lighten her mood. "He had on three tee shirts and a pair of two hundred dollar sneakers."

Eden gave him a grateful smile for letting her off the hook for judging Hector Garcia so rashly.

Dane's response was a smile of camaraderie.

*****

"Why are you going to his place?" Randall asked. "The man is supposed to pick his date, up not the other way around."

"If he came here and saw that I live in a two million dollar loft he might start to wonder about where I got all of this money. A director of case management, even a graduate from Harvard, couldn't afford this."

"Okay, but you're picking him up in an Infiniti hardback convertible. How do you explain that?"

"Oh, I can get away with that," she laughed. "People buy cars that they can't afford all the time."

"You're right," Randall chuckled. "I'm a testament of that."

Less than an hour later Eden nervously ran her hands down the sides of her dress. She rang the bell.

Immediately it was flung open and Dane stood at the threshold. "I have good news," he grinned. He stepped aside to give her entry.

"What is it?" she asked curiously.

"The Garcia baby is out of the woods. They're letting her go home tomorrow."

"That's great news," Eden said in a relieved voice.

Kane was dressed in a pair of khaki shorts, flip flops and tee shirt. Giving him an appraising look she said, "I feel overdressed for the occasion."

"If you want to take off your clothes so you can be more comfortable don't let me stop you," Dane teased with a wicked grin.

"Yeah, that's going to happen," Eden said mockingly. Her attention was drawn to the large oversized glass doors on the far side of the room. Hardwood floors matched a maple kitchen table that was placed in front of the windows. The living room area housed a sofa, coffee table, and huge flat screen television with stereo equipment. Jazz music played softly in the background.

"This is nice," she said, sitting on the sofa.

"It'll do," he said. "Would you like a glass of wine? White, yes?"

She gave him a look. "That's fine."

Dane quickly joined her and handed her a glass. "Now that I have you trapped in my lair," he said teasingly, "tell me all about Eden Savoy."

Her body stiffened.

"So that's why you asked over here." She said with forced lightness, "You intend to interrogate me?"

"No, I got you over here because I want to get to know you better."

Eden gave him a cynical look.

"I know that you graduated from Harvard but don't know much of anything else."

"I don't like to talk about my childhood. I was raised in foster care and it's a time that I choose to forget." The lie made her throat dry. Suddenly a vision of Nanny's face flashed in front of her and her expression was stormy. Eden quaffed the rest of her wine in one gulp.

Noticing her discomfiture but misunderstanding the reason Dane said quietly, "I understand."

"Why don't you tell me about your family?" She held her glass out and Dane immediately replenished it.

"My father lives in Dallas and my mother passed away three years ago."

"Oh, that's too bad," Eden said sincerely.

"Yes, it took me a while to cope with the loss." A sober look settled on his face from the memory. "We were very close."

"Where did you go to college?"

"A small one in New London," he said.

"Did you have a girlfriend?"

Dane's face grew pensive. "I wouldn't say that I had a girlfriend, but I met someone very special."

Butterflies fluttered in her stomach.

"You remind me of her."

Eden's heart skipped a beat. She asked casually, "Why?" Eden asked with pretended surprise, "Is she African-American?"

"Yes," Dane said. "But that's not why. I mean you two look nothing alike." He paused. "I think it's your laugh."

"So that's why your brother said that you like dark meat?"

"Probably," Dane said. A flush of red stained his cheeks, giving credence to his embarrassment at the memory.

"Do you keep in touch with her?" Eden knew that she was playing with fire but she had an insatiable desire to know what he would say. "I mean, are you two still friends?"

"No, we're not," he said slowly. "Let's change the subject."

"You sound guilty as hell." Eden studied him over the rim of his glass. "What did you do to her?"

"I was a boy and let my family do my thinking for me." He emptied the contents of his glass then quickly refilled it. "She just kind of got caught in the crossfire."

"Did you apologize to the woman that you hurt?" she persisted.

"I tried," he said. "But the issues were never resolved."

"And now you're trying to hurt another woman." Eden gave him a look of reproach. "I'm sure that your wife isn't quite over you yet and you're already trying to move on."

"First of all, my wife isn't hurt by our split," Dane said quietly. "She's been dating another man for months."

Aghast she asked, "Are you having her followed?"

"No. But sometimes information has a way of presenting itself."

The ringing telephone shattered the silence.

With a snort of frustration, Dane grabbed the receiver. "Of course," he said. "I'll leave the spare key with my doorman. See you then."

He slammed down the phone. "Sorry about that," he said. "It was Kane."

A look of displeasure that she didn't try to hide crossed her face.

Dane gave her a knowing look.

"He's not thinking of moving up here, is he?" She was sickened at the thought.

"He's coming to attend a seminar at the convention center."

"Oh," she said relieved.

"You never have to worry about Kane moving up here. He's Texan born and bred. Besides, his wife would never go for it. Whitney hates New York."

"So he did marry Whitney," she mused quietly to herself.

239

"What did you say?" Dane asked with a penetrating look.

"Nothing," she quickly denied. "How long have they been married?"

"Since a month after he graduated from college," Dane said in a sour tone.

"Do they have any children?"

"No, they've had two miscarriages." Now his voice was tinged with sadness, "It's too bad because Whitney would be a wonderful mother."

"That might be a good thing in the long run. Your brother didn't exactly strike me as daddy material."

Dane shot her a look. "Don't judge Kane solely by the one time you met him. He could be a wonderful father if he gave himself the chance."

"So you two are very close?" Eden asked.

"We used to be." Another solemn look crossed his face. "But now, not so much."

"Why not?" she probed.

"I don't know," he said. "After college we just sort of drifted apart. I never really wanted to work in the family practice and then," he hesitated, "after I married Felicity things got a little tense."

"Why? Don't they like her?"

"We went about it the wrong way."

Eden gave him an inquiring look.

"A lot of the time presentation is everything. I only knew Felicity a month before we got married in Vegas."

Shocked, Eden stared at him.

"From the time we were children it was sort of understood that I was going to marry Whitney's sister, Tara." He gave a dry smile. "She was the family choice. Our parents had been friends for over twenty years."

"How quaint," Eden said dryly.

A look of penitence crossed Dane's features. "After I graduated from college I knew that there was no possible way I could marry Tara. I broke it off and it seemed as if all hell broke loose."

"So you parents didn't like the idea that you upset the apple cart?"

"Yeah. And everywhere I went I saw Tara. She was part of our group and people were still partnering us off. I left for the summer to make sure that everyone understood that we were finished. I hooked up with one of my frat brothers who had a condo in Greenwich Village. That's when I met Felicity."

"Oh," Eden said.

"Í liked her right away. She was sort of a free spirit and we had a lot of fun together. One weekend we flew to Vegas and got married. Then when I returned to Dallas with her reality sunk in. My family was cold to her. And Felicity hated Texas.

"We decided to move up here hoping things would get better, but before long we knew for sure that it wasn't the location that was the problem. It was us."

Eden and Dane sat on the loveseat. He took his hand and began to knead her taut neck muscles. "You're always so tense," he murmured. "What has you in such turmoil all of the time?"

Lulled by his touch, and the background music of their past, Eden couldn't speak.

Dane's other arm was resting on the couch behind Eden. With the palm of the other hand he gently pulled her head towards his.

She lifted her hands to push him away, but instead they crept around his neck holding him close. Memories of the time, when terrified, they'd clung to each other in the darkness of the library at their college flooded her entire being. His touch ignited something inside her that she hadn't felt in years. And when his mouth touched hers she melted.

At first his kiss was soft, but then he parted her lips with his and his tongue leisurely explored her mouth, tasting all of her.

Dane took his warm hands and slowly pushed up her dress. He slid his fingers through the side of her thong and probed.

Instinctively, she spread her legs invitingly, giving him full access to her.

Suddenly, Dane dropped to his knees in front of her. He quickly divested her of her thong. Then he took her legs and placed them over his shoulders. He buried his head between her thighs and inhaled. Dane inserted his tongue in her center and worshipped her.

And then she lost her head.

Dane cupped his hands underneath her buttocks lifting her so he could drink in as much of her as he could.

Eden writhed on the couch. Her head was flung back and she cried out his name as his tongue played havoc with her pinkness.

Suddenly his tongue left her.

Miffed, Eden opened her eyes.

She now saw that Dane stood in front of her. His breathing was ragged, but his body was poised at attention. He scooped her into his arms and he purposefully strode to the bedroom. Kicking the door closed with one foot, he gently laid her on the bed.

With a smoldering look, he pulled at the hem of her dress.

Eden sat up and lifted her arms.

He let her dress drop to a heap on the floor with her thong.

She unsnapped the front clasp of her bra and her breasts stood out proudly yearning to be licked.

His eyes never left her face and he seemed to drink in every aspect of her. Once she was naked, he breathed a large sigh of relief and cupped his dick. Then he slid in bed next to her, drawing her close. Dane nuzzled led her neck.

His action transported her back in time, and weak from desire, she gladly gave in to him.

243

Eden moaned only because she couldn't hold it inside any longer.

Dane took his mouth and suckled Eden's breast. His fingers on his hand played with the moistness of her center. Then he stilled his movements. He carefully covered her body with hers and entered her in one fluid movement.

Once again, she drew him into her circle and clung to him. She wrapped her legs around his waist, clamping him to her. Eden met thrust for thrust with a fierceness that punished and pleasured his dick at the same time. As he screamed her name, she felt complete.

Eden was awakened by Dane's wandering hand.

She felt the warmth of his breath from behind her.

Dane loomed over her and gave her a soul searching kiss. Gently he positioned her on all fours, and then he entered her thrusting with a fierceness that shook the bed frame.

Eden clutched him with the walls of her vagina and stilled her body as he rode her. When they exploded it was in unison.

Eden pulled away from him, turned and with the flat of her hand pushed him onto his back. She straddled him and the wetness between her thighs as it rested on his stomach excited him into attention. She lifted herself slightly and grabbed his penis. It hardened like a missile in the palm of her hand. She closed it in her fist and gripped it hard. Then she inserted it into her. Eden slowly moved down. Then she began to rock forward. With her hands she pinned him to the mattress, curtailing a lot of his movement. Eden slid up and down on his stick until they exploded.

Dane lay on his stomach sleeping. His arm was slung possessively across her stomach.

She edged her body from under his. Dressing swiftly in the darkness, she grabbed her purse and left.

When she reached her apartment, Eden got off the elevator and came face to face with Randall and Colin. Randall was dressed in his bathrobe and had a lit cigarette in his hand.

She quickly masked her surprise at seeing them together. "Hello," she said to both of them before she walked to her door.

"Give me a minute," she heard Randall say to Colin.

"How did it go?" Randall asked quietly. "When I got your text message earlier, I could hardly stop myself from calling during your rendezvous to get an update."

"The whole game plan has changed," she said with a bemused expression before she went inside and shut her door.

*****

The next morning Randall sat at her table sipping a cup of coffee.

"Well," he said with a speculative gleam. "How was it?"

"I could kill you," Eden wailed as she towered over Randall. Her arms hung at her side and her fists were clenched.

"Me?" Randall said with his index finger to his chest. His eyes were open wide with fake surprise. "What the hell did I do?"

"You pushed me into going out with him."

"Hell, I didn't tell you to sleep with him. That was all you," he said with a knowing smile.

"I can't believe that I gave him some pussy," she shouted in mortification.

"I can," Randall said. "Hell, you were long overdue. He was just in the right place at the right time."

Eden shot daggers at Randall.

"If that's all it is," he added brazenly.

"What do you mean?" she demanded.

"Was it as good as it was all those years ago?"

Eden dropped her head.

"So it was," Randall chuckled.

"Actually," she said looking back at him. "I think that it was even better with some age on it."

"Are you going back for seconds?" Randall asked.

She sat in the chair across from him. "No," she ground out the words.

"I would. Just to make sure that I wasn't imagining how good it was."

"I don't know about that, Randall." she answered.

"Don't be afraid of life, Eden. There's a reason why Dane Hamilton ended up working at the same hospital that you did. Remember, God is always in control."

"I can't think about this right now. Let's talk about something else." Eden said, "Oh yeah! What the hell was Colin doing sneaking out of here at one o'clock in the morning?"

"He wasn't sneaking," Randall gave her a cocky smile. "He was happy to be here."

"I thought that you were through with him after the way he acted at the wine tasting."

"I'm through with him now. I just had to let him know who the boss is. Now I can let it go."

"I wish that I were like you."

Randall took his hand and placed it comfortingly on hers. "I don't want you to be like me, Eden. You'd like to be callous but after everything you've been through, you're not."

*****

When Eden arrived at work Monday she recognized the nosy look Ryta directed at her.

"Good morning, Ms. Savoy." Ryta grinned.

Eden stopped in her tracks. She asked guardedly, "Why are you calling me that?"

"Oh, no reason," Ryta denied without even attempting to act as if she meant it. "What did you do this weekend?"

Eden's eyes narrowed as she thought about how to answer the trap that Ryta was obviously laying for her. "Why?" she said slowly.

"Oh, nothing," Ryta said slyly. "It just seems as if you've been a very good girl."

"Okay." Eden planted her hands on her hips and said, "What's going on?"

Ryta held her hands out to her side. "It's not up to me to ruin a surprise for anyone. Just go on about your day and you'll find out soon enough what I mean."

Eden shook her head from side to side and walked off. As she made her way to her office she noticed the nurses at the station she passed giving her sidelong looks. When she opened her office door she stepped back in surprise. A vase that looked like it held at least two dozen of yellow roses with baby breath was on the corner of her desk.

Eden walked over a picked the small card. She recognized Dane's scrawl from college. *Friday night meant a lot to me, Dane.* Mesmerized, she held the card in her hand. Suddenly she felt a presence behind her. She turned and found herself only an inch from Dane's sturdy frame.

He leaned over and kissed her on her cheek.

She drew back.

Dane's eyes narrowed in surprise at her reaction.

Without speaking Eden walked around Dane and shut her office door with a decisive click.

"How could you?" Eden said with forced coldness.

Nonplussed, Dane asked, "What do you mean?"

"You're a married man," she continued in the same tone. "Do you want people to know what happened between us?"

"I don't care who knows about us," he said quietly.

"Well, I do," she declared emphatically.

"Are you ashamed of me? Is that what this is about" Obvious hurt was mirrored in his eyes.

"If your father-in-law hears about this…"

"I don't care what he thinks," Dane said.

"If you didn't care about what he thought you'd get a divorce," she said with a challenging look on her face.

A heavy silence enveloped the room.

"I would think that you too would be worried about your image," she said quietly.

"My personal life is my personal business," he said in a defiant voice.

"Then why bring your personal life to work? You shouldn't even be in my office unless it's something to do with a patient. Is that the reason for your visit?"

Dane stuffed his hands in his pockets and rocked back and forth on his heels. "I can't figure you out. What happened to that hot, vibrant, woman that I made love to the other night?"

"Maybe she was caught up in the moment and temporarily forgot the past."

Dane gave Eden a look filled with understanding. "So you've been hurt before." He said in a meditative voice, "Everyone has, Eden. But you have to move on and try not to repeat the mistakes of the past."

She gave him a wary look.

"Eden, give us a chance to know each other," he said quietly. "I bought tickets for *The Lion King*. I would be honored if you would go with me."

There was complete silence in the room as Eden digested Dane's words. Finally she said, "I'll think about it."

As she was sliding her lunch tray down the conveyor belt, she had the sensation of being watched. Eden swung her head around and met the penetrating stare of the vice president of the hospital, Andrew Lancaster.

She lifted her chin and held his gaze until he looked away.

Chapter 13

Randall stood in Eden's bedroom and watched her slide into her heels.

Suddenly she sat down on the bed. "Why am I doing this?" She cradled her head in her hands.

"To finally know for sure. You haven't been living your life."

He held his hand up when he saw Eden start to protest. "I know that you love your job at the hospital and volunteer work at the clinic, but your love life needs work."

"I'm too busy to have a relationship."

"You keep yourself busy so that you don't have to examine your lack of a love life. You've got to start living again, Eden."

"But not with Dane," she spat. "He's already had his chance and blown it."

"Eden," he said with heartfelt meaning, "life is for the living and its there for the taking."

"What do you mean?" she whispered.

"When you speak of Dane your eyes flash with such animation. I admit that it's an angry fire but at least its emotion. In all the years I've known you I've never seen you so animated when you speak of any other man."

"There's a thin line between love and hate," she offered lamely.

"But you need to figure out which pertains to how you really feel. Find out what he's all about. Date him as if you are really Eden Savoy. From what he's told you about his perspective on things that matter this guy may have really changed. If he has, then he's a good man. If he isn't, you have the power to get even."

"How long should I play the charade?" she asked.

Randall was quiet as he mulled over the situation. "Give him six months. If you still hate him after that tell him who you are and dump him."

"What if I don't hate him?" she asked in a tiny voice.

"Then at that time reassess the situation. Decide whether you want to be Eden Savoy or Sybil Masterson."

"I don't know about this, Randall."

"You hold all the cards, my dear. Use them."

*****

Dane's door was flung open and Kane stood there.

Eden froze.

Kane gave her a long, lazy look before he stepped back. "Dane's in the bedroom getting dressed. He had an emergency at the hospital so he's running late."

Eden's only response was to give him a curt nod before she went and sat at the table on the other side of the room, trying to get as far from Kane as she could.

"Dane said that you graduated from Harvard," Kane drawled.

"Do you find that hard to believe?" she asked frostily.

Kane studied her in the red dress that was the perfect foil for her dark skin.

"You're a very beautiful woman," he said abruptly. "Do you have a twin?"

"No."

"Too bad," he said. "Since Dane and I are twins, I think that it would be perfect if we did a Doublemint twin scenario. But since there aren't two of you, Dane and I have been known to share," he whispered suggestively.

Any thawing of the ice that had begun to melt around Eden's heart for Dane froze up again once she processed Kane's words and the memories of what they'd done to Peyton surfaced.

Dane entered the room. Immediately his eyes narrowed when he saw Kane posed over Eden.

"What's going on here, Kane?" he asked curtly.

"Nothing," he said, innocently moving away from her. "I was just trying to get to know your friend but she doesn't talk much."

"She doesn't like you," he growled. "So leave her alone."

Kane put his hands in the air in mock horror. "Excuse the hell out of me."

"Are you ready, Eden?" Dane asked.

"Yes," she said as she gracefully stood.

"Leave the spare key with the doorman, Kane."

"Will do, Dane," he said brusquely.

As Dane drove to Broadway Theatre, she felt him sliding looks at her out of the corner of his eye. "Did Kane say something inappropriate to you?"

"Why was he there? I thought that he'd be gone by the time I arrived." She spoke in a chilly voice.

"He changed his plane flight until this evening. He said that he needed an extra day to himself," Dane said, obviously relieved, "He'll be gone by the time I get home."

Throughout the play Eden never looked at Dane. *You idiot! How could you forget? I almost did forget.* She warned herself, *Don't forget again.*

On the ride home Dane said, "You've hardly spoken to me all night. What's going on?"

"I never talk during plays," she responded quietly. "It disturbs others around you."

"But you barely talked during intermission either. What has upset you?"

"I felt uncomfortable being out in public with a married man," she responded in a stiff voice.

Dane stiffened at her choice of words. "I've already explained that to you."

"And I don't buy it," she retorted caustically.

Dane put his hand on Eden's knee. "You can trust me."

"Humph," she grunted and crossed her arms in front of her.

"You don't seem the type who would care what strangers that you'll probably never see again think."

"I don't think you know me well enough to be able to gauge what I'm thinking, Dane. Just because we fucked it doesn't mean that you know me."

He pulled his car into a parking space and shut the engine off.

"Will you come up?" Dane asked with a sober expression.

Suddenly Chloe's words surfaced. 'Remember, the power's in the pink stuff.' "Just for a little while," she answered.

Dane asked as he strode to the kitchen, "How about a glass of wine?"

"That will be fine, Dane." Dane picked up a remote and the voice of R Kelly floated in the air. He went into the kitchen and poured two glasses of wine. When he reentered the living room he stopped dead in his tracks.

Eden stood in the center of the room naked except for her candy-apple red stilettos.

Dane dropped the glasses he was holding. Ignoring the shattered glass and liquid on the hardwood floor with lightning speed he rid himself of his clothes. His penis was hard and ready for use.

Eden Savoy watched her prey. The nipples on her plump breasts were dilated from a combination of complete control and excitement. She spread her legs and taking her index finger slid it inside the lips of her vagina. Then holding her finger out she sauntered over to Dane and placed it on his lips.

Hungrily his tongue snaked out and licked it before he drew her finger into his entire mouth. Then eagerly he grabbed her.

Eden reveled in the onslaught of his mouth.

Dane's hands cupped her full buttocks and pulled her closer to his body. His penis lifted and poked her navel and its tip lifted her belly button ring.

Suddenly Eden freed herself from his roving hands and stepped back. "We need to talk," she said and the deliberate throatiness of her voice sounded foreign to her own ears. "Listen to R Kelly. He's telling you what will happen when a woman's fed up."

Dane's Adam's apple throbbed nervously.

"This can't go on forever and you know what you have to do to keep fucking me."

"Eden," he croaked his own voice husky from frustration, "I'll give you anything you want, but I need time to clear up some personal matters."

Eden's eyes cast a glint of steel. Her voice held a slightly condescending tone as she said, "I'll not wait forever. If you don't free yourself, I'll fuck Kane."

"What did you just say to me?" Did you say that you would fuck my brother?" Dane's eyes bulged angrily in his head and his dick suddenly lost all of its rigidity and shrank to be less than half the size it had been only a minute earlier.

"If you leave me no choice I would," she said deliberately. "After all, he looks very much like you, but he seems to know what he wants. And goes after it."

Dane's nostrils flared angrily and he spat out, "I'll not let you do that."

"With every thrust, I'd pretend that it was you," she said.

Then she walked to his bedroom with him almost stepping her heels.

Once inside, Eden lay back on the bed. She drew her knees up and let them fall open.

Fully erect again Dane joined her on the bed and eagerly buried himself between her legs.

Then she took the palms of her hand and pushed him away.

"What?' he said questioningly.

"I won't be content as the other woman, Dane." Her eyes glittered in the darkness. She saw the look of agreement in his eyes before he entered her moist body, yet she drove her point home. "This may be the last time we're together," she whispered in his ear as he pummeled her body with long even thrusts.

Eden clawed his back and her nails were like talons yet Dane never winced from the pain.

Dane felt as if he was teetering on a cliff, but he held his climax until he felt her body completely saturated from her own sex. He grunted, "Eden," and came.

They lay still in the darkness. Suddenly Eden delivered a stinging blow to his buttocks and the sound was like a whiplash.

His body grew very still, not from pain but from a very distant memory.

After his labored breathing subsided he turned on his side and made to pull her into the folds of his body.

Before he knew what was happening, she maneuvered her body from underneath his, got up and walked back into the den.

Dane followed her.

She gingerly stepped around the debris on the floor and grabbed her clothes. Deliberately taking her time, she stretched her arms up and slid the red shift over her head, down her waist, and around her curvy hips.

Eden watched Dane.

Dane watched Eden.

"Don't leave," he whispered. "Stay the night."

The only light in the room was what seeped through the square windowpanes and sliding glass doors.

The light cast a shadow across Eden's face as she sized him up. *I've got him right where I want him.* Deliberately she pivoted on the four inch heels she'd worn since she'd entered his apartment and strutted over to the door. "I can't stay here," she said in a deliberately unemotional voice.

As Dane watched his obsession sashay out of sight a feeling of *déjà vu* consumed him.

Overcome by a feeling of raw desperation, Dane plopped down on his sofa with a thud and buried his face in his hands.

*****

Eden opened her e-mail and read the message. "You have an e-card." She manipulated her mouse and clicked on it. *Meet me in Central Park West at one o'clock. I'm bringing lunch. Please confirm.*

After a slight hesitation she clicked the yes box.

At twelve-thirty she locked her office and headed out the building. Instead of going to the trouble of taking her car out of the parking garage and losing her spot, Eden hailed a cab. Once inside she told the driver, "Central Park West, please."

"Yes, ma'am."

Once she arrived at the park, she walked the winding path. She swung her head around in all directions looking for him. *According to his directions he should be around here somewhere.*

Even with sunglasses on the bright sun was blinding. She tried to shield her eyes with her hand as she surveyed the grassy knoll. There was a father and son flying a kite. There were many mothers pushing their babies in strollers on the winding path, and there were quite a few young people playing sports. There was a vigorous volleyball game. Others were playing catch with either a baseball or football.

In the distance, she saw a large bunch of balloons. Holding them was Dane.

Eden unsuccessfully tried to tamp down her pleasure at his gesture.

Once she reached him he leaned over and kissed her on her cheek. Then he handed her the balloons.

She said, laughing, "Now what am I going to do with all of these?"

"Treasure them until all the hot air is out of them."

"I think that you're the hot air, Dane," she teased.

"Ouch." He placed his hand over his heart. "That hurt my ego."

"Well, at least you're admitting that you have one."

"Don't we all?" Dane cleared his throat. "I wanted to have lunch with you today so that we can talk. And I want to make sure that you understand something."

"What?"

"You know for sure that my wife and I aren't together. You're not coming between a man and wife because there's nothing there. I feel obligated to give Felicity the time that I promised her. But I don't expect you to wait forever."

Dane's eyes narrowed with an intensity Eden hadn't seen since the night they'd hidden in the media center at college "What you said the other night about sleeping with my brother," he paused, "that was mean. It was also untruthful because you wouldn't do something like that." He gave a negative shake of his head. "You're not that kind of woman, and it's beneath you to suggest that you are."

She countered his assessment of her character by asking, "Have you and Kane ever done *ménage e trios* with a woman?"

A guarded look settled on Dane's face. "Why would you ask me that?"

She shrugged in a deliberately nonchalant manner. "I don't know. I just heard that often twins like the same women."

"Kane and I don't have the same taste in women. I like mine spunky."

"So I guess that means no." She watched him closely.

"It means that I've done things in my past that I deeply regret," he said in an evasive tone. "And that's all I'm going to say about that. What you need to focus on is us and you giving us a chance to get to know each other. Please don't prejudge me, Eden."

She hesitated for a minute, digesting his words. "I'll think about what you've said." Then in a more upbeat tone, "I'm hungry. What'd you bring for lunch?"

"I didn't quite know what you like so I got subs from the deli around the corner. I eat there quite a lot and have never been disappointed."

"You've gone to a lot of trouble, Dane." She cast him a sideways look. "What if I'd said no to a lunch date with you?"

"Then I would have cried in my iced tea. Shall we sit?"

Once they were situated on the blanket, Dane reached inside the basket and pulled out two large sandwiches. "One is a turkey with Swiss and all the trimmings and the other is roast beef. You get first pick."

"I'll take the turkey," she said. "The only beef that I eat is mine."

Dane gave her a look of longing. "So I take it you make a mean roast beef?"

"Yes I do," she said right before she bit into her sandwich.

"May I'll get lucky one day and you'll cook for me."

"Maybe," she responded in a light tone.

"Here you go," he said handing her a bag of potato chips.

"Thanks," she said, taking it.

They ate their food content to watch people in the park.

Dane finished his meal first and once he downed his ice tea, he belched loudly enough for the people seated on the nearby bench to hear him.

An immediate look of chagrin settled on his face.

She flung her head back and burst into laughter.

"Excuse me, Eden. I'm trying so hard to impress you and I blew it."

Once her laughter subsided she asked curiously, "Why are you trying to impress me so much?"

He shrugged still a little embarrassed by his gaffe. "I don't know," he said, "but for some reason I want your approval."

"So that means all this, the picnic, the theatre, is an act and not the real you?" she said, watching him carefully.

"No," he said with obvious sincerity, "it's me all right. I'm just always nervous that you might not agree to see me again so I try to make each time that we spend together meaningful."

Dane lay stretched out on his back basking in the sun.

She propped her head up on her hand and peered down at him. "You look like you're in hog heaven," she said.

"I am," he replied. "It doesn't take much to make me happy."

"Really?" she asked.

"I'm a simple man who enjoys simple things. A picnic in the park with good company, a good movie with a bottle of beer, or a lazy Sunday with family. Those are the kinds of things that I enjoy."

Eden stared in Dane's green eyes and again felt the stirring of past emotions. She blinked several times in an effort to shake off the memories.

"What are you thinking right now?" Dane whispered.

She was at a loss for words. Not wanting to reveal her true feelings, she said, "I'm thinking that after all that food it'd like to walk."

"That sounds like a plan," Dane acquiesced.

Dane looped one arm through the picnic basket and draped the other around her shoulders. "I enjoy Central Park," he said as they strolled. "It's the one place in New York that makes me feel close to nature."

"You sound like you miss the country life."

"Sometimes. But I'm really starting to enjoy living here." He gave her a look full of innuendo. "It has perks that Texas doesn't."

She smiled at him.

263

"You have a beautiful smile, Eden. You should use it more often."

After a while, Dane looked at his watch. He said in a mournful voice, "I hate to do it, but I have to leave. I have an appointment with the hospital cardiologists at three o'clock."

"Yipes," she said, now checking the time. "I can't believe we've been here so long."

"I'll walk you to your car," he said.

"I didn't drive because I didn't want to lose my parking spot. I'll have to take a cab."

"Nonsense," he said firmly. "I'm going the same place you are. We'll ride together."

"I don't know, Dane," she mumbled. "Someone from work might see us."

"I'll not take no for an answer." He looked at her stubborn expression. With resignation he said, "I'll let you out farther down the street and you can walk into the main building's entrance."

"Okay."

Once they reached Dane's car, he opened her door. Before she was able to get in, he grabbed her and spun her around. "I know you won't let me do this once we get back to the hospital."

Dane took his hand and lifted her face.

Without knowing it she opened her mouth invitingly.

The feel of his lips on the side of her neck surprised her.

Dane nuzzled her neck, simply holding her close in his arms.

After what felt like an eternity he gently turned her around and gave her a slight nudge.

Eden basically fell into her seat.

They were quiet for most of the drive back to the hospital. Eventually she said, "Why am I not surprised that you're driving a BMW? I think that's every doctor's choice."

"How about you and that fancy ride you're driving?" he said, pulling out in traffic. "I'll trade you mine for yours."

"I got it on sale," she said. The lie she told besmirched the pleasant lunch they'd had and she stared guiltily out the window.

When Dane pulled over before they reached the hospital, partly out of regret that she had again lied to him, she turned to him and planted a solid kiss on his mouth.

He beamed. Then he reached for her.

Hastily she opened her car door. "I better get going." She reached into the back seat and grabbed her balloons.

Instead of the elevator Eden opted for the stairs. When she reached the floor where her office was located she ignored the curious looks as she strutted by with enough balloons to keep a clown in business for a couple of days. Once in her office she put them in a corner and as she worked her last couple of hours of the day, every time her gaze rested on them she felt a small thrill.

*****

When Eden entered the clinic she looked around in amazement. The usual mayhem that greeted her was absent. There were no screaming children, frustrated parents, or any of the personnel who were usually bustling about. Her first instinct was to back slowly out the door, afraid that there was some sort of hostage situation and everyone was bound and gagged in the back.

She relaxed when she saw Dane striding down the hallway towards her.

"What happened?" she said, holding her hands out. "Where is everyone?"

"I left you a message at the hospital. The water main broke so we have to shut down until it's fixed."

"Oh," she said. "That's too bad. What are people going to do?"

"I was in the back making a sign. I'm going to put instructions on the door for patients call for an appointment at the clinic on 35th Street."

"That's a good idea," she said. "Would you like me to help?"

"I'm almost done with the sign but you can watch me put it up," he said.

Eden followed Dane to his office.

Once he completed writing his message with a red marker on a white poster board he said, "Even though I'm sorry for the people that usually come here, I don't mind not working tonight. I'm dead tired. And I'm starving."

"I hear you," she said. "That's why you weren't able to reach me at work. I tiptoed out early and stopped by my place. I had a taste for some pot roast and put it in a crock pot to eat when I get home."

"Pot roast." Dane licked his lips in a salacious manner. "I haven't had homemade pot roast since my mother died," he added.

Eden's heartstrings tugged at the wistful look on Dane's face. Before she could stop herself she said, "You're more than welcome to come over and have some."

"Eden," he said gratefully, "you are a lifesaver. Did you drive?" he said.

"No," she answered in an almost fearful voice. Now that she'd invited him she couldn't retract the invitation and she felt cornered. "You know that I take the subway down here."

"That's perfect. My car's right outside. Let's put the sign up and get out of here."

All the way to her loft, Sybil's fingers drummed the console between them.

When she felt Dane observing her movements, she forced herself to stop. *How am I going to explain my expensive loft?*

Once they got to the intersection where she lived she said pointing, "That's my parking garage. I'm on the fifth floor."

"I know," he said.

Eden stared at him questioningly.

"Do you really think that I would make love to a woman and not know where she lived? Come on, Eden, you should know me better than that by now." On the ride in the elevator, the wheels in Eden's head were turning furiously. Once they reached her place, she unlocked her door with trepidation.

Dane gave an approving whistle once inside. "How can you afford this on your salary?"

Eden gave him a quelling look. "Don't you think that's gauche of you to ask me that?" she asked in a haughty voice.

"I'm sorry, Eden, I didn't mean to offend you. I just know that they rob you blind in New York for any decent-sized apartment and this is immense with a view that anyone would kill for."

"Well, I got lucky," she said, avoiding his eyes. "This is rent controlled and I sublet from someone else. They split the rent with me so they don't lose it."

"God certainly rains blessings on you, Eden."

She felt stung by his comment. "Not really. Are you so materialistic that you think that money is the only blessing that a person can have? How about a family with a mother and a father? Or maybe a sibling or two. I have none of that."

A real look of apology was evident on Dane's face. "I'm sorry, Eden. I know that you must have had a rough time in foster care."

Sudden shame washed over her. "Let's change the subject."

She walked into the kitchen and lifted the lid of the crock pot. The mixed vegetables and potatoes lay steaming on top of the roast. She turned around to get a fork out of a drawer.

Dane was standing almost on top of her. "I'm sorry for what I said, Eden. Please don't let it spoil our night."

After a very long pause she managed to squeak out, "I'm sorry too, Dane. More than you can possibly know."

He took his hand touched her cheek.

She instinctively turned her face and rubbed it against his palm. "Go into the den and relax while I finish dinner," she murmured.

As she watched Dane's retreating back a feeling she couldn't make sense of washed over her. Dragging her gaze away from him, she turned and took her rice canister out of the refrigerator and measured two heaping cups and put it in a pot. Then she washed it thoroughly and put it on the stove to boil. Next she took she mixed a box of Jiffy cornbread and placed it in the preheated oven.

Eden kicked her shoes off and walked back into the den.

Dane was sitting on the couch with his head thrown back, his eyes closed. He had muted the television and the only sound in the room was his light snore.

Tiptoeing over, she looked down at him.

Sensing her presence, his eyes slowly opened. A strange look stole across his face. Dane stared at her as if seeing her for the first time. His eyes started at the top of her head. His perusal drifted past the sheer ruffle blouse that pulled tightly across her full breasts and the navy peasant skirt that nipped her tiny waist. Then he gave a slight smile when he saw her bare feet.

Knowing that she was desperately in need of a pedicure, she put one foot on top of the other in an effort to hide her chipped polish.

Seeing this he grinned. "It's too late," he teased.

"I'm long overdue for a pedicure," she whispered self-consciously.

"I don't think you need to bother, Eden. Everything about you is beautiful to me." He took her hand and kissed it.

Quicksilver shot through her at his touch.

They sat at her dinette set. Eden had opened a couple of bottles of Smartwater and poured it into their glasses.

Dane looked at it doubtfully. "Don't tell me you believe that water is going to make you 'smarter than the average bear'?"

Hearing Dane use the same phrase he had while they were at college made her laugh out loud.

He looked amused. "Don't tell me that you never heard that quip before. It's from one of my favorite cartoons when I was a child."

"No, I know it all right." She grinned. "I'm just not used to hearing adults use it."

"Being childish keeps me young," Dane answered, uncaring that she had bordered on calling him childish.

He took his fork and dug into a piece of meat. He swallowed it whole. "Eden, this is the tastiest pot roast that I've eaten in years. I would say that it is the tastiest but my mother may be listening and I don't want her turning over in her grave."

Eden laughed. But then she asked in a serious voice. "Do you care a lot about what your family thinks?"

Dane mulled over her question. "I used to. I think that when you're young it's natural to have the desire to please your parents. That can be a problem because no one has parents that are perfect or always make the right decisions. My father has softened in his old age."

"He has?" she asked, swallowing a mouthful of food.

"Yeah, and I'm proud of him. Back in the day, if I had told him that I was moving to New York he would have pitched a fit and threatened to cut me off."

"What changed him?" she asked.

"Life," he said soberly. "The sudden passing of my mother devastated him. He was out of town at a medical conference and she had a brain aneurysm. It was a total shock because she had just been to the doctor and been given a clean bill of health." Dane shook his head gravely. "I think dad blames himself for him not being there. Too this day we don't know if she could have been saved."

"That's a sad story."

"Ever since then father's been more about keeping the peace. The things he used to take for granted he doesn't anymore."

"Such as?" Eden asked.

"Well, for one thing, now he can't seem to get enough of our company. When we were young every summer he sent us somewhere. We went to Europe, Greece, or a rich kids' camp. We learned to navigate boats, Jet Ski, horseback ride, tennis; the whole nine yards. It was great fun, but sometimes I used to wish that he didn't want us gone for the whole two months of vacation. Or maybe once we left I hoped that he'd missed us enough to send for us to come home early, but he never did. Now he almost insists that we come home every holiday."

"That can become bothersome. Especially since flying has now become the unfriendly skies with all those checkpoints and so forth."

"Yeah, but it's worth it. The minute he sees me he lights up like a Christmas tree."

"So now you're one big happy family?" Eden said.

"No, not really. I mean, there's always Kane."

Eden smothered another laugh as Dane rolled his eyes before he bit into a big chunk of cornbread.

*****

Eden was standing in the doorway seeing Dane off. She startled herself by saying, "You can stay the night if you want."

"I wish the hell I could." Dane ran his hand through his jet black hair. "I'm scheduled to operate first thing in the morning and I know that if I stay here tonight I won't be rested enough to do my best job."

"Oh," she said.

"I would be too excited to sleep lying next to you. I might have to get a sleep aid so after we make love I can get some sleep instead of doing what I'd want to do."

"And what is that?" she asked in a sexy voice.

"To do a happy dance for hours all around the bed." He grinned.

Eden grinned back.

Dane looked at her full lips and a peculiar look crossed his face. "When you smile like that, you look..."

"I look what?" The dread that he'd figured out who she was shook her to the core.

Dane shook his head as if he was trying to rid it of something. "Nothing," he said before his eyes slid away. "I need to go. Good night, Eden."

Dane leaned over and kissed her on the cheek.

She moved closer.

Dane leaned in and when their lips met Eden lost track of time.

Dane explored her mouth with his, and after he freed her she had to gasp for air.

With unsatisfied sexual frustration Eden watched him until he disappeared on the elevator. Then she closed the door and leaned on it.

She had just finished stacking the dishwasher when she heard someone cough behind her.

She turned around and saw Randall. "When did you sneak in here?"

"I've been standing here observing you for a minute. Why do you have that look of contentment on your face?"

"No reason."

"Could it be the fact that I passed Dane Hamilton in the parking garage?"

Eden's mouth dropped open in surprise. "How did you recognize him?"

"You've describe tall, dark, and handsome to a tee. Too bad you didn't tell me he was so grumpy looking."

"Dane wasn't grumpy. He's just real tired and he has an important operation in the morning."

"No," Randall drawled. "The minute he saw me he started glaring. The look he gave me was real cantankerous." He held his hands up in mock horror. "I was almost frightened."

"I think that you're imagining things," she shot back. "Dane is one of the easiest going men I've ever dated."

"Well, well, well," Randall said musingly. "This is refreshing. Now you're defending him."

"I'm not defending him," she denied hotly. "I just think that you're wrong."

"Hmm," he joked. "And you're sensitive too."

"Randall," she said crossly. "I've had a long day. Do you mind not trying to needle me?"

"You're smitten," Randall said smugly.

Eden glared at Randall.

He grinned back.

"I'm going to take a shower," she said. She flung the words over her shoulder as she stomped to the bedroom, "You know your way out."

Randall's raucous laughter followed her and in an effort to shut it out she slammed her bedroom door.

Later that night Eden tossed and turned in bed. For the first time since Dane had blown back into her life, when words or phrases that pertained to their college days were brought up she hadn't flinched.

Chapter 14

Eden made an entry in her calendar. When the elevator doors opened she looked up and was taken aback.

Andrew Lancaster and Dane flanked a petite redhead.

Eden's mouth got dry.

Dane's face turned beet red. He nervously stammered, "Hello, Eden."

Eden was unable to respond.

Dane's father-in-law watched the scene with obvious disapproval. His mouth had a hard line to it and his jaw looked rigid. He looked at Eden, Dane, then his daughter.

Felicity was staring at Eden with a blank look on her face when the elevator doors started to close.

Andrew stuck his arm out and held the door for his daughter to precede him out. Then Dane, with unwavering eyes on Eden, stepped out of the elevator.

She looked through him and nimbly stepped inside the elevator.

When she turned around Dane was inside the elevator with her. The doors closed and in a something of a trance she noticed the shocked looks on the faces of Andrew Lancaster and his daughter.

"Get out of here!" she demanded.

"I wasn't going with them with you looking the way you do."

"How do I look?" Rage and jealousy battled throughout her body.

"Like you lost your best friend," he said quietly.

"You ain't no damn friend of mine," she spat.

Dane turned around and pushed the red button so the elevator stopped descending to the floor where Eden worked.

"What the hell are you doing?" she yelled.

"Calm down," he ordered quietly.

Eden was irate. "You don't tell me what to do."

"Calm down and let me explain," Dane choked out. By the look on his face he was apparently having a hard time forming the words.

"Explain what?" she ground her words. "That I'm not only fucking a married man, I'm fucking a liar."

Dane blanched. "Don't say that, Eden."

"It's not like I didn't know," she whispered. "I should have known." She talked as if she were alone.

"Eden," he said, "nothing has changed. Felicity and I have no marriage. She comes here every week to have lunch with her father. I simply ran into them in the hall."

"Go away," she said in a drained voice.

"No, I will not go away," he said heatedly. "I'll prove to you that I'm not the liar that you think I am." Dane turned around and punched two buttons and the elevator began ascending instead of descending.

"What are you doing?" she asked her voice overwrought with apprehension.

"I'm sure that Felicity and her father are in his office," he said grimly. "We'll settle this right now."

"No the hell we won't." Eden shrank against the wall. "I don't want this confrontation, Dane. Maybe you don't give a damn about your reputation or how you hurt people but I do."

"No," he said, grabbing her by the arm and pulling her close to his body. "I'm going to prove to you once and for all that what I say is the truth. I'm an honest man, Eden, why can't you see that?"

When she heard his words Eden slumped against him. "You have to stop and think clearly, Dane. Maybe you can survive this sort of messy affair but I can't. I've worked long and hard to get where I am and I don't want to lose my job."

The elevator continued its ascent to the twenty-fifth floor.

"Please don't, Dane," she begged.

With restrained violence Dane slammed the button and stopped the elevator again. He put his arms around Eden and with the palms of his hands cradled her head.

"Pull yourself together, Eden," he murmured softly.

They remained still for a while. "I'm going to send the elevator back to your floor. You go into your office and get hold of yourself."

"Where are you going?" she whispered.

"I have a meeting with my nurse practioner and then I'm leaving for the day. I'll be at your place at six o'clock and we'll talk this out. Okay?"

Eden shook her head no.

"I'm bringing dinner," he said in an insistent voice.

The elevator doors opened and in her haste to get away, Eden stumbled.

Dane reached out and grabbed her, steadying her on her feet.

She pushed him away and darted past Ryta who watched them with a knowing smirk plastered on her face.

Once inside her office Eden covered her face in her hands.

*****

Eden was unlocking her apartment door, and as usual, Randall opened his door when he heard her.

He took one look at her distraught face and gasped, "What's the matter?"

"I saw Dane's wife today," she said.

"How? When?"

"Supposedly," she held her fingers up in the quote unquote mannerism, "she was there to have lunch with her father."

"That's plausible since he works there. Don't you believe him?"

"Yes I do. The problem is that I feel like the world's biggest hypocrite for accusing him of being a liar when that's all I am," she whispered in a broken voice.

279

*****

Eden lay on her bed with a cold compress on her forehead. She'd had a piercing headache since early that afternoon and the two Aleve tablets she'd taken over thirty minutes earlier were just starting to kick in.

The sudden ringing of the doorbell made her sit up straight in bed. Pulling on her green kimono wrapper she walked down the long foyer. Looking through the peephole she recognized the breadth of Dane's shoulders.

"What do you want?" she hollered through the closed door.

"I need to talk to you," he said in a strained voice.

"Go away," she said. "Can't you see that what we're doing is wrong?"

"Eden," Dane said, "please let me in."

"No," she stated vehemently.

"The least you can do is let me in and not keep me standing on your doorstep like some axe murderer."

She didn't answer him.

"I'm not leaving and the people using the elevator are staring at me." He said in a warning voice, "Your neighbors are going to have a lot to gossip about tomorrow."

Eden opened the door and dragged him inside. She slammed the door shut.

Dane held bags of food in his hands and she could discern the smell of chicken.

Dane stared at her as if in a stupor. His mouth hung open.

Eden's kimono hung open from the force of her slamming the door and one of her boobs was exposed.

Embarrassed, she pulled her robe closer around her.

Dane said hoarsely, "Don't cover yourself from me."

"Dane," she began.

"Let's eat," he said in a stressed voice. "Are you hungry?"

She whispered, "Yes."

Dane strode into the kitchen and placed the bags on the table.

Eden went to the cabinet.

Dane took her arm and gently led her to a chair at the table. He pulled it out for her.

She sat down and once Dane saw that she was situated he said, "Relax. Let me take care of you."

Dane opened a bag and took out several paper plates. Then he opened several cartons of food. There was an array of dishes. Garlic sesame chicken, sweet and sour pork, shrimp fried rice, and egg rolls. He spooned generous helpings on each of their plates and then went to the refrigerator.

He grabbed two bottles of Smartwater and filled their glasses. Handing her one he said, "Because I need it."

Eden attempted to give Dane a blank stare, but she failed.

They ate their meal without talking and once they were done, Dane started cleaning up the kitchen.

Eden rose to help him.

He ordered softly, "Sit down. You've had a rough day."

Once again Eden sat.

She watched him as he filled the sink with water and wiped down her countertops.

After he finished rinsing the sink out he turned to her. He leaned back against the counter and surveyed her. "I understand how upsetting that must have been for you to see me with Felicity today. But I promise you she was not there to see me.

"I don't hate Felicity so I saw nothing wrong with riding the elevator at the same time as she and her dad." Dane searched Eden's inscrutable expression yet he couldn't get a read on what she was thinking.

"I was more than willing to prove to you that there is nothing between me and Felicity, but you stopped me. And I wish that you hadn't."

Eden jerked when she heard these words.

"I was so riled up at the thought of losing you everything would have come to a head and it would have been a welcome relief."

"If you really want to divorce her you don't need me to do it," she whispered. "You don't need an excuse."

"I haven't pursued a divorce because in the past there wasn't a need to. Eden, I feel so guilty about my marriage. I married the wrong woman and I knew when I was promising to love, cherish, and be with her for the rest of my life that I was lying. I hate that I did that and maybe destroyed her belief in happily ever after."

"You sound almost too good to be true, Dane," she mumbled in a lackluster voice.

"I'm just trying to be a better man. I've hurt people or been a party to someone hurting another and I don't want to walk that road again."

Eden gave him a searching look.

"Please don't leave me, Eden," he said with a pained look on his face. "Give me time to close the doors on my past."

Her shoulders slumped dejectedly and she bowed her head in submission.

Seeing this, Dane came to stand in front of her. He took his hands and helped her to her feet before disrobing her. The green pool of satin swirled around their feet.

Dane clutched hungrily at her breasts.

Eden became soaked from desire.

"Do you want me, Eden?"

"Yes," she whispered. "There are no blurred lines about that Dane."

He took his tongue and traced the midnight around one of her nipples. With the other hand he gently squeezed the other breast.

Eden moaned and thrust her hands in his hair.

Without taking his mouth of her breast, he scooped her into his arms and instinctively strode down the hallway cradling her.

After he gently laid her on the bed, he stripped naked and joined her. As they rocked together in pleasure their bodies climbed new heights. After they climaxed their desire, Dane spooned her.

When Eden woke the next morning, she spied a note on the vacant pillow. "I have an early surgery this morning. I'll e-mail you."

She took the pillow and hugged it to her, breathing in the lingering scent of Dane's aftershave.

*****

"Did you get the e-mail from Human Resources?" Ryta asked.

"No," Eden said. She looked at the stacks of folders on her desk. "I'm just getting here. Why, is there something earth shattering on it?"

"No," Ryta said. "It's just a generic letter to all hospital employees about liaisons and socially fraternizing with each other."

"What!" Eden said. Her heart beat rapidly as she thought about the timing of the e-mail.

Ryta came into the room and quietly closed the door behind her. "I like you, Eden. And I have a lot of respect for you. You are fair to all of us. But I think that you should know about the rumor. They say that you're having an affair with Doctor Hamilton."

"Who says that?" Eden asked with a closed look on her face.

"More people than you want to know," Ryta said in a cautious voice.

"Why would anyone think that?"

"Evidently someone peeked at the card with the flowers that were sent to you. It happened before they reached me."

"Oh." Eden asked her, "And what do you think?"

"I think that people should mind their own business. But I did want to warn you."

"Thank you for telling me," Eden murmured gratefully.

"I don't care if it's true or not. But I do know that if you are seeing Doctor Hamilton no one can do a thing about it."

"What do you mean?"

"There are three other doctors at the hospital that are dating someone they work with. It's been going on for years," Ryta said in a cynical voice. "At least you're qualified for your job. Some of them got promotions and big hefty raises to boot."

Ryta let Eden digest the news for a minute. Then she added, "Also, I happen to know that vice president Lancaster has a girlfriend on staff at the hospital. She's also twenty years his junior."

Stunned, Eden leaned back in her chair. "How would you possibly know that?" She added doubtfully, "It could be just a rumor."

"Nope," Ryta said with a smirk. "Let's just say that I know because the woman is my ex-husband's niece. She's always been precocious. So, in other words if they tried to fire you or anything like that you could sue them and you'd win too." She looked at her earnestly. "In the event that should happen *I* for one would be more than willing to corroborate what goes on around here."

After Ryta left, Eden booted up her computer. She quickly scanned her e-mail inbox and read the letter from Human Resources. The hypocrisy of the letter that had Lancaster's handprints all over it burned her. She printed it and put it in a folder in the bottom drawer of her desk in case she needed it in the future. As she was reading the rest of her e-mails one popped up from Dane. It was an invite to lunch. Instead of replying to it, she picked up her cell phone and called Dane's mobile.

"Hello." He sounded sexy yet tired showing that he'd been up all night.

"Have you read your e-mail?" she asked brusquely.

"No, I only had time to send you that one before I went to surgery. Why what's up?"

"Human Resources sent out a generic letter that basically states that we shouldn't be dating."

"We who?" Dane said.

"I think with the timing of it that it's meant as a warning to us," she said dryly.

"Hmmm," Dane said. "That's unfortunate. I must say that I'm pleasantly surprised that you don't seem more upset."

"I don't like oblique threats, and I certainly don't like people to think that they can push me around."

"That's my girl, Eden." Dane said gently, "However, you were right yesterday. I don't want to be the reason that you're the source of gossip at your place of work. I'll show a little more decorum when you're around. It's just so hard for me because you're so damn hot."

"Then stay away from me and neither of us will get burnt," she offered in a teasing voice.

"Yes, ma'am," Dane said in a deliberately peevish voice.

A couple of days later, Randall was helping put Eden's suitcases in the trunk of her car. "This is sudden."

"I got an e-mail from Haley that she's the lead in the school play, so I want to pop down there and surprise her," Eden explained.

"She'll absolutely love that." Eden let herself be enveloped in Randall's strong embrace.

Once he let her go he said, "Let me know when you get there."

"I'll text message you," she promised.

*****

Dane sat at his desk and dialed Felicity's cell phone number. It went straight to voicemail.

"Felicity, I need to speak to you. When you come to the hospital to meet your father for lunch I'd like you to stop by my office before you see him. It's very important." After he disconnected he dialed his nurse practitioner. "Pamela."

"Yes, Doctor Hamilton."

"I'm expecting a Mr. Rittenhouse. When he arrives, send him right in."

"Yes, Doctor Hamilton."

After he hung up the phone Dane stared thoughtfully into space. *Eden Savoy. What is it about her that makes me do anything to have her? I'm going to demand that Felicity agree to a divorce pronto.*

A cough made him stop his musings.

Lloyd Rittenhouse leaned on the door jamb. He held a black leather binder in his hand.

Dane motioned him inside. He got up from his desk, walked past Lloyd and closed the door. He gestured for him to sit in one of the leather chairs across from his desk. "Why did you want to see me this morning, Lloyd?"

As Lloyd sat down he plopped the binder on his lap. He said with a smug grin, "I found out what happened to Sybil Masterson."

Dane's heart pounded. "After all this time?" he said quietly.

"Well, she did a damn good job of covering her tracks." Lloyd leaned forward and licked his lips in a salacious manner.

"I'd given up hope of ever finding her," Dane mumbled. "And now the reason that I wanted to has somewhat diminished."

Lloyd's eyes practically bulged out of his head. "Are you trying to tell me that after all this time you don't want this information?"

"No," Dane said and a nerve in his cheek pulsed nervously. "I want it. I'm about to embark on a new chapter in my life so it's best that I settle the past."

"Good because when you hear what I have to say you'll be dumbfounded."

"Dumbfounded?" Dane asked in bewilderment.

Lloyd leaned back and watched Dane closely. "You never really explained to me why you've searched for this woman for so many years. Maybe it's none of my business…"

"I need to settle my past so it doesn't continue to ruin my future." Dane gave him a haunted look. "Where did Sybil go after she dropped out of school?"

"That's the thing. She didn't drop out of school. She was in a car accident and in a coma for weeks."

"Oh my God!" Dane exclaimed, horror-struck at the thought. "That's terrible. All this time I thought that she'd just decided not to finish school."

"Quite the opposite. After she recuperated, she finished through Harvard."

"How did you find that out?"

"I had to grease a lot of palms to get that information. But sometimes a recession can be your friend. People get angry when they lose their job as a clerk while others are getting million dollar bonuses for doing a bad job.

"I found a contact in the registrar's office willing to work with me. While Sybil was in the hospital, she petitioned for her grades to be sent to her in Wilmington."

"Harvard," Dane said with admiration. "Sybil always wanted to get a degree from there. Why was she in Wilmington in the first place?"

"She was on her way to Boone, North Carolina, when she had her wreck."

"Boone," he said. He scratched his head as he tried to remember why that town struck a nerve with him. "Why does that sound familiar to me?"

"Her roommate Peyton was living there. She was going to see her."

"Peyton?" A look of sorrow crossed his face. "I wondered what happened to her."

"She died," Lloyd said flatly.

"Oh my God, man. Have you no good news? And to put it so bluntly."

"I'm sorry," Lloyd said. "But that's my way. I know this is a lot of information to get at one time, but as soon as I tied it all together I called you."

"I did ask you to find out," Dane acknowledged. "But it's so tragic."

"Maybe," Lloyd said secretively.

Dane paused before he said, "What do you mean?"

"That small town of Boone is full of gossips." He scrutinized Dane, wondering how he was going to take the news. "You have a niece. A beautiful ten-year-old named Haley." Lloyd opened his leather binder and handed Dane a photograph.

It was one of Haley as she stood outside a school chatting with a group of girls.

Dane knew which one was his niece because she had Kane's big, blue eyes. He stared in awe at the vision. "I thought that Peyton never had the baby. Kane told me she got rid of it."

"Well, she didn't," Lloyd said.

"I can see that!" Dane glared at Lloyd. "Does Kane know about her?"

"I have no idea what your brother does or doesn't know," Lloyd said. "You'll have to ask him."

"I will," Dane stated harshly.

Lloyd sat quietly waiting for Dane to come to terms with the fact that he had a niece out there that he'd never known about. Finally he said, "There's more, but I don't know how you'll take it."

A feeling of trepidation crawled up Dane's spine. "Is it about Sybil?"

"Yes."

"What is it?" Dane asked. "Is she okay?" he said, fear making his voice slightly shake.

"Oh yeah, she's okay." Lloyd said watching Dane's face closely. "And she's living in New York."

"She is?" Dane said in a stunned whisper.

"Yes," Lloyd said. "The accident almost left her disfigured."

"I feel horrible knowing that she had to go through that," Dane stammered painfully. "After I graduated from college I went to Scranton to find her." Dane got up from his desk in agitation and paced the floor. Finally, he stopped in front of Lloyd. Stuffing his hands in his pockets he said, "That's when I found out that her grandmother had died. I always thought that was why Sybil disappeared."

"Sybil had some plastic surgery," Lloyd said quietly.

"That's too bad because she certainly didn't need it." He half-smiled at the memory. "She was absolutely stunning."

"She still is," Lloyd said.

"You have a photograph of her too?" Dane stammered.

Suddenly an air of foreboding filled the room.

"Yes. I have a photograph of Sybil Masterson and one of Eden Savoy from the New York Driver's License Bureau."

"Eden Savoy?" Dane exclaimed. "Why do you have a picture of her?"

"Because they're the same person," Lloyd answered with quiet authority. "Sybil changed her name and physical appearance as much as humanly possible." Lloyd handed him the pictures. "I have a feeling that you already know her," he added sardonically.

Dane's eyes were wide with disbelief, his breathing erratic. The pictures dropped out of his hands as if they were too hot to hold. He used his hands to prop himself up on his desk to not fall. The eyes of Eden Savoy, one hazel and one honey stared at him. "Why would she change her name?" he uttered in dismay.

"Because she didn't want to be found," Lloyd said in a matter-of-fact tone.

Once Dane was alone he stared at the photographs of Sybil and Eden. Holding them side by side he compared the two pictures. He scrutinized the one of Eden Savoy. *She's wearing contacts. How could I have not seen it? And she grew her hair long.* Then it came to him. The way she'd felt as he'd buried himself inside her. The way she'd tasted. Her laugh, and the way she'd slapped him on his buttocks after they'd made love. The reason she thought that his wife's name was Tara instead of Felicity. All of these things flooded into his consciousness. *No wonder I fell for her so fast and hard. I've fallen desperately in love with the same woman twice.*

Dane methodically went through the portfolio that Lloyd had left him. Once he'd memorized every detail about what had happened to Sybil he put it in his desk drawer and locked it. Then he buried his face in his hands and soon his palms were wet from his tears for the love of his life.

Chapter 15

Dane was shaken from the demons that plagued him when his phone rang.

"Yes," he barked into the receiver.

"Your wife is here to see you," Pamela said cautiously.

"Send her in."

Once she entered the room, Dane looked at Felicity. As always she was impeccably dressed. Today she wore a white pleated skirt and a striped green Polo shirt. Her red hair was pulled back from her face and secured with a white ribbon.

She lifted her face to him.

Dane dutifully kissed her on her upturned cheek. Then he made a motion for her to be seated.

"What is so urgent?" Felicity asked in a plaintive voice. "You know how Daddy hates to be kept waiting."

"Then you should have arrived earlier." Without preamble he said, "I want a divorce."

Felicity drew in a sigh of irritation. "I thought that we already discussed this," she said in a tired voice. "I need more time."

"You've dragged your feet long enough. Break the news to your father today or I will." His tone held a mixture of warning and stubbornness.

"What's your hurry all of a sudden?" Felicity said with exasperation written all over her face.

Dane remained silent.

"You found her," she blurted out. Then she gave a snort of resentment. "You finally found her."

Dane simply stared at her.

"Well, tell me!" Felicity screamed.

"Lower you voice," Dane ordered in an even tone. "But I can tell you, this isn't all about Sybil."

"That's bullshit, Dane. I know you too well to for you try and fool me." She said in an unbelieving voice, "After all this time she still wants you?"

"This divorce needs to happen. We both need to move on and be with people who can make us happy." he said quietly.

Felicity screeched, "You and that bitch are trying to recreate some fleeting, college, lust, shit that won't make it in the real world," she said cruelly. "You'll see."

Dane's eyes narrowed contemptuously. "She's not the bitch, Felicity, so don't call her that! And do you think that relationship that you're having is going to last? Felicity, you surprise me. I never figured you for a Cougar."

Felicity gave him a wary look. "What the hell do you mean by that?" she spat out.

Dane calmly reached inside his desk and took out the binder that Lloyd had given him at a previous meeting. He'd taken the pictures out of the safe at his apartment that morning and put them in his briefcase in anticipation of their meeting. Handing them to her he said, "You're screwing a twenty year old boy that works at the country club."

Felicity's hands shook as she took to photographs.

He shook his head regretfully. "It's such a tired cliché, Felicity."

She gave him a look full of hostility.

"I've felt guilty because I never really put into our marriage what I should have so I understood your need for other company."

"You don't like to fuck enough," she said condescendingly.

Dane chose to let that pass. "We got married on a whim. We realized our mistake immediately, but you wanted to try and I did the best I could."

"You never made any real effort because of that Sybil woman! Her shadow was always in our marriage."

"You may be right," he agreed solemnly. "But whatever the case, I will no longer be a smoke screen for your torrid affairs."

"Look who's talking," she said. "Daddy told me that there's a rumor going on in the hospital that you're doing some woman named Eden." She sneered, "That must be that chick you followed into the elevator that day. And you talk about clichés."

"Eden is no torrid affair," Dane said candidly. "I really love her."

Felicity blanched.

"I don't want to play the game any longer." Dane trapped Felicity's eyes with his. "Admit it, Felicity. You don't love me anymore and part of that *is* my fault. You only want to stay married to me because I'm a doctor and it suits your image of what your life should be. But the bottom line is we need to get a divorce before we start hating each other." He added softly, "Any more than we already do."

Felicity swallowed the lump of bile lodged in her throat.

Now Dane's tone brooked no argument. "You will sign the divorce papers that I'll have sent to your home no later than Wednesday. Even though you have family money, I want you to have some of mine. I'll give you twenty percent of our assets. I think you deserve that."

Felicity glared at him with a burning animosity.

"It wouldn't be a good idea for your father to try and punish me through my job because of our divorce," he added succinctly. He tugged his wedding band off his hand and gave it to her. "I'm done being punished."

After Felicity stormed out in a huff, Dane sank to his chair, feeling as if the weight of the world had been lifted off his shoulders.

*****

Eden stood undetected in the back of the school auditorium and watched Haley. She was singing her last number in the musical of *Annie*.

After Haley took her last bow and the curtain closed, Eden made her way backstage. Stage mothers and fathers bustled around their children. She saw Haley sitting quietly away from the fray as she untied the saddle shoes that were part of her costume.

Eden planted herself in front of her.

Haley saw her shadow and looked up. "Godmomma," she screamed. Then she threw her arms around Eden.

Laughing, Eden hugged her. "You're going to crush your flowers."

"I can't believe you're here! Why didn't you tell me that you were coming?"

Handing her the flowers, Eden said, "Because then it wouldn't be a surprise, silly."

"Haley, are you still coming with us?" The question came from a short, stocky boy that Eden recognized as a member of the cast. He was part of a group crowding the stairs.

"No, my godmomma's here," Haley shouted.

"Go ahead with your friends. I don't want to ruin your plans," Eden said.

"I can hang out with them anytime," Haley said.

"But I'm going to stay for a couple of days."

"You are?" Haley beamed.

"Yes, so go along with your friends. I'll sit with your Uncle Conrad tonight and catch up on what's been going on with you. That way I'll have a lot of ammunition to yell at you about when we do talk tomorrow."

"But I have school," Haley pouted.

"Hmm. I believe a little birdie told me that he'd let you play hooky while I'm here so that we can spend some real time together."

"You're the only person Uncle Conrad would do that for," she said with an impish grin.

"Come on, Haley." The boy looked apologetically at Eden.

Haley rolled her eyes. "I'd better go. His mother is the one driving us to Dairy Queen and she can be…"she bit off the rest of her sentence out of respect for her.

Holding back laughter caused by Haley's expression Eden said, "Go on. I'll see you at home."

*****

Eden and Conrad sat in the sitting room drinking cider. "You're doing a great job with her, Conrad. She was awesome in the musical."

"I know," he said sheepishly. "I go and sit in the front row and clap every time she sings a song. The other parents get annoyed, but I don't care."

"She's so full of vitality."

"It was touch and go with her for a while. After my parents died one right after the other like that Haley started acting out. There were times that I started to call you and ask you if you would come get her. I thought that she needed a woman and all."

"Why didn't you tell me?" Eden asked quietly.

"We got through it. And to be honest," he said, staring frankly at her, "I didn't want to lose her. Without her, I don't know how I would have gone on."

"She's so much like Peyton it's eerie."

"She is. Haley's headstrong, beautiful, and smart. She wants to experience everything at once."

"Do you think that she really wants to be an actress?" Eden asked nervously.

"She does right now," Conrad said. "But it probably won't last. Last month she wanted to be an astronaut. Six months ago it was a stewardess."

"Well, at least she has goals," Eden chuckled.

"That's the difference between Haley and Peyton. From the time I can remember, all Peyton wanted was to live in a big city and have a rich husband take care of her. Haley wants to get things on her own. After Peyton came back home pregnant she had happiness staring her right in the face, but she wouldn't take it," Conrad said morosely.

Eden gave a start of surprise. "What do you mean?"

"Alfred Jones wanted to marry Peyton and raise Haley as his own."

"Alfred Jones?" Eden screwed her face up in concentration. "He was Peyton's high school sweetheart, wasn't he?"

"Yeah, and he still loved her. But all she did was dream about Kane Hamilton," Conrad said resentfully. "Now Alfred is married and he treats his wife real good."

"You can't blame Peyton for not marrying a man she didn't truly love," Eden said with fervor. "Marrying someone you don't love is no solution."

"But Peyton cared for Alfred. While she was big and pregnant with another man's child, he'd take her on dates and they'd have a good time together. She just couldn't let go of the past and it ruined her future."

Eden froze upon hearing these words.

"We had a really hard time growing up. The kids at school used to pick on us because of our clothes. Cheerleading was the only place Peyton felt that she shined. We thought it was a godsend when she got that cheerleading scholarship," he said morosely, "but it turned out to be the beginning of the end of her. She tried to bully her way into a life that wasn't meant for her.

"Once she got back here, she continued to wallow in self-pity about what had happened to her and refused to see things for what they were. She was as much to blame as this Kane maybe even more. I sneaked and read a letter that Kane sent her. He wrote that she'd told him that she was taking the pill and had lied. When I confronted her she didn't deny it. He could have done better by her," Conrad said in a taut voice. "But it wasn't all him."

*****

"Why do you have to go home tomorrow?" Haley whined.

"Because I have to go to work and you have to go to school."

"Why did you change your name? I asked Uncle Conrad and he said that he didn't know."

"I was stupid," Eden answered bluntly. "I was running from something and that's impossible to do. No matter what happens, Haley, you can't run from life."

Haley stuffed another French fry in her mouth. She swallowed it. "Uncle Conrad is sick."

"What makes you say that?" Eden asked, pretending an intense interest in the menu on the wall.

"He kept going to the doctor so when the nurse called I listened on the extension in the other room."

"Shame on you, Haley," Eden quickly scolded her. "That was a private conversation."

"I wanted to know what was going on and he wouldn't tell me."

"He probably didn't want to worry you," Eden said soothingly.

"He has cancer," she whimpered. "The doctor told him he has six months to a year." Haley's eyes filled with tears. "Did you know?"

"Yes," Eden said truthfully. "He and I talked about what his wishes are."

"What are they?" Haley cried softly.

Eden handed Haley a napkin to wipe her eyes. "When the time comes he wants you to come and live with me in New York."

"Do you want me?" Haley asked in a small scared voice.

"Of course I want you." she answered firmly. "You're my daughter, Haley." She gave her a look filled with love. "You'll always have a home with me."

*****

With purposeful strides Dane boarded the elevator and rode it to the twenty-fifth floor.

Once he reached his father-in-law's office he smiled at the secretary. "Hello, Kaitlin. Is Andrew available?"

"He sure is." She smiled at him. "He just got back from a meeting. Do you want me to let him know that you want to see him?"

"No, thanks," Dane responded in a deliberately offhand voice. "I can announce myself."

When Andrew Lancaster looked up from a pile of papers he was shuffling around and saw Dane entering the room the initial look he got on his face was one of anger, but he quickly masked it. Standing, he came around the desk and held out his hand to Dane.

"How are you doing, Dane?"

"I'm doing well, thank you," he said, sitting down in the chair in front of the desk.

Andrew leaned on his desk and studied Dane. "What brings you up here?"

"I was in the area and thought that it would be a good idea for us to have a private chat."

"Really, what about?" Now the tone of his voice changed and it bordered on rudeness.

"Has Felicity said anything to you about the problems we've been having?"

"Yes, she talked to me," he said in an obviously disgruntled tone. "But even before she did I knew that she wasn't happy."

"I'm sorry for my part in that," Dane said truthfully. He drew in a deep breath. "I'm sure that she told you that we've been living apart for quite some time."

Andrew nodded his head.

"Felicity is a lovely woman and she should be married to a man who loves her the way she should be loved."

"I'm sorry to hear that you feel that you aren't that man, Dane." He added sarcastically, "Maybe you could have been if you weren't so distracted by outside influences."

"Nothing has distracted me from my marriage to Felicity. It was really over before we moved up here from Texas," he said firmly. "We wanted to give it one last shot before we called it quits. We didn't last a month after we got here." In a no nonsense tone he said, "My other reason for stopping by is that I wanted to make sure that we're on the same page. Even though I will no longer be your son-in-law, I intend to remain on staff at the hospital. I can tell from the way I've been treated thus far that I'm appreciated here and considered an asset."

Andrew glared at Dane with barely concealed hostility. "So it's true! You're having an affair with Eden Savoy," he spat with disgust.

"I know that you understand that it's not always possible not to become involved with someone who works at the same establishment. I'm sure if that was the case *you* of all people would understand how that could happen." Unflinchingly he held Andrew's disgruntled stare. Dane stood and held his hand out.

Andrew also stood to his feet but ignored Dane's gesture.

With a nonchalant air Dane said, "It was nice talking to you, Andrew. If not before, I'll see you at the monthly board meeting."

Andrew curtly nodded his head.

*****

Eden and Randall sat in a small pizza parlor around the corner from where they lived.

"When are you going back to work?" Randall asked as he bit into another piece of pizza.

"Oh, Monday probably. I need a couple of days to recuperate from that drive."

"I'm glad you're back. I miss you when you're not around."

Eden gave him a look of love. "I always miss you too. You're my big brother."

"Well, speaking as your big brother what are you going to do about Dane?"

"I'm going to end things with him. I can't stomach the charade anymore."

"But it's turned into something more than charade, hasn't it?"

"Yes. But I mustn't lose sight as to how he's a married man sleeping with me."

"Life isn't black and white like that, Eden. Married people can live in the same house and have absolutely no relationship. Dane and his wife don't even cohabit. From the outset, he was upfront about being married and he's not trying to hide your relationship."

"I understand that," she said quietly. "But the history that we have... We could never get over the past."

"You two have that elusive something that every couple craves for. It's whatever that thing is that can't keep people away from each other. You don't know it, but your eyes soften when you say his name. Your love for him has withstood the test of time. And as for him, I think that he loved you before and he loves you again."

"Dane doesn't even know who I am," Eden denied. "If he did he'd hate me for lying to him."

"Maybe not once he knew the whole story. You created an alter ego because you couldn't deal with your past. Dane came on to you. Not the other way around. After all that time he was a stranger and you didn't owe it to him to explain to him what you'd gone through. That's the sort of thing that takes time."

"But I waited too long to tell him," she choked out. "And now I'm too embarrassed. The lies behind my eyes bar me from telling him the truth. I've ruined any future chance of happiness with Dane."

"If a person deeply loves someone, then they try to forgive them for almost anything. You need to tell him who you are."

"I need to break things off with him," she whispered. "And the sooner that I do the better off he is."

Twilight had settled on the city. As Eden and Randall walked back to their apartment building they held hands.

Neither noticed the man who sat in the black BMW watching them.

*****

Conrad's words echoed in her head. 'She just couldn't let go of the past and it ruined her future.' Feelings of regret overcame Eden's spirit. She stared at her reflection in the mirror as she took her contacts out and put them in cleaning solution. *I've got to tell Dane the truth...*

She closed the lens holders and put them in the cupboard under the sink. Then she stepped into the hot steaming shower. Eden thoroughly scrubbed her body from head to toe. She doused her head under the spray. *I wish that I could wash away my sins as easily.*

Wrapping a towel around her, she walked to the counter and put astringent on a cotton ball and whisked it across her face, then rubbed sesame oil over the rest of her body. Naked, she walked into her bedroom but just before she climbed into bed she heard her doorbell.

"Coming, Randall," she hollered. She grabbed her silk kimono off the hook behind her door and flung it open.

Dane stepped into the dark foyer.

Eden closed her eyes and turned her back to him. "What are you doing here?' she asked with bowed head.

"Why do I keep seeing you with that man?" he growled.

"What! None of your business," she exclaimed. "Now I know that you are stalking me!"

Eden heard the door behind her slam shut with a decisive click.

"How dare you come here uninvited," she said in a quaking voice. She was afraid to face him. She wasn't read to be exposed for the liar that she was. She searched her mind for something to say. "You're a married man."

"I was a married man. Felicity signed the papers today. The divorce will be final in thirty days."

Eden gasped in astonishment.

From behind Dane reached and untied the sash to her robe. It fluttered into folds at her feet.

Dane moved her hair out of the way and began to gently nibble the base of her neck. He whispered between bites, "I love you, Eden. I love you so much and now we can be together."

She felt weak in the knees.

Without turning her around, Dane fondled her breasts and Eden gasped.

Dane pulled her back against his body and she felt his hard member sandwiched between the crease of her buttocks. "Feel how much we want you," he muttered.

Heat rose in her abdomen at the feel of him. Eden was unable to stamp down her desire for him.

"Take me to bed," Dane demanded in a voice husky from desire.

With bent head, Eden grabbed his hand and led him to her bedroom that was bathed in blackness. She climbed onto the bed and positioned herself on all fours.

Once Dane was behind her, he gently entered her. He paused for a moment, giving her time to adjust to his girth and then he began to move.

Eden held his manhood prisoner, taking in all of him, making sure it's slickness never left her body.

Dane moved slowly and each time he moved backwards she screamed.

They moved sinuously for an eternity. The only sound in the room was a one that sounded like the waves of the ocean lapping around rocks on the beach.

He whispered gently in her ear, "I love you so much I ache for you."

Hearing those words made her release the flood. "I love you too, Dane," she grated out.

When Dane felt her come, he released his joy and shouted, "Sybil."

Hearing these words, Eden collapsed on the bed and lay silent.

Dane dropped his arm around her waist, and snuggled up behind her, planting his head between her shoulder blades. Then he began whistling off key.

Eden felt her heart constrict when she realized that it was the melody to Usher's song, 'You Remind Me.'

"Why did you call me Sybil?"

"I didn't call you, Sybil," he whispered drowsily. "You must be imagining things. I love Eden Savoy. Now go to sleep."

Long after Eden heard Dane's heavy snore she stared blankly into the darkness.

*****

The next morning Dane awoke to the sound of the shower running. The beeping of his IPhone made him reach into his trouser pockets. Dane read the message and panic clutched his heart.

Eden entered the room clad only in a towel. Her brown eyes spied Dane's stricken face. She looked at the IPhone still in his hand. "What's happened?"

"I got a text from Kane. My father has had a heart attack."

"I'm so sorry to hear that, Dane." Concern was written all over her face.

"I just made plane reservations. We need to be at LaGuardia by one o'clock to make the flight."

"We?" she squeaked. "Dane, I can't go."

"Can't go?" He stared at her brown eyes with anguish in his. "I can't do this alone, Eden. I need you by my side."

"Dane." She sank down on the bed next to him and put her arm around his shoulders comfortingly. "You have to see that it wouldn't be appropriate for me to go with you."

"I don't see why not!" he shouted. Bounding to his feet, Dane pulled her flush to his body. The heavy air between them was suffocating. "You said last night that you love me. Is that the truth?"

There was a grave silence in the room.

"Yes, I do," she replied truthfully. "But, Dane, you don't have all the facts." She exhaled. "I need to tell you something."

Dane cut her off gruffly, "That can wait. My father may die and I don't want that to happen without me being at his side or him having met you. I need you with me, Eden."

She looked away.

"Why can't you be there for me?" he asked in a hurt voice.

Eden stared at Dane's face.

It was full of angst and lines of worry creased his forehead.

A feeling of love for him overrode her fear and she made a decision. She attempted to smooth out the lines of worry that creased his forehead. "I can."

Dane's body slightly relaxed and he released her. Then he took that same hand and kissed the palm. "I have to go home and pack," he said. "I'll meet you at the airport no later than eleven-thirty."

After Dane left, Eden went to her dresser drawer and dug out the list of things that she'd jotted down at the beginning of her quest to get revenge on Dane. She read the words 'Hurt Dane by separating him from his family.' With a feeling of disgust she tore the paper up into little pieces and dropped them into the wastepaper basket.

Then she sat down and took out a piece of stationary. She began the letter with, 'My dearest Dane.'

Once it was done, she added a picture of her and Peyton. Then she sealed the letter and slid it inside the pocket of her luggage that she hadn't yet unpacked from her last trip.

*****

Dane had stared stoically out the window since they'd boarded.

Once they were in flight, the stewardess approached them. "Would you like something to drink?"

"No, nothing for me," Dane said and stared back out the window.

"I'll have a Long Island Iced Tea."

The stewardess glancing at Dane's morose profile gave Eden a look of understanding. "Coming right up," she said.

Eden slid her hand in his.

Dane squeezed it. "Thank you for coming."

"Thank you for feeling that I'm worthy of making this trip with you." Apprehensively she began, "Dane."

"Be quiet, please." His tone was inflexible.

Eden dutifully sank back into her seat.

When the stewardess came back with her drink, Eden took it, quaffed it in one swoop, and handed it back to her.

She hovered in the aisle. "Would you like a refill?"

Eden felt Dane's disapproval. "No," she said. "That ought to do it."

After she'd refused the second drink, Dane resumed his interest in the clouds.

The combination of lack of sleep and alcohol lulled Eden asleep.

When she awoke she found herself slumped onto Dane. Her eyes fluttered open and she found herself automatically blinking several times because one of her contacts had moved during her nap. She had to blink hard several times more until she felt it slide back into place. Then she looked up to find Dane's penetrating stare observing her.

He leaned over and pressed his lips firmly on hers.

The warmth of his caress made her feel as if she was floating on air.

"Come on, Eden," he drawled, "it's time to disembark."

*****

When they walked into Baylor University Medical Center they were hand in hand. Dane stopped in front of the receptionist's desk. "What room is Clint Hamilton in?"

"He's in I.C.U." she replied after she looked at her ledger. "Only family is allowed visitation."

"We're family," he said.

Eden's heart did a somersault.

Dane took the two badges and after handing her one half dragged her behind him to the elevator.

"He's in I.C.U.," Dane muttered.

"Probably to keep infection away from him," she said hopefully.

Dane nodded his head in agreement.

When they reached the fifth floor and stepped off the elevator there was a group of people standing outside the I.C.U unit. Eden immediately spotted Kane in the crowd speaking to the doctor. She recognized Whitney from a picture of her and Kane at Dane's apartment.

When Kane saw them his jaw dropped in shock. Everyone turned to see what had diverted his attention from what the doctor with the clipboard was explaining.

Dane said in a clipped tone to the doctor, "What's the status of my father?"

"I was just telling your brother that he had a blockage around his artery and we put a stint in. He's gonna be okay. As a matter of fact, we're moving him to a private room."

"Thank God," Dane breathed.

"I'm going to go and write up the paperwork. If things continue the way they are, he'll be released in a couple of days. As long as he remains relatively quiet he can convalesce at home."

"Thank you very much, doctor," Dane said gratefully.

314

"I'm just glad this is a happy ending. It isn't always the case." And with a brief nod he strode off.

Dane looked at Whitney. "Whitney, this is Eden. Eden this is Whitney."

"Nice to meet you." The welcoming smile on Whitney's face seemed authentic as she held out her hand out.

Eden took the proffered hand and as she shook it said, "It's very nice to meet you. Dane speaks of you quite often."

"Good things I hope." She gave a small laugh.

"Yes," Eden offered. "He only says kind things about you."

"We need to discuss some things in private," Kane said briskly. "Dad's new room is 806. I'll meet you there." Abruptly he stormed off.

Eden and Whitney sat in the small visitors' lounge on the fifth floor. "So you're Dane's girlfriend." It was a statement not a question.

"It's complicated," Eden whispered.

"It's always complicated with the Hamilton family."

Eden didn't respond.

"He must think a lot of you to bring you," Whitney said with conviction. "Did you know that Dane used to be engaged to my sister?"

"Yes, I knew that," Eden said quietly.

"I felt sorry for my sister when he broke off the engagement, but I understood."

Again Eden didn't say anything.

"Now Tara's happily married to a lawyer and living in Los Angeles."

"I'm pleased that things worked out for her," Eden said, not knowing what else to say.

"I knew that Dane's marriage to Felicity wouldn't last. He only married her to separate himself from the hold his family had on him."

"That sounds like a pretty drastic move, don't you think?"

"Not if you knew Dallas and all the intricate family generational crap that goes along with it. When push came to shove, Dane was strong enough to battle it, but Kane wasn't."

Eden gave her probing look.

"I wish Kane was more like Dane. Then he'd go ahead and divorce me and we'd both be happy."

"I'm not encouraging you to leave your husband or anything, but you don't have to wait for him to divorce you. You can divorce him."

"I love Kane too much to initiate a divorce. But I wouldn't contest one if he decided that's what he wanted. I've just gotten used to turning a blind eye to his dalliances because I can't give him children."

"That's no reason for you to put up with a cheating man," Eden protested.

"I look at our relationship as if the glass is half full instead of half empty. I recently lost another baby." Her voice tailed off. "And I just found out that for health reasons, I can't try anymore."

"I'm very sorry," Eden said gently.

"I'm sorry to unload on you like this," Whitney said with a catch in her voice. "I mean, after all, we just met. But I can't tell my *friends*. I don't want to see the pity in their eyes at every charity event," she said in a voice tight with tension.

Long afterwards they sat quietly each lost in her own thoughts.

Chapter 16

Eden separated herself from the family. She wandered the hospital halls sneezing from the smell of antiseptic. After stopping briefly by a restroom, she resumed her search for the chapel. She was screwing up her face in concentration, when she saw signs pointing to the hospital chapel. She followed them, and soon was pushing open the door to the chapel. She breathed a sigh of relief when she found that it was empty.

Eden sat in the last pew, which was bathed in quiet darkness. The altar was lit with small candles that shone on the walnut pews adorned with red cushions. A large portrait of Jesus and the twelve Disciples took up a large part of the wall behind the pulpit. Huge mock stained glass windows flanked the walls on each side of the room. She slid to her knees and faced the altar. With head bent she prayed. Eden prayed for the Hamilton family, Chloe and her family, and Nanny. Then she poured her heart out reciting her troubles.

I thank you for sparing Dane's father. I know how hard it is to lose a parent and he's already lost his mother.

Lord, as you know, I have done a terrible thing. If I could undo it I would. My heart was so broken, terrible behavior spewed out of me. I went out of my way to hurt people. Instead of remembering that vengeance is yours I behaved in the exact opposite way of how I was raised. I tried to destroy Dane. Because of that I have destroyed any chance that I may have had of having a meaningful relationship with him.

After he reads my letter, please make it possible for him to forgive me. If he can't do that I understand, but please allow him be able to forgive himself. He will feel like he's a fool once he finds out my true identity. Please give him the strength to go on with his life and not make the mistakes that I have. That means not being able to forgive someone for how they hurt you and allowing it ruin any future relationship. Dane deserves to be happy. Lord, I'm coming back into your arms. Please make me whole again.

When Eden got up and turned around she gave a start of surprise. A chaplain was quietly watching her.

He walked towards her with a welcoming smile. "I was going to try and tiptoe out but I was afraid that I might make too much noise and disturb you."

"That's okay, Father," she said looking at his collar. "I'm finished."

"Call me Chaplain Michaels," he said with a smile. "You're concerned about a family member?"

"Sort of," she whispered. Then not wanting to split hairs because of her new found decision to be honest in all things, she said, "My friend's father is here. The doctor said that he's going to be okay, though."

"That's a blessing. I'm sure your friend is relieved."

Eden sat down in a pew.

The Chaplain took that as an invitation and sat down next to her. He wasn't so close that she felt her personal space invaded, yet she felt his comforting presence.

"Dane," she confided, "is very relieved about his father. But I'm afraid his peace is going to be short lived."

"Oh," he said with a look of query. "Why is that?"

"I have to deliver some really bad news that's going to upset him."

"Can't it wait until he's better able to handle it?"

"There will never be a good time to tell him what I have to," she gulped. "And it can't wait any longer. If I did it would only make things worse."

"Oh, I see," Chaplain Michaels said.

"I have done something awful to him," she said in a broken voice.

"Hmm," he said gently. "You don't seem the type."

"But then you don't know me. I'm a phony and really good at putting a mask on."

"I don't think so," Chaplain Michaels denied. "If you were truly like that you wouldn't have even made such a statement."

"You don't know what I've done," she said in a woeful voice.

"But you're in the right place to start over. You don't know how many people are here at the hospital visiting loved ones and it never occurs to them to come to the chapel. Yet you found your way here."

"Maybe because I'm so laden with guilt."

"At least you know how to feel guilt. Some people never feel bad when they hurt others."

She gave him a look of gratitude inspired by the fact that he saw something decent in her.

Seeing this he smiled. "Go to your friend and tell him what you've done. Ask for his forgiveness. It might take a while, but be patient, give him all the time he needs. I think that eventually he'll come around to seeing the person that I do, a warm, loving, individual who made a mistake as mankind often does."

As Eden headed back to the lounge she saw Dane standing in the hall. He was swinging his head around, apparently searching for someone. When his eyes rested on her coming towards him he visibly relaxed.

"I've been looking all over for you."

"I was in the chapel."

"Oh." He smiled his appreciation. "So you prayed for my father? That was very kind of you, Eden."

"I had quite a list, but he did get first dibs."

"I think that your prayers helped. The doctor thinks that they may end up releasing him even earlier than they thought."

"That's excellent news, Dane."

"I'm going to send for Miles. He's going to take you and Whitney to the house. Father can't have too much company so I think that it's best for you to meet him after he's released."

"Whatever you think is right, Dane," she agreed softly.

"I'm happy that you're here with me, Eden."

Dane leaned over and planted a kiss on her lips. What he meant to be a brief caress of thankfulness turned very passionate.

Eden clung to him, not wanting to let him go. Her arms crept up to a vise-like hold around his neck. When they finally broke their embrace it was bittersweet.

Dane growled in a teasing manner, "Why would you kiss me like that here and now when you know that I can't do anything about it?"

She merely gave him a soft smile as an answer.

"I'll take a rain check for following up on that kiss." Dane slapped her lightly on her backside. "I'm going to check in on Father."

Eden and Whitney were once again alone in the lounge as they waited for the family car.

Suddenly Eden broke the silence. "I need you to do me a favor." She reached in her handbag and took out the letter that she'd written to Dane. "Give this to Dane in about an hour."

Whitney stared, clearly mystified by the powder blue, bulging envelope, but she solemnly took it and put it in her purse.

"I have to use the ladies' room." Eden said genuinely, "It was really nice meeting you."

"Likewise," Whitney replied. She watched Eden leave with confusion written on her face.

After Eden left the bathroom, she took the side stairs, and walked out of Baylor University Medical Center and hailed a taxi to the airport.

*****

Dane and Kane faced each other as adversaries at the foot of their father's bed.

"Why did you bring that woman, here?" Kane demanded. "You're still married to Felicity. Father doesn't need this."

Dane cast a worried look at his father's sleeping form. "Then why bring this up at his sickbed?" He added derisively, "That's not too bright."

"He's sedated," Kane scoffed. "He can't hear anything."

"First of all, I don't answer to you. But just for the record, my divorce from Felicity will be final in a month. I'm going to marry Eden ASAP."

Kane made a snort of derision. "That's tacky."

"Felicity and I haven't had a real marriage for years. Besides, who the hell are you to talk?" Dane took his index finger and poked Kane's chest. "You need to clean up your own life before you start criticizing mine."

"You really have a penchant for the sisters, don't you, Brother?" Kane sneered.

Dane's face turned beet red from anger. "I like what I like. And unlike you," he sneered, "I know what I want. When we were in college, your behavior helped me lose someone who meant the world to me. I won't let it happen again. Because of you my whole adult life has been off kilter."

"Don't blame me!" Kane spat out. "I did you a favor. Sybil wasn't good enough for you." Kane asked in exasperation, "What the hell's the matter with you? One marriage right after the other, it's disgusting. When Father hears that you're marrying a black chick you'll find out who he thinks needs to grow up."

"I can't believe how arrogant you are." Dane looked at his brother with real pity. "I keep waiting for you to become a better person, but with time you only get worse."

"You're making a mistake."

"I'm so tired of saying it." Dane shook his head sadly. "I feel like a broken record. I make my own decisions. I love and respect Father but neither he nor you can stop me from marrying Eden."

"Why do you *have* to have *her*?"

Dane's eyes sparkled and he said truthfully, "From the time I met her I knew she was the one. When she's not with me, I think about her all of the time. And when I'm with her I dread the thought of us parting. I yearn for her."

"There's something about her." Kane's face screwed up his face. Puzzled he said, "I can't put my finger on it but something isn't quite right about her."

Not ready to reveal Eden's true identity Dane ignored his comment. Instead, he addressed the most pressing issue at hand. "If you want to be a part of my life you will treat her with the utmost respect whether I am around or not. I won't lose out on true love again."

"True love?" Kane said harshly.

"Yes."

"Dude, you are really sprung."

"I'm glad that I know how to love somebody," Dane said with honesty. "I certainly don't want to be like you. You're so self-absorbed, Kane, it's pitiful," Dane sneered.

"Self-absorbed?" Kane's eyes narrowed in anger. "What do you mean by that?"

"For one thing, I'm talking about the way you treat Whitney. You openly cheat on her. You should have never married her. Then maybe she could have ended up with a man who would give her the love and respect that she deserves."

"Don't you worry about my relationship with my wife. Besides, Whitney knew what she was getting into when she married me."

"But people sometimes change. Sometimes they even mature. Father and I hoped that you would. Whitney probably thought that with time you'd settle down, but you haven't. There's nothing more pathetic than a middle aged playboy, Kane," Dane finished disdainfully.

A long hostile silence filled the room.

Dane drew in a deep breath and stared at his twin. "Do you know about Haley?" he demanded.

Kane averted his eyes. "Who is Haley?" he mumbled.

"She's your daughter by Peyton Monroe. She lives in Boone, North Carolina and is being raised by her disabled uncle."

Kane backed away from Dane, wanting to put some distance between the two of them. "How do you know about that?" he demanded rudely.

"So you did know," Dane uttered in a contemptuous voice. "I prayed you didn't. That way I could have a vestige of hope that you're not a complete asshole."

A flush started at Kane's hairline and flowed down his neck disappearing under the collar of his shirt.

They heard a stirring in the bed.

Dane and Kane plastered fake smiles on their faces, and went to their father's bedside. They peered at him.

Clint Hamilton's face was pallid. He crooked his finger at his sons for them to bend closer. It was obvious that he had to struggle to form words. He glared accusingly at Kane. "I can't believe you let your mother leave this earth not knowing she had a grandchild. I'm embarrassed to call you my son." His eyes shifted to Dane. "Bring this granddaughter to me immediately."

Dane and Kane's eyes locked over their father.

Shame was evident in Kane's eyes.

Dane's wore a look of relief.

*****

Eden and Chloe sat on the front porch. Their chairs made squeaky sounds every time they went backwards and it reminded

Eden of the many summer nights they'd sat there and dreamed of what their futures would be like.

Chloe said, "Did I ever properly thank you for my car?"

Eden looked at the yellow Corvette under the carport that looked as if Chloe spit polished it on a weekly basis. "Yes," Eden dragged the words out. "You've thanked me several times. You don't need to again."

"Well, it's not as if everyday someone has your favorite car delivered to your doorstep," Chloe chuckled.

"I enjoyed doing that for you, Chloe. You've been like a sister to me all my life. Besides, you have earned it." Eden gave her a look of gratitude. "You take care of things on my behalf. I like the houses built on Nanny's property and I have you to thank for that."

"They are nice, aren't they?" Chloe said with satisfaction. "I couldn't believe it when they told me that there was enough land for two houses to be built."

"I'm not surprised," Eden said. "Back in the day a person had more land than house. Now it's the other way around."

"You know, the whole neighborhood got involved when Habitat for Humanity was building them. People volunteered to cook for the workers. There was a fish fry and a picnic with hot dogs and hamburgers. They really did it up."

"That was really nice of them. I'm glad that something Nanny struggled to keep through tough times is worthy of her memory."

"The families living there also seem real nice. They're two sisters with kids. They lost everything in Hurricane Katrina so they didn't mind relocating here at all. One of them is a clerk at the school where I work and she's always helpful when I need something."

"Good. I like it when things work out for people."

"Angela, that's her name, said that the house she's living in now is better than the one she lost. But she's still upset that all her family treasures were swept away when the dams broke."

"You can never fix the past," Eden murmured, "no matter how hard you try."

"Eden, I'm so glad that you came for a visit. When you left here last time it looked as if you had the weight of the world on your shoulders." She gave her a critical look. "But you look some better. I guess you're healing."

"Maybe I'll start to heal now." She absently fingered the locket that now she never took off. "But you don't know the horrible person I'd become."

"Horrible person? You could never be that," Chloe objected.

"Wanna bet?" Eden countered. Then in a very glum voice of acute humiliation she recounted step by step what she'd done since she became Eden Savoy.

"Damn!" Chloe exclaimed. "Girl, you put the "R" in the word revenge."

"That's not a compliment." Eden hung her head in a disgraced manner.

"I knew your ass was up to some shit when you changed your name and all, but this is some crucial mess," she said, stunned.

"Chloe…" Eden said as her eyes filled with tears.

"So let me get this straight. You made him leave his wife?" She gave a pointed look at the area between Eden's legs. With a raised eyebrow she said, "Damn, your shit must be tight."

Eden gave Chloe a look of exasperation.

Ignoring it Chloe continued, "Then you went to Texas with him. Then you sneaked out of the hospital without telling him goodbye. Why did you pick that time to leave?"

"Because I knew that if he knew who I was he wouldn't want me there." She wiped the tears that were cascading down her face off her cheeks with the back of her hand.

"I don't get it. Why are you now so upset at what you did?" Chloe gave her an encompassing look.

"Because I deliberately went out of my way to hurt someone."

"Yes, you did," Chloe replied with her usual candor. "And you knew what you were doing right from the beginning. You're not some young kid anymore. Sybil, Eden, or whatever you want to be called today. You thought of a plan," she paused, "and I must say you executed it meticulously."

"Are you trying to make me feel worse?" Eden asked glumly.

"No," Chloe denied. "I'm just trying to get you to put things in perspective. You got what you wanted. You got even."

"Now I wish that I hadn't hurt him."

"I really think that you wish that you weren't hurt," Chloe shot back in her outspoken way. "You've been here five days and I've heard you cry yourself to sleep every night. That's a woman who's been hurt by love."

"So you think the only reason that I'm sad is because I fell in love with him? You think I'm that self-centered?" she said, stung by her friend's assessment of the story she'd told her.

The tragic look in her eyes softened Chloe's demeanor. "I don't really think that. It's just that I don't understand why you went after Dane like that in the first place? I think that Kane is the real culprit in all this mess."

"He is. But Dane didn't have to go along with everything Kane told him to do."

"They're twins! There's always a dominant one and they battle for control. But it seems to me that now the power has shifted and Dane is in complete control of his life."

"Now he is. But the bottom line is he was part of a ménage a trois with my roommate and Haley could have ended up being his child. That's icky."

"Oh, Eden," Chloe said in a tired voice, "grow the hell up! Dane was young. People make mistakes. Ménage a trois are more common than you obviously know. You two weren't fuckin' so it's not as if he cheated on you with your best friend."

Eden knew that everything Chloe said made sense, but she made one last attempt to state her case so her friend didn't think that she was a complete idiot. "After we were intimate he could have said something," she muttered.

"Why? I don't go around telling my current boyfriend who I've been with in the past. Shit, he better not ask me either."

The indignant look on Chloe's face made Eden smile for the first time that day. "I certainly feel sorry for the man that might have the nerve to ask your hard ass."

Chloe switched gears. "So how long are you going to hide here? You know that you're welcome to stay as long as you want, but you know also that you have to go back at some point and face the music."

"I have years of vacation time built up so I told them that I'd be out for two weeks."

"Are you going to contact Dane?"

"No," she mumbled. "After what I did to him, he probably needs Doctor Phil."

"You don't want Dane to have a session with him." Chloe laughed uproariously. "Doctor Phil might tell him to not take you back, and I don't think you want that."

"I don't," Eden whispered.

"You must love him a lot to go to such lengths to get revenge on him."

"I do."

"Unfortunately love and hate can sometimes go hand in hand. But let me tell you somethin'," Chloe paused and said sternly, "too much craziness will run a man off. Start using your head. When you get back to town go to him. Don't hide behind a letter."

"Yes, Chloe," Sybil answered meekly.

They looked up and saw a black SUV driving down the dirt road that led to Chloe's house.

"Who is that?" Eden asked.

"I don't recognize the car," Chloe said, craning her neck as she tried to make out the driver.

Once the vehicle stopped, the driver's side door opened, and Dane stepped out. He was wearing jeans and the cowboy boots he'd worn the day she'd been introduced to him at college. He planted his hands at his waist and he looked ready to rope a steer.

"It's Dane," Eden squeaked nervously.

"I figured that out the minute he got out the car. Damn, girl, he's fine. He has lips like Harry Connick Junior." Chloe ran the tip of her tongue around her lips. "Well, instead of you having to go to him he's found you." Chloe gave Eden a speculative gleam. "But he looks really pissed. Ooh," she whispered, "your ass is gonna get it."

Tongue-tied at the sight of Dane, Eden sat there mutely.

He stalked towards them in his panther-like gait. "You must be Chloe," he said, nodding briefly at her.

"I am." She looked at Eden. "Do you want me to leave or stay?"

"You can go," she answered in a tremulous voice.

"I'll be in the house if you need me." Before she left she gave Dane a look that he was on notice and if anything happened to her friend he'd have to deal with her.

Once they were alone, Eden asked quietly, "How did you find me?"

"Randall told me where you were. Nice guy. He has a new boyfriend named Javier. They're a cute couple." Dane sat down on the first step close to her.

"Oh," she mumbled.

"I got your letter."

"Then why are you here?" She looked at him. Her eyes were filled with torment and repentance. "You know who I am, and you know what I did to you."

"I didn't quite understand your entire letter. Mind you, I should have." He added sardonically, "It *was* thirty pages long, front and back."

Eden gave a self-deprecating shrug. "I felt the need to really try and make you understand that I'm sorry for what I did."

"That I got." He gave her a piercing look. "Why did you slap me before you left school?"

"I overheard you denying to Kane that we were lovers. I felt that you were ashamed of our relationship."

"Eden," he said and gave her an exasperated look. "I have never been ashamed of being in love with you. If I remember the conversation correctly, Kane accused me of fucking you. I've never fucked Sybil or Eden. I've made love to them. Besides," he added roughly, "I wasn't going to discuss our sexual relationship with Kane because it was none of his business. You were my woman and what we had was very special."

"Also..." Her heart palpitated wildly. She gave him a look out the corner of her eye, "I also found out that you had a threesome with Peyton."

A look of acute humiliation consumed Dane's face. He focused his eyes on the pendant he'd given her. "I thought that might be one of the reasons you refused to talk to me." He paused and gave her a soulful look. "If Peyton was alive, I'd apologize to her for allowing myself to be coerced into a situation where she was taken advantage of." He took Eden's hands and held them in his. "I can't fix that, but maybe I can fix us. When that happened I had been out drinking all night with my frat brothers and was pretty ripped when I got home. Alcohol isn't an excuse for what I did, but it is the reason."

She shot him a dark look filled with jealousy. "At the same time I found out that you were engaged to a woman named Tara and sleeping with me."

"From the moment I looked into your gorgeous eyes, I emotionally checked out of that relationship. I hadn't had sex with her since we were together. She was away at school at Texas A & M. I just felt that I should break the engagement in person. I owed Tara that." He paused. "Eden, I'm begging you to forgive me."

"I've already forgiven you." She held her hands out in despair. "Who am I to judge anyone's behavior?" She gave him a tortured look. "Dane, how can you be so kind to me after what I did to you?" she wailed.

"Part of what happened to you is my fault."

"Why would you say that?" she asked in an uncomprehending voice.

"I should have made Kane be more responsible. Peyton wouldn't have taken off if Kane had at least shown her some respect during her pregnancy. If he had it wouldn't have been all on you to shoulder the responsibility of looking out for her." Feelings of repentance were apparent on Dane's face. "At the very least I should have told Father what was going on. But I was so conditioned to covering for Kane it never occurred to me to betray him."

He shook his head in self-recrimination. "Even though Father couldn't have made Kane marry Peyton, as a family we could have been supportive. If we had done that you wouldn't have been traveling alone to Boone and almost killed in that bizarre accident," he ended in disgust.

"I don't want you to feel in any way responsible for my accident. Sometimes things happen, Dane, and there's nothing anyone can do about it."

"Like me falling in love with you twice," he said in a wondering voice. "It hadn't even occurred to me to put in for a divorce until I met Eden Savoy because I still loved Sybil Masterson. Then after I found myself wanting to spend every waking moment with you I was confused. I was still in love with Sybil Masterson. But now I was equally in love with Eden Savoy. I doubted my ability to make judgment calls." He gave her a sharp look. "Why did you leave Texas the way you did?"

"I knew that I didn't deserve to be there," she said miserably. "I felt that if you knew who I really was you wouldn't want me to be a part of such a family crisis."

"I already knew who you were when I insisted you go to Texas with me," Dane explained. "My private detective had stopped by the hospital the previous day and revealed your true identity to me."

Eden's mouth dropped.

"I'd had him looking for Sybil Masterson for years. I wanted to settle things once and for all. I thought that since we were more mature we could try to recapture what we'd had.

"But then I met Eden Savoy and fell madly in love with her. I still wanted to find Sybil because our past haunted me throughout my marriage with Felicity and I didn't want to go through that again.

"I didn't ask you for time before divorcing Felicity because I had still had feelings for her. I was just so confused by what was happening it was like I was in limbo.

"By the time you gave me that ultimatum, I'd already fallen hard for you. So I decided that I was blessed with having experienced two great loves in a lifetime and I better get my act together before I blew it again." He shook his head in amazement. "I had no idea that I was in love with only one person, not two different women."

Mortification washed over her for her part in making Dane doubt his ability to understand his own heart. She looked him deeply in his eyes, searching. "Dane, do you really see me for what I am?"

"Yes," he affirmed. "I see a very young woman named Sybil Masterson who went through a traumatic experience and conjured up a totally new life as a coping mechanism for all the turmoil she'd been through. I also see a woman named Eden Savoy who is smart, faithful to her friends, and fantastic in bed. I loved her from the moment I set eyes on her."

"The person you love or who you think you love may not exist," she said miserably.

"Oh," he said. "So you're not really a director of case manager who graduated from Harvard?"

"Yes, that part's true."

"So you don't really like pizza?" he asked.

"I love pizza."

"So you don't really like to give a blow job?" His lips twitched in amusement.

"Dane," she mumbled, embarrassed.

"Oh, because I thought that if you were going to deny that then I really do need to get back in that rental and get the hell out of here."

"I would if I were you," she said in a pathetic voice.

"Would you really, Eden?" He searched one hazel eye and one honey brown one and was satisfied by what he saw. "I had almost lost all hope that I would ever look into those beautiful eyes again. I've missed them and you. Besides my mother, I have only loved two women in my life," Dane said in his low throaty voice.

Eden gave him a penetrating look.

"They are Sybil Masterson and Eden Savoy and I'd be happy living the rest of my life with either one of them."

A sudden transformation flooded her body. Now Sybil Masterson's heart flip-flopped. "Do you really think that we can get past this?" she asked in a voice filled with incredulity.

"We can only try," he answered. "And I think that I know how to make certain we do."

Dane got up and walked to the SUV. He fumbled around inside the interior and then he walked back to her, hiding something behind his back. Once he got to the porch he ordered softly, "Sybil Masterson, Eden Savoy, please stand up."

For the first time ever hearing her two names together she smiled as supreme happiness filled her. Sybil stood.

Dane dropped to one knee.

Sybil gasped as he showed her what he'd been hiding behind his back. It was a black velvet box. He opened it and a beautiful square cut diamond sparkled at her. She placed her hand over her heart in awe.

"I love you so much it aches. I want you in my life, now, tomorrow, and forever. Will you marry me?"

Tears of joy streamed down her face. She gasped excitedly, "Yes, Dane, I'll marry you."

He reached over, took her hand, and slid the ring on her finger. It was a perfect fit. He brought it to his mouth and kissed it.

*****

The next morning Chloe stood in the kitchen whipping pancake batter.

Dane, dressed in a pair of shorts and tee shirt, shuffled in and sleepily rubbed his eyes.

"I'm glad that my mother is in Atlanta visiting her sister," Chloe teased. "You and Eden made so much noise last night I had to wait until you finished before I could fall asleep."

Red flooded Dane's cheeks. Then his expression lightened when he figured out from Chloe's expression that she was only teasing him. "Besides, with you two not being married and all, Mother wouldn't have ever let the two of you spend the night in the same room."

"Well, I'm sure that the next time we come down here we'll be man and wife so she should have no problem with us sharing a room."

"So are you two planning on tying the knot soon?" She nodded at him to take a seat at the kitchen table.

"As soon as the ink dries on my divorce," Dane responded vehemently. "Our wedding is almost eleven years overdue."

"So you really love my girl?" Chloe asked.

"More than words can say. It's obvious to me and should be to anyone else who knows our story that Sybil and I are soul-mates."

Chloe smiled at his description.

"She's such a strong woman," Dane said. "I admire that."

"Yes, she's all that and I love her to death. But Sybil can really carry a grudge. She's always been like that and I don't see her changing." She gave him a look full of caution. "You're going to have to give her time to learn how to be cordial to your twin. What happened between him and Peyton isn't something that she's ready to forgive."

"If she can just figure out that Kane's paying for his mistakes then maybe she'll be able to at least learn to be tolerant of his company."

"What do you mean? How is he paying for his mistakes?" Chloe said as she poured batter into the hot, buttered frying pan.

"He's unhappily married. I know for a fact that's a miserable state to live in. Yet he's not smart enough to figure out what he needs to do about it. He and his wife have been unable to have children and that's very important to him. I feel that he's being punished for his past deeds and the way he's treated his only offspring. Kane feels that not having a child means that you're not a man."

"Do you feel that way?" Chloe asked, trying to get to know as much about Dane as she could. She flipped the pancakes in the frying pan over.

"No," he said. "But I do want to have children with the right woman. My ex-wife and I never even tried to start a family." He shrugged matter-of-factly, "I guess neither of us wanted to be tied together forever."

"But Kane has a child," Chloe said.

"Yes he does. Even if they eventually have a relationship he's missed out on so much with her. She's already ten years old. Childhood is when kids are formed as to the kind of person they're going to be. Kane lost that time because he's a selfish, arrogant, man," Dane said in a sad voice.

Chloe put a plate of pancakes in front of Dane. Then she handed him a bottle of syrup. "He's your twin," Chloe said, watching him closely. "How does that make you feel?"

"His behavior appalls me. But I still have love him. After all, not only is he my brother," Dane paused and said quietly, "he's my twin brother."

Chapter 17

Dane expertly handled the SUV on the narrow, winding roads.

Sybil sat back at ease. For the first time since her accident she wasn't nervous as she traveled to Boone. She placed her hand reassuringly on Dane's knee.

He looked at her. "I'm scared to death. What if Haley hates me on sight? You know guilt by association."

"I'll talk to her first. I'll explain to her that you didn't know about her until last week."

"That's going to hurt her," he said in a sober voice.

"I know," she said. "But the fact that you're so eager to have her in your life should ease some of her grief."

"My father is anxious to meet her," Dane said fretfully. "I've got to get her to agree to travel to Texas with us. Even though Father's doctor said that he'll be okay if he watches his diet and takes care of himself, you never know about these things."

"Once Haley finds out how much I love you and we're going to be married I think that she'll come around. Conrad is who you need to worry about."

"And I don't blame him. I'm the twin of the man who has behaved in an unconscionable manner. All my life I've had to deal with people lumping Kane and me together," he moaned. "It's been the bane of my twin existence."

"I'll smooth things over with Conrad. I started working on him on the telephone yesterday."

"You did?" Dane asked a little apprehensively. "What did he say when you told him that Kane's brother was coming to meet him and Haley?"

Sybil was quiet for a minute. Then she said diplomatically, "I'll work on him."

When they pulled up in Conrad's yard, he sat in a chair with a rifle laid across his lap. Leaning behind him on the wall was a bullwhip. On his face was a ferocious scowl.

Dane stared at him. "Damn! Are you sure we're not in Texas?"

"Sit tight," she said as she opened her door and climbed out.

Forcing a look of bravado she didn't feel, she walked up to Conrad. She reached down and hugged his unresponsive body. Then she sat on the step at his feet. "He didn't know, Conrad."

Conrad didn't look her way. He continued to glare at Dane as he sat in the car.

"The minute he found out he tried to set things straight."

Finally Conrad looked at her. "He hurt you, too, Eden."

"I know," she agreed. "But he didn't mean to."

"How is that?" Conrad asked in an inflexible voice. "How can you hurt people and not mean to?"

"Sometimes people are caught in the middle of a situation and their hands are tied."

"So you've forgiven him?" Conrad asked.

"Yes," she answered truthfully. "I've forgiven him for everything." She held out her hand. "You see, we're going to be married."

"I saw that ring the minute you got out of the truck. Are you sure about this, Eden?"

"I'm going by the name Sybil again," she said softly.

Conrad gave a start of surprise.

"I love him, Conrad." She gave him a measured look. "He's a good man and he loves me in spite of my many faults."

"Damn!" Conrad said in a miffed voice. "I'd intended to shoot him. You can bury someone in the swamps out here and no one would ever find the body. I'd at the very least planned on using my whip."

"But you'd be using it on the wrong brother," she declared emphatically.

They looked up as they heard Dane's car door opening.

Dane showed no outward sign of the trepidation that Sybil knew he was experiencing. He took the steps two at a time. Once he stood in front of Conrad, he stuck his hand out. "I'm Dane Hamilton and it's a pleasure he meet you."

Conrad slapped it away and grunted, "You may as well follow me inside. Mosquitoes run you out of here once the sun goes down."

Conrad struggled to his feet.

Sybil knew not to reach out to help him up.

As he struggled to grab his crutches, Dane made a motion to help him.

Sybil gave him a look of warning.

Dane let his hand fall back down to his side.

Once they were inside, Sybil fixed everyone a cold glass of Kool-Aid. "Where is Haley?" she asked.

"After you called and said that you were in town I sent her off to the movies with her friends because I wanted to talk to the two of you alone first. She was surprised that she got to go because she's been acting up lately."

"Acting up how?" Sybil asked in a worried voice.

"She won't clean her room," Conrad said crossly.

Sybil laughed. "She's like her mother in so many ways."

"Don't I know it," Conrad said gruffly. "And you'll be finding that out sooner than you thought."

A morose silence entered the room. "What do you mean?" Sybil asked.

Conrad shifted his gaze to Dane. "Has Sybil told you that I have terminable cancer?"

"She mentioned it," Dane responded carefully.

"I don't have long. We've already made arrangements for her to take over the care of Haley. Now that ya'll are gettin' married, are you okay with that?"

"Yes," Dane answered truthfully.

"You'll be the father figure in her life."

"I'll treat her as if she was my own."

"You better treat her better than that," Conrad warned in a deadly voice. "Because if you don't I'll come back from my grave and haunt you day and night."

Changing the subject to something she felt that she could handle better than the thought of Conrad dying she asked, "Does Haley know what's going on?"

"No," he said. "I left that up to him." He cocked his head at Dane. "Let him clean up his brother's dirty business since he's not man enough to do it himself."

Dane nodded his head in acceptance.

Sybil reached over and grabbed Dane's hand. "But I'm going to soften the blow." She looked at Dane then back at Conrad. "We're a team."

They were watching the news when Haley burst into the room. When she saw Sybil she screamed and flung her arms around her neck. "Godmomma, why didn't you tell me that you were coming back so soon?"

"You know how I like to sneak up on you," she said, returning her hug with a force that almost took Haley's breath away.

After they finished Sybil stepped back and twirled her index finger.

Haley dutifully turned around in a circle.

"You look good, honey." Then she swatted her on her behind. In a voice full of censure she said, "Start cleaning your bedroom. If Uncle Conrad gives me one more bad report about that I'm going to cut your monthly allowance in half. I'd like to see what kind of job you're going to keep if you don't know how to do what's expected of you."

Haley shot Conrad a look that spoke volumes. "Yes, ma'am," Haley muttered. Then in an effort to try and change the subject her eyes focused on Dane.

Dane sat as if in a trance as he stared at his niece.

Pointing at him she said in a demanding voice, "Who's that?"

"Haley, this is my fiancé, Dane," Sybil explained carefully.

Haley screamed again. "Fiancé?" she shrieked. "I didn't even know that you had a boyfriend."

Dane stood up and not being able to contain himself any longer gathered Haley into his arms. He held her tightly.

After suffering the embrace for a minute, Haley pushed him away and looked in bewilderment at Dane.

During the embrace Dane's eyes had filled with tears.

"What's the matter with him?" she asked in a puzzled tone. Sensing that there was something momentous going on, she stared at all the adults in the room.

"I'm in need of some ice cream," Sybil said. "Why don't you and I go to the Dairy Queen in town?"

"Okay," Haley said following her without questioning her. "But if you don't watch it, you're going to get fat."

*****

They sat in a booth at Dairy Queen. Sybil watched Haley wolf down a banana split.

She'd ordered a small dish of chocolate chip ice cream but was so nervous she'd barely managed to touch it.

Haley finished her ice cream and after daintily wiping her mouth said, "Now why did you want to get me off to myself?"

Sybil played for some time. "How do you know that I just didn't want some alone time with you?"

"If that's all it is you wouldn't be so nervous."

"What makes you think that I'm nervous at all?"

Haley pointed at Sybil's hand. "I know because you keep tapping on the table with your acrylics." She grinned.

Sybil took her hands and clasped them in front of her. "I guess I am nervous," she said truthfully. "I wanted to talk to you alone about Dane."

"Okay," Haley leaned back. The expression on her face reminded her of the days when she had some gossip to tell Peyton and the memory almost made her cry.

"As you already know we're getting married."

An expression of alarm settled on Haley's young face. "Does that mean that you don't want me anymore?"

"Of course that's not what I mean," Sybil denied in such a heated voice she attracted the attention of the people sitting at the next booth. "Dane and I have discussed it and when the time comes," she paused, "we'll be more than happy to raise you as our own. As a matter of fact," she added softly, "we'd be honored."

"Is this Dane really a nice guy?" Haley asked, searching Sybil's face.

"He's the best."

"Then I'm sure that I'll like him. Besides, if you love him that's all that matters."

"No, Haley. It's a little more complicated than that."

"Why?"

Sybil drew in a deep breath. "Dane is your uncle."

"What? I don't understand."

"Dane is your father's brother."

"What father?" she asked in a suspicious voice. "I don't get it. You mean this Dane is some long lost brother of Uncle Conrad?"

"No, Haley. He's the twin brother of your natural father, Kane Hamilton."

Haley echoed Sybil's words. "Some guy named Kane Hamilton is my father?" She whispered, "I never knew my father's name. Uncle Conrad said that it didn't matter because he was dead."

"I'm sure that he told you that in order to spare your feelings, honey." She added in a contrite voice, "I'm sorry, Haley."

"You mean to tell me that my father is alive?"

"Yes, and he lives in Dallas."

"So Uncle Conrad has been lying to me all my life?"

"He did it to protect you, Haley."

Haley glared at her with accusing eyes. "And you kept it from me too. You've been a part of the lie."

"I felt that I had no choice," Sybil whispered. "Maybe I should backtrack and start from the beginning."

Haley folded her arms and leaned back. Her blue eyes were narrowed and she looked just like Kane did when he was riled about something.

"You mother and I met the Hamilton twins, Dane and Kane, our senior year of college." Then Sybil recounted to Haley step by step what had occurred during her and her mother's senior year of college. Eden tried to soften it a little when it came to her mother's indiscretions but she didn't change any of the facts.

Once she was done there was at first silence at the table.

Then Haley burst into tears.

Sybil handed her a fistful of paper napkins and Haley mopped her face.

Sybil felt the waitress and manager's eyes on them and she gave them a negative shake of her head, relaying the message that Haley was fine and they wanted to be left alone.

After her face was dry Haley said, "So Kane Hamilton is the person that I'm supposed to hate?"

"You can hate him if you want to, Haley. You certainly have the right. But I've found that when you harbor hatred in your heart that the vengeance will in the end tear you apart."

"You're only saying that because now you've settled your differences with that family!" Haley's eyes bored into hers and

Sybil felt another shiver because she looked so much like Kane. "They've ignored me for ten years." Her young voice raised several decibels. "How dare they think that they can walk into my life? I have all I need. I have you and Uncle Conrad."

"Haley, neither your grandfather nor Dane knew about you." She said in a beseeching voice, "Please don't punish them and deny them the chance of getting to know you. You're such a wonderful kid; I know that I'd be a worse person not ever having had you in my life."

"So I also need to hate this Whitney person?" Haley stated in an uncharacteristically cold voice.

"Now why would you say that?"

"Obviously she stole Kane from my mother."

"I don't think that she knew anything about your mother, Haley," Sybil said gently. In a soft voice she continued, "And you need to remember, no one can steal a person from another."

"Well, as far as I'm concerned, since Kane didn't want me in his life I'm going to keep it that way," she retorted in an unbending voice.

"How about the others?" Sybil scrutinized Haley's face. "They're victims just like you are."

"I guess Uncle Conrad did what he thought was best for me. I'd probably have done the same thing if I was him. After all, he couldn't make this Kane want me."

"Haley, it's not as if Kane rejected you. He's never even met you."

"But he didn't want my mother, right?" Haley shot back.

"He wasn't ready to be a father."

"What did we do to be treated like that?" she said in a wooden voice. "He didn't even give us a chance to be a family." Haley's blue eyes mirrored fresh pain.

"He was young."

"Not so young that he couldn't sire me and then dump me. He knew what he was doing." Her eyes flashed angrily.

"It's not about you," Sybil said.

"Why are you taking up for him?" Haley demanded in a scornful voice.

"I'm not taking up for him," Sybil denied. "I'm defending you."

"What do you mean?"

"I won't let you carry the burden of thinking that there's something wrong with you because there isn't. Kane rejects all women." She hoped her words sank in and Haley understood the difference. Wanting to ensure that Haley got it, Sybil said, "Haley, I want to let you in on something."

"What is it?" Haley asked.

"Kane isn't good to his wife Whitney either. She's very unhappy. Your mother was very lucky that he didn't marry her because he would have made her miserable." After her statement a long silence ensued. Eventually Sybil broke it. "Honey, now that your grandfather knows about you he desperately wants to meet you."

"He does?" Haley asked distrustfully.

"Yes. Will you give him a chance to get to know you?"

"I'll commit to meeting with him one time," Haley said without enthusiasm.

"Okay," Sybil said relieved. "I'll call your school tomorrow and tell them that you'll be absent for a couple of days."

When they arrived back at the house it was dark. The porch light was on and Sybil knew that Dane and Conrad were anxiously waiting for them. The minute she cut the SUV engine off the front door opened and Dane stood on the threshold.

Haley flung open her car door and stormed up to him. She planted her body in front of him. Haley stood with one leg thrust out in front of the other with her thumbs hooked into the pocket of her jeans. "Did you know about me?" she demanded crossly.

Dane was set back on his heels as he watched her stance. She had every one of his brother's mannerisms. "No," he answered honestly.

Haley pushed past him.

"Where are you going?" Dane asked in a careful voice. "I'd hoped that we could sit down and have a talk."

"I don't have time." Looking at Sybil she said, "I have clean my room. Then maybe I can figure out what to pack for my trip to Texas." Then Haley stomped into the house letting the screen door clatter behind her.

They heard her say, "I'm going to clean my room, Uncle Conrad. And by the way, I love you."

At the same time, Sybil and Dane drew in deep sighs of relief.

The mentally exhausted Sybil climbed the porch steps and once she reached the top she fell against her fiancée's rock, hard body.

Dane propped her up against his long limbs.

*****

The yellow warning light on the plane lit up. The next thing they heard was the stewardess' voice. 'The aircraft is beginning its descent into Dallas. Please turn off all cell phones and electronic devices.'

Sybil looked at Haley who was bobbing her head to whatever she was listening to on her IPhone. Sybil tapped Haley on her knee.

When Haley looked at her Sybil said, "Turn your IPhone off."

"Okay," she turned off her machine and looked at Dane. "I'm hungry."

"My father has a meal waiting for us when we get home."

Haley didn't make an answer.

"If you don't want to wait we'll pick something up in the airport once we land."

"I can wait," she replied.

The stewardess came and with a quick smile at Haley changed the position of her seat from the reclining one she'd been in for the duration of the trip.

Sybil looked at Haley and whispered with an anxious look, "Are you nervous?"

"Why would I be nervous?" Haley replied in a flippant tone. "I didn't mess up, they did."

Sybil looked at Haley. She knew from the way she chewed on her bottom lip that she was putting up a front. She was terrified at meeting the man who had denied her existence her entire life.

Sybil looked at Dane to see if he'd overheard what Haley said. His watchful eyes as he looked at Haley made her know that he did.

"Dane, does Kane know that Sybil and Eden are the same person?" she asked Dane.

"Yes, he knows," Dane answered in an expressionless voice.

"What did he say when you told him?"

"Not much," he said, glossing over the long telephone conversation he'd had with his brother. "He needs to worry about his own past." Dane added, "My father also knows."

Oh," she said in a small voice.

"When I explained to him that Haley's godmother, Sybil, who happens also to be my fiancé was coming with me he wasn't surprised."

Sybil looked at him questioningly.

"Evidently Father knew of our not so secret relationship when we were in college so it was no shock to hear of an impending marriage."

Once they retrieved their luggage and went outside, a blast of dry air almost made them stagger. Dane swung his head around and then found what he was searching for. "Father sent the car for us. Come on, ladies."

As they followed Dane to the long, black limousine with a chauffeur standing next to it, she glanced at Haley who appeared quite unimpressed.

Dane grinned at the tall man with salt and pepper hair. "Miles, it's good to see you."

"Mr. Clint asked if I would come and meet your plane." He grinned. "Ever since you called yesterday and said that you were coming he's had the whole house turned upside down getting things ready."

"I'm not surprised," Dane said. "But I wish he wouldn't excite himself. The doctor told him to relax."

"Humph," Miles said as he loaded their gear. "He hasn't followed one instruction the doctor gave him. He won't eat the food that Idalis cooks for him and if she scolds him he threatens to fire her."

"He won't fire her," Dane said dryly. "She's been his cook and housekeeper for over thirty years."

"She ain't worried. But after an argument she gives in to his demands and cooks him what he wants or he won't eat at all."

Dane shook his head. "I'll talk to him and her."

"You always talk to him, but when you leave he just goes back and does what he wants to." Then, expectantly, Miles turned his attention to Sybil and Haley.

"Miles, this is my fiancé, Sybil Masterson and her goddaughter and my niece, Haley Monroe," Dane said proudly.

"I'm so pleased to meet you," Sybil and Haley replied in unison.

Haley unflinchingly met Mile's stare as he thoroughly looked her over. Looking into Haley's blue eyes he muttered to himself, "You're his all right." Then Miles gave a toothy smile. "I'm much honored to meet both of you."

"Let's get out of this heat," Dane said. After he held the door open for Sybil and Haley to get in, he walked around to the other side and sat in the front with Miles.

The two men chatted about what the latest gossip in town was or what they'd seen on the news.

Sybil was content to sit back and listen to their conversation.

Haley seemed lost in thought as she stared out the window.

After they drove a while Sybil leaned over. "We've only committed to staying for two days. If you want to leave earlier, just say the word and we're out of here."

"Thank you, Godmomma," Haley whispered and clasped her hand.

Sybil squeezed it comfortingly.

After another twenty minutes the limousine slowed, took a wide turn and pulled up next to a steel gate with a gold *H* centered on it. Miles rolled down the window and punched some numbers. The gate opened.

A huge sprawling white house with columns was centered in the middle of a perfectly manicured lawn.

Out of the corner of her eye she looked at Haley.

She still appeared unimpressed.

The front door opened and Kane and Clint Hamilton came out.

Sybil had seen pictures of Dane's father but even if she'd seen him on the street she'd have known who he was. His sons looked exactly like him. The only difference was that he was practically bald.

"Let's go," Dane said before he opened his car door.

Once they exited the limousine Haley hung back. Her blue eyes were fixated on Kane.

Kane viewed her across the expanse but he made no move towards her.

Clint's gait was slow but purposeful as he descended the steps. Once he reached them he looked at Dane. "Thank you for bringing her to me." Then he looked at Sybil. "I will always be beholden to you for the part you played in making this happen. Thank you."

Sybil nodded her head in appreciation of the gratitude emitting from Dane's father.

Then he looked at Haley. It was quiet enough to hear flies buzzing around them. "You're Kane's child," he said gruffly. "There's no doubt about it."

"Did you know about me?" Haley's voice croaked.

"Of course not," he said in a stern voice. "But I know about you now. You're my grandchild and you're a blessing."

Kane finally moved and came down the stairs, his eyes never leaving Haley. Once he reached her he said quietly, "I'm your father, Kane."

Haley shrank against Sybil. "You're not my father," she said in a cold voice.

Clint grinned. "There's absolutely no doubt in my mind that she's a Hamilton. No need to take a blood test here. Y'all come on inside. Idalis has made a huge lunch for us."

Sybil put her arm around Haley and guided her towards the house. She looked over her shoulder and saw that everyone but Kane was following Clint.

Kane remained planted in the same spot. His hands were thrust into his pockets and he stared at the ground.

For lunch, they were seated at a long, cherry wood table that could easily seat eight. Clint sat at the end. Haley sat between Sybil and Dane. The only tension at the table was between Haley and Kane.

Kane had positioned himself across from Haley and tried to get her to make eye contact with him. Every time he attempted to draw her into conversation she pointedly ignored him. Eventually he quit trying.

Clint asked Haley a lot of questions. They were mostly about school and what she liked to do in her spare time. She politely answered them but when she told him that she wanted to be an actress, Clint put his third piece of chicken down.

"You're too smart for that. You should be a doctor."

Dane said to his father in a warning tone, "Don't start on her."

"Okay," Clint acquiesced.

"Now I know you're getting old," Dane laughed. "You would have never given up so easily five years ago."

"It's a waste of time to try and influence people. They do what they want to anyhow."

"Is Whitney going to be joining us later?" Sybil asked Kane.

"No. She had to take her mother out of town to see a sick relative."

"Oh, I'm sorry to hear that." Sybil said to him with real regret, "I'd looked forward to seeing her again."

Kane gave her a grateful look acknowledging that he knew she was at least trying. "There's always next time."

"Should you be eating that?" Haley asked her grandfather with a critical look. "I heard that the doctor told you not to eat fried foods. That's your fourth piece of chicken."

"You mind your own business, young lady," he growled. "By the way, your skirt is too short."

"So is your hair," Haley shot back.

"Haley!" Sybil exclaimed in an admonishing tone. "Don't say that to him."

Clint looked at his granddaughter. "Let her be." Then he laughed until his eyes were filled with tears. Holding his stomach he said, "That's the best comeback I've heard in a long time. I'm so enjoying you, gal."

After lunch Kane said, "Haley, I would appreciate it if you would meet with me in the library. I'd like to talk to you."

"Okay," Haley said, "but I want Grandfather and Uncle Dane with me. That way you can't lie."

A frightened look crossed Kane's face. "All right," he said in a defeated voice. Then he shuffled towards the library.

The others rose from their chairs to follow suit.

Dane walked up to Sybil and gently kissed her on the lips. "She'll be fine," he said.

An hour later, they all exited the library and dispersed in different directions. Haley climbed the stairs to her bedroom two at a time. Kane strode out the front door, slamming it, and Clint veered towards the kitchen.

Dane plopped down on the couch next to her. He said in a slightly sympathetic voice, "Kane tried to explain away some of his bad behavior but Haley wasn't having it. She chewed him up and spit him out."

"What did your father say?"

"Nothing," Dane answered. "He didn't make any excuses for Kane. I think that he rather enjoyed the way she hammered at him. I know he feels that Kane deserves it."

"Maybe I should go to her." She started to get up.

"Leave her be," he said gently. "She needs time to herself."

"Do you think that she'll ever forgive Kane for abandoning her?"

Dane looked at her. "Have you ever forgiven your father?"

"Not really," she answered. "But maybe if he had tried to reach out to me before he died I would have."

"The burden is all on Kane. He's the one that has to make it work."

Then Dane stretched out and laid his head on her lap.

From the hallway Clint observed the peaceful look on his son's face as Sybil stroked his head.

With a smile he quietly crept away and climbed the stairs to go to his bedroom for his afternoon nap.

Epilogue

Thirteen-year old Haley walked out in the den and did a twirl in front of Sybil and Dane. "I love the outfit you guys bought me."

"I didn't have anything to do with purchasing that." Dane eyed the short-shorts and tank top.

Ignoring that remark Haley asked Sybil, "Mom, what's my curfew?"

"Twelve o'clock."

"But its Saturday night and it's my birthday," she protested as she pushed her ash blonde hair out of her face.

"Which is why I thought that you'd be home with us tonight," Dane said in a pretend hurt voice.

"Ugh! I mean you guys are real cool parents and all but Kelly's throwing me a little get together at her house. I'll be with you guys tomorrow."

"Thanks," Sybil retorted dryly.

"Are Uncle Randall and Uncle Javier coming over?"

"Yes, they confirmed," Sybil said.

"I wish that Aunt Chloe was here," she said wistfully.

"She was just up here for Christmas. You know that she's busy planning her wedding so it's impossible for her to get away."

"I know," Haley acknowledged. "My party sounds like fun even though we'll be stuck inside all day."

"Not all day. We're going to eleven o'clock services at church," Sybil said.

Haley groaned. "I think that we should skip it. You're too big to go anywhere."

"Hey!" Sybil exclaimed. "That's not nice."

"Just kidding, Mom. I just don't want your water to break during service."

"The babies aren't due for another month."

"I can't wait for the twins to get here. I'll baby-sit for you all the time."

"I think not," Dane muttered, making sure he was overheard.

Haley chose to ignore that comment. "Mom, twelve o'clock is too early to have to be home."

"Then Kelly should have planned her event for the daytime," Sybil said firmly.

"Oh my gosh!" Haley rolled her eyes in the same manner that Sybil always did. "That would be so lame."

Dane hid a smile.

"Your grandfather and Whitney called while you were in the shower," Sybil said. "They wanted to wish you a happy birthday. They also wanted to know if you got their gifts."

"I sure did." She smiled gleefully. "I'll call them tomorrow and thank them."

"Your dad was on the line too," Dane added.

A tense atmosphere entered the room.

"What did I say that I prefer you to call him?" she asked.

"I am not calling him your sperm donor, Haley," Dane said in a chiding voice. "Kane really wants to talk to you and wish you a happy birthday."

"Blah, blah, blah," she said. She glanced at her phone. Then she bent down and kissed them each on the cheek. "Kelly texted me that she and her mother are downstairs waiting for me in the lobby, I have to go." Haley rushed out the room.

Sybil observed the pensive look on Dane's face as he stared at the door through where Haley had exited. "Give it time." She absently fingered her locket. "We're a testimony of how time heals all wounds."

Dane gave his wife a tender smile and laid his head in her lap. He snuggled as close as he could to her protruding belly where his boys slept peacefully. "Yes we are," he said with heartfelt relief.

Michele Cameron

In memory of my father,
Philip Swails Cameron

of Camerontown/Lake City, South Carolina

Sunrise: Sunset:

May 9, 1935   September 26, 2012

Author's Website:

http://michelecameronauthor.com

Facebook aggieauthor@cfl.rr.com

Coming Soon